W9-AYL-354

Avoidable Contact

Books by Tammy Kaehler

The Kate Reilly Mysteries
Dead Man's Switch
Braking Points
Avoidable Contact

Avoidable Contact

A Kate Reilly Mystery

Tammy Kaehler

Poisoned Pen Press

Copyright © 2014 by Tammy Kaehler

First Edition 2014

10 9 8 7 6 5 4 3 2 1

Library of Congress Catalog Card Number: 2014931733

ISBN: 9781464202360   Hardcover
        9781464202384   Trade Paperback

Poisoned Pen Press
6962 E. First Ave., Ste. 103
Scottsdale, AZ 85251
www.poisonedpenpress.com
info@poisonedpenpress.com

Printed in the United States of America

To my mother, Gail,
For convincing me I can do anything.

Acknowledgments

I tell stories about a real racing series, real cars, and real tracks, and I do my best to make the technical and racing details as accurate as possible. But I generalize, exaggerate, and flat out make the rest up. Where the line between reality and make-believe blurs, I hope readers and race fans will forgive some liberties. Only a couple character names aren't make-believe: Tommy Kendall, Christine Syfert, and Leon Browning, thank you for donating generously to the Austin Hatcher Foundation and allowing me to make you part of Kate's world.

I owe a great debt to Kevin Buckler, Bob Dickinson, Jeanine Curtis, and everyone else at The Racer's Group. You made this story possible by helping me understand what it's like to be part of a team for this incredible race. Thank you also to drivers Kuno Wittmer, Dominik Farnbacher, and Oliver Gavin for generously explaining the track and checking to make sure I'd done it right—any mistakes are mine. And to Doug Fehan (who really does have charm as his superpower), thank you for putting up with my questions.

It takes a village to make sure I get things right, and I owe thanks to the rest of my racing world experts: Beaux Barfield, Pattie Mayer, Drew Bergwall, Steve Wesoloski, Shane Mahoney, Dawn Bell, Lauren Elkins, Scot Elkins, Dr. (and spotter) Chris Murray, and Tyler Tadevic. You gave me access, information, answers to weird "what if" questions, and helped me at every step.

To my writing peeps and critique partners, Christine Harvey and Rochelle Staab, thank you for encouragement, commiseration over every step in the writing process, and a lightning-fast beta read. To Simon Wood, thank you for the guidance, Obi Wan. Thank you to my agent, Lucienne Diver, for reviews, feedback, and believing in me and Kate. To everyone at Poisoned Pen Press—especially Annette, Barbara, and Rob—and my fellow PPP authors, thanks for the support and for letting me play along.

In the world of my family and friends: thank you to Lara Kallander for reminding me I needed to use the character named after her in this third book. Extra special thanks to friend and subject matter expert Dr. Jason Black for helping me figure out how to kill (or at least horribly injure) people. To Stan Laughlin, thank you for the stories, and to Scott James, thanks for the wonderful photos. To Barb and Mary, thanks for being so enthusiastic, for helping me with names, and for being my race buddies—it's an honor to be part of your lives. Finally, thank you to my parents (real, by marriage, and honorary), Gail, Roger and Aggie, Linda and Jerry, and An. Thanks for calling when I forget to and living with my grunted responses when you ask how the writing is going.

Last but not least, to Chet, my person. Thank you for giving me space when I need it and hugs or tissues when I need those. Thank you for the many years (they feel like a hundred).

Daytona International Speedway

Daytona Beach, Florida

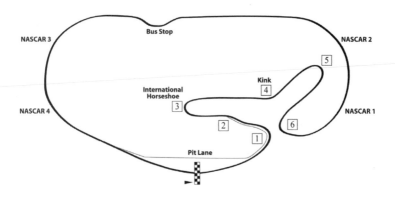

Chapter One

Nothing surprised me about pre-race festivities anymore. Skydivers, samba dancers, Clydesdales—we saw them all. Uniformed cops and security guards generated no excitement. But two police officers with their serious faces on, heading my way? Unusual.

I stood in pit lane, enjoying the view of overcast skies, an enormous racetrack, and some ten thousand people, all of us buzzed on anticipation and adrenaline. Drivers, teams, and fans savored the buildup to the green flag. Everyone focused on the world inside the giant bowl of Daytona International Speedway. Everyone was ready for the marathon that is the legendary 24 Hours of Daytona endurance race. Then the sight of badges, gunbelts, and somber faces, flanked by Series staff, shot my heart rate into race-stint territory.

I straightened up from my slouch against the side of our number 28 Corvette. Tug Brehan, the number two guy in operations for the new United SportsCar Championship series—and, hands down, the most stylish guy at the racetrack—led the officers to me through the sea of people.

Tug put a comforting hand on my shoulder. "Kate Reilly, this is Detective Latham with the Daytona Beach Police." He gestured to the tall, slender man with a shaved-bald head and mocha-colored skin. "And Officer Webster, Daytona

International Speedway Police." That was the older guy, shorter and rounder, with graying red hair and pale skin.

Webster nodded, then turned to scan the crowd around us.

Latham looked from me to Tug. "Is there somewhere quieter or more private we could talk?"

I shook my head. Dread curdled my stomach. "Tell me." When the cop didn't respond, I pointed to the front of the grid. "We could fight our way to my team's pits, but it's at the far end of chaos. What is it?"

Tug beckoned to someone. Holly Wilson, my best friend and new manager/assistant, appeared next to me.

I panicked. "My grandparents?"

"Your family is fine." Tug started to say more, then stopped. Relief left me lightheaded.

Latham cleared his throat. "I understand you know the Series Vice President of Operations Stuart Telarday well."

"Stuart?" *Twelve hours ago I'd have said he was my boyfriend. I'm not sure what he is now.* "He's a good friend. Is he in trouble?"

"I'm sorry to tell you he was involved in a hit-and-run accident a couple hours ago." Latham watched me intently. "He's in critical condition."

My mind went blank. I shook my head. "Hold on. What?"

"Stuart Telarday was injured in a hit-and-run shortly before eleven this morning. He was crossing International Speedway Boulevard, possibly on his way to a restaurant."

"Outside the track? He wouldn't leave the track on race day. It can't have been him."

"He carried three kinds of photo identification."

The news slammed into me with the force of a couple Gs. I must have swayed, because Holly put her arm around my waist. Tug stepped forward again.

"A restaurant?" The details didn't make sense. *Stuart. Hurt. Critical.*

"A security guard at the track exit said Telarday mentioned the Mexican place," Latham responded. "On the corner of Bill France Boulevard."

I looked at the detective, but pictured Stuart instead. Black trousers, crisp white Series shirt, horn-rimmed glasses, and a slight frown on his face as he scrolled through messages on his phone. He saw the green light and stepped into the crosswalk with his typical determined stride. Then a car careened through the intersection, inspired by the racetrack nearby, tires squealing—bam. I closed my eyes on the horror of impact and a person—Stuart—flying and hitting the ground.

The pedestrian and car were easy to imagine. I'd witnessed nearly the same accident yesterday, in the same location. Then, however, the car braked and swerved in time, and the pedestrian jumped out of the way.

I opened my eyes, astonished to find a vibrant world around us. I looked at Detective Latham. "How bad is he?" It came out as a whisper.

Latham spoke first. "The official word is critical."

"We're not releasing anything more than that," Tug—Stuart's employee—put in. He pitched his voice low, though the cacophony around us made it unlikely anyone else could hear. "But I think it's appropriate to tell you, Kate—" he eyed Holly.

I exhaled sharply. "She won't repeat it."

He nodded. "Stuart has compound fractures of multiple limbs, broken ribs, internal bleeding, a broken collarbone or shoulder. But the concern is the skull fracture and possible brain injury. He's in surgery right now."

I had to concentrate to make sure I was breathing. "Is he going to—" I couldn't finish the question. Not out loud.

Tug took my hand. "Kate, we don't know. He's got the best team of doctors around." I stared at him, trying to process his words. Tug was short for a man—which still meant taller than me—with dark hair, perpetually tan skin, and something around the eyes that hinted at some kind of ethnic ancestry—part Native American was my guess. The charm he always oozed was mixed now with sympathy and concern.

I need to sit down, pronto. I pulled free of Tug and Holly. I curled up on the pavement next to my car, my arms and head on my bent knees. I tried not to think about the pain and terror Stuart must have felt. Tried to think positive thoughts about the work surgeons were doing. How Stuart would heal. I processed the idea of him fighting for his life in a hospital room. Not being at the race. Maybe ever. I tried not to cry as I argued with myself.

I should be there. You can't do anything. I should be there anyway. You have a job to do here. How can I be here with him hurt? Are you willing to let two dozen people on your team down or damage your career to sit in the waiting room? Would my boss let me? Would Stuart want me to?

Slowly the buzzing in my head faded, and I looked up. Detective Latham and Officer Webster were talking with Jack Sandham, my team owner and boss, and Tom Albright, our team media, computer, and everything-else-unassigned guy.

Holly crouched down next to me. "You going to make it, sugar?"

"No alternative." My voice shook.

"This going to stop you from driving?"

"Not getting in the car won't help him. He wouldn't want me to stay out of the car and sit at the hospital." I grabbed Holly's hand. "Would he? Should I be there? I feel like I should be there."

She shook her short, red curls. "He'd tell you not to let your job be another casualty of his accident."

I looked at my feet.

"Time for you to stand up, though." She tugged on my hand. "Come on. They're starting to clear the grid."

When I pulled myself to my feet, everyone closed in again, physically and emotionally. I turned first to Jack. I had to look up a foot and a half to meet him in the eye.

"You okay, Kate?" His voice was low, gruff. At my nod, he blew out a breath. "Do you need—if you need to go to the hospital, I won't stand in your way, but it's problematic. I wouldn't say that, except he's in surgery, and it's not like you can see him anyway." Jack was uncharacteristically flustered.

"I'll stay here now. Later…" I swallowed hard.

"We'll see what happens later," he agreed. "For now, you're third stint in the car. Do you want extra time?"

"Let's stick to the schedule. Let me do my job."

"Business as usual then. Keep me posted on how you're doing." He moved away.

I turned to Tug and the cops. "Thank you for bringing me the news. Tug, who can keep me updated on his condition? Who's at the hospital?"

"Let me have your cell number, and I will call or text." He handed me a business card. "His family is en route, and in the meantime, Polly's there."

I recited my cell number, feeling a flicker of relief. Polly was the office manager for the operations team, helping Stuart and Tug ensure every team, supplier, and sponsor had the information or tools they needed to race. I knew Polly viewed Stuart as a second son. Even better, she knew I was dating him, and I could contact her directly.

Latham recorded my number in his notebook. "We'd like to ask you a few questions."

I had a terrible thought. "Was it an accident?"

"Based on witness accounts, we believe it may have been a deliberate attack."

No one would want to kill Stuart. I had to pause to be sure my voice was steady. "I have no idea what I can tell you, Detective. It doesn't make any sense to me—and I certainly didn't run him down in a jealous rage." I faltered, remembering my last conversation with Stuart wasn't all sunshine and roses.

Webster, the track cop, raised an eyebrow. But before he or Latham could follow up, Tom interrupted.

"Kate, get ready, Zeke's on his way to you." He bounced on the balls of his feet.

I didn't give the cops a chance to argue. "That's SGTV with a live shot. You'll have to wait."

I walked to the front of the Sandham Swift Corvette where Tom had cleared a space for a good camera angle. I took a deep breath. My mind churned with Stuart's condition, the argument I had with him that morning, and what the cops wanted to ask me.

"Tom," I shouted. "Topic?"

He shook his head at my unasked question. "Race only, not Stuart."

Thank God.

Zeke and his cameraman were on final approach. Fifteen feet away. Ten. Five. I took another deep breath.

Showtime.

Chapter Two

"Another benefit of this year's merger between the former American Le Mans Series and Grand-American Road Racing is the appearance of stalwart ALMS teams in not only this race, but also at other iconic tracks and races that were previously part of the Grand-Am schedule." Sports Group Television reporter Zeke Andrews walked slowly backward in my direction, facing the camera.

"One such team," he said, only two steps away now, "is Sandham Swift Racing, a longtime privateer in the ALMS. They're a team that's had their troubles in the past, but has been turning their luck around in recent years, perhaps in part due to the arrival of one Kate Reilly."

He reached me and turned, the camera swinging to capture us both. We stood side-by-side, at roughly equal heights, his talking head blond and tanned, mine black-haired and even more pale-skinned than usual because of the news I'd received.

"Kate," Zeke began, "what do you think are the factors in the team's improved competitiveness over the last couple years—culminating in a second-place finish in the championship last year? And what's the team think about the chance to compete here at the Daytona 24?"

I turned on interview autopilot, smiling at Zeke as the camera moved to focus on me alone. "The only credit I'll claim for Sandham Swift's recent success is for being part of a team that works hard and works well together. In the last year and a half, we've come together and really meshed—from drivers, to crew and mechanics, to the bosses and support staff. We enjoy being out here racing, enjoy the competition, and we're on fire to beat all of them."

Zeke smiled with me. I registered one of my co-drivers for the race, Miles Hanson, approaching from my left. It figured SGTV also wanted to talk to NASCAR's tall, handsome golden boy.

"As for being here at this race?" I looked left and right at the assembled teams and cars on pit lane. "We're excited for what we hope is the first of many, many years. The next twenty-four hours…" I froze as fear crashed down on me. *What's going to happen to Stuart?*

Zeke's eyes widened at my uncharacteristic on-camera fumble. I could see him forming another question as I attempted to speak past the lump in my throat.

Miles stepped into the breach, slinging an arm around my shoulder and drawing the camera's attention. "We're so ready for the next twenty-four hours, we're speechless." He smiled, and we all laughed at his joke before he went on. "They're going to be intense. Exciting. Stressful and probably scary. But amazing. I think that's how the whole team feels. And I'm honored to be here for the first time with such a strong team—strong in team dynamics and on the track. Y'all watch out for us."

Zeke asked Miles a follow-up question about the difference between the stock cars he raced all year in NASCAR and the sportscar he was driving this weekend, and I struggled to keep a pleasant, happy look on my face. I was only partly successful.

Zeke tossed the live feed back to his broadcast partners in the booth and turned to me immediately. "Kate, what's wrong?"

I sagged against Miles' side, and my eyes filled with tears. *Stop it, Kate!*

"Kate?!" Zeke had known me for a dozen years, and he'd rarely seen me cry—tears weren't allowed in Kate Reilly's rulebook.

I took a deep breath and straightened. "Sorry, Zeke. Sorry, Miles, and thanks."

Miles squeezed me in a brief hug and returned to the other side of the car. Zeke's eyes widened in shock as Tom spoke in his ear.

I grabbed Zeke's hand. "If he's telling you about Stuart, don't broadcast it."

He looked hurt. "Don't offend me, Katie-Q." He hauled me in for a quick hug and whispered in my ear. "He's an ass-kicker, Katie. He'll fight this. Hang in there."

I nodded. *Don't cry, don't cry, don't cry.*

Zeke stepped back. Every trace of my pseudo-big brother was gone, replaced by my racing mentor and coach. He put his hands on my shoulders. "Katie, you focus on the race and on doing your best. That's all you can control, so be great. Use your emotion to perform. You hear me?"

I smiled for real this time. "I owe you one."

"Katie-Q, you owe me more than that." His sunny, outrageous smile took up half of his face. "Text me if you need anything else. I'll be in the SGTV broadcast booth for the race." With that, he ran down the pit lane after his cameraman.

I turned back to my team and the car and saw Tom and Holly standing with the police detective and the speedway cop.

Tom waved me over, his curly brown hair already looking unruly and disheveled. "If you sneak out now, you have a few minutes to talk—maybe over in Victory Lane?"

Latham shrugged agreement. I led the cops and Holly past teams forming lines next to their cars. We crossed through the pits into the gated area with a podium wide enough for two dozen people. I stopped and faced the officers, fear and anxiety dragging at me. I wished I could sit down.

"Ms. Reilly, we'll keep this brief." Latham flipped open his notebook.

"Kate," I corrected, studying the two officers. Latham, the DBPD detective, was mid-forties, polished, and obviously in charge. Track-cop Webster was at least fifteen years older and fond of jingling the change in his jacket pocket.

"Kate. Can you walk me through your day?" Latham saw my surprise and held up a hand. "A formality. We ask everyone."

I should have remembered the drill from past investigations I'd been part of—including the one in Connecticut where I'd been prime suspect for a while. "Holly and I drove over from the hotel about nine this morning. Aside from the social media thing in the Fan Zone at ten, we were in the team lounge—the room on the end of the building next to the rear garages—or in the garage until I went to the series driver meeting at eleven thirty-five. After that it was directly to the autograph session in the Fan Zone and out here to the grid."

Webster spoke up. "You were in those places only? Never went anywhere else?"

"The bathroom at the end of our lounge building, that's all."

"Twenty minutes," Holly said. "That's as long as she was ever out of my sight all day. Even then, you were halfway between the garage and the lounge talking to fans, right, Kate?"

"Talking to fans and Stuart," I confirmed.

Holly jammed her fists on her hips and looked at the cops. "She didn't have time to get a car outside the track and run him down."

"Easy, Ms. Wilson," Latham said. "We don't think either of you did. Mr. Sandham and Mr. Albright have already confirmed neither of you could have left the track today. But we do want as full a picture as possible. Kate, when did you see Mr. Telarday and what did you talk with him about?"

My breath hitched and my chest felt constricted. I didn't want to relive the argument that could be the last interaction I'd ever have with Stuart. I heard the on-track announcer introducing the mayor of Daytona Beach, "here to say a few words," as the cops and Holly waited me out.

I swallowed. "It was a few minutes before eleven. He was annoyed with me for canceling dinner with him last night."

"Why did you cancel?" Latham asked.

"I was tired, worried about today. Concerned going out with him would result in more exposure than I wanted." Both men looked confused. "It's not publicly known we've been dating. I like keeping my private life private."

Holly rolled her eyes. "Worst-kept secret in racing."

"I didn't want to deal with it last night."

Latham nodded. "He was angry this morning?"

"Angry is too strong. Annoyed. Irritated." I paused, remembering. "But you know? He was also self-righteous."

"*You* were angry?" Latham asked.

Webster chimed in. "You said something about a jealous rage this morning?"

I opened my mouth for a denial, then reconsidered. "I was angry, hurt, keyed up for the race." I shivered. The chill was only partly from the breeze and cloud cover. "Stuart warned me about misleading photos on a racing blogger's site. He'd gone to the restaurant last night anyway, and a woman involved with a racing team joined him for a drink. At some point, she kissed him—uninvited, he claimed. Someone took photos. He assured me it wasn't what it looked like."

Webster jingled change. "You described him as self-righteous?"

"Maybe I imagined it. But I got a vibe of 'this wouldn't have happened if you hadn't canceled.'"

I answered "no" to the next four questions they asked: did I know the woman from the photos, did I know anyone who had a grudge against Stuart, was there anyone who'd want to hurt him, and did I know why he'd have been off-track at a restaurant this morning. I felt useless.

"You're telling me everyone likes your boyfriend?" Webster looked skeptical.

I looked from Webster to Latham. "My turn. Who's in charge here?" *Why is the Speedway security guy grilling me?*

Webster rolled his shoulders. "We like to handle our own problems at the track. Bigger situations? We call in the City PD, but stay in the loop. Besides, I taught this guy everything he knows."

"Webster was my partner at the police department until he retired last summer," Latham said. "Officially, I'm in charge." He grinned at the older man. "Webster has a hard time letting go."

Webster flushed. "The Speedway's my turf. We've got a short period of time to get answers. No sense sugarcoating everything."

Latham kept smiling. I got the sense it was a well-worn argument.

With a flourish, the announcer introduced the national anthem singer, a minor country-western star. The familiar music rang out.

I checked the time on my phone. "We've got two minutes to a flyover, then the cars start up and roll off. I can't tell you much, and if I'm not going to the hospital—" I took a breath to stop my quivering chin. "I need to get to the pits. Shouldn't you be out trying to find the car or something? Figuring out who did this?"

"We're working on it." Latham flipped his notebook closed. "You know Stuart well. You probably know who he interacts with, works with, likes, and doesn't like—that information can help us. Think about it more." He handed business cards to me and to Holly. "Call or text if you have any thoughts at all."

"Also, any of the security guys can reach me on their radios," Webster added.

My face heated. "I don't mean to put the race above Stuart, but I can't—"

I was drowned out by the early arrival of a C-17 military cargo plane making a low pass above us.

Latham spoke when we could hear again. "It's a lot to take in at once. Give it some thought, and get back to us with any names, ideas, or anything you've got."

Holly patted my shoulder and spoke to him. "We'll be in touch soon."

We left the officers conferring in Victory Lane. As we hustled down the pit lane walkway, we heard the four famous words over the PA, "Drivers, start your engines!"

Sixty-eight cars roared to life. The sound of all that horsepower broke through my anxiety and fired my blood.

Chapter Three

Holly and I joined the flood of drivers and crew washing down pit lane to their team spaces. Each car in the race was assigned one pit space to pull into on the active or "hot" side of pit lane, as well as a corresponding, pole-framed, tented space for team operations on the other side of a low pit wall. We hurried down the crowded walkway behind the tents, sidestepping racks of equipment and golf carts full of people. The buzz in the air was all about Stuart.

"That was fast," I muttered.

"The paddock grapevine is mighty effective."

Four spaces down the lane, Duncan Forsythe from the factory Corvette team, running a pair of new C7.Rs, stopped me with a hand on my arm.

"You take Stuart our best wishes, when you see him, Kate." Duncan leaned close to be heard over the noise of the cars pulling off the grid. "We're all praying for him."

I managed to smile weakly before moving on.

I spoke in Holly's ear. "How does everyone know about Stuart's accident already? And how does Duncan know about my relationship?"

"It's not the secret you think it is, Kate."

"I really hate that."

We saw the answer to my first question in the next pit space we passed. Tug spoke with a small knot of people, dealing out business cards. His somber expression wasn't helped by the gleam of excitement in his eye.

I made a disgusted sound.

The last of the cars exited pit lane. Holly spoke softly in the sudden quiet. "The logical explanation is he's telling people why they won't be able to contact Stuart and to contact Tug instead." She dodged around a flatbed cart loaded with tool chests and car body parts.

"I suppose that's reasonable. But he doesn't have to look like he's enjoying it."

We reached what seemed like a mile of tent for a team running seven cars. One more team space, then Sandham Swift. The pit space would be the team's nerve center for the next twenty-four hours—and the center of my world, even if my heart and thoughts strayed to an unidentified hospital operating room.

Once inside the tent, I joined the other Sandham Swift drivers in front of the array of monitors behind the command center, our largest pit cart—an eight-foot tall, rolling toolbox with two levels of seating on top. Hanging from the upper levels of the cart were fifteen screens, twelve of them showing a camera feed from different corners or vantage points on the track. The remaining three showed the timing and scoring list for the field, the live feed from SGTV's broadcast, and the in-car camera mounted in my number 28 Corvette.

The monitors were vital. All we could see from the pits was a section of the track between the start/finish line and Turn 1. The bank of screens allowed us to track the progress of Sandham Swift's cars around the track almost continuously.

Sandham Swift's three-car pit space was packed tent-wall to tent-wall with crew, drivers, support staff, and guests. We were four-deep in front of the monitors. I wiggled forward to stand next to two of my three co-drivers in the 28 car, Miles Hanson and Colby Lascuola. The fourth member of our driving team—Mike Munroe, my regular co-driver for the full racing season—was behind the wheel, preparing to take the green. Each of Sandham Swift's three cars would be piloted by four drivers taking turns behind the wheel. The car and crew went the full twenty-four hour duration, but individual drivers got to rest between shifts.

Miles patted my shoulder, and Colby smiled as the field paraded by on the front straight. I saw Mike's hands on the in-car camera feed as he swung the wheel back and forth, making the car swerve and hopefully keeping debris off the tires. The ambient car noise died down again as the field processed into the infield portion of the track. One of the other Sandham Swift drivers turned to me.

"Kate, we'll get this out of the way, shall we?" Leon Browning, a twenty-one-year-old Scot who matched me in height and outshined me in sartorial flair, had raced with Mike and me the previous year. He was part of the foursome in the 29 car for this race. While Leon could usually be counted on for a ready joke, he was subdued now. He glanced at the other Sandham Swift drivers, then back at me. "I'm speaking for all of us when I say we're praying for Stuart, and we're ready to support you any way you need."

I looked from Leon to the others, most of whom were watching me and nodding. "I—thanks, but—"

Leon stopped me. "We agreed the best thing is *not* to natter on about updates and such. We'll expect to hear from someone if there's news and expect you to tell us if you need anything at all. Otherwise, we'll speak to you only about racing. Right?"

They understood. Relief and gratitude welled up inside me, and I blinked the corresponding tears back. "Thank you. Sincerely."

A few of the other drivers reached out and patted my shoulder or gave me a thumbs-up. I smiled my thanks.

"Right, then." Leon gave a sharp nod. "Let's one of us go and win this thing."

"I'd settle for survival." *On more than one front.*

The field of cars stretched across four monitors as they made the transition from the infield to the banked turns of the speedway on their second of four laps behind the pace car.

With the cars on the other side of the track, I could hear Tom behind me, obviously answering questions for visitors. "The United SportsCar Championship has two classes of prototypes—those are cars built for racing, not for the street—competing at the same time as two classes of GT sportscars—those are versions of recognizable street vehicles."

I heard a murmur in response, and Tom spoke again. "This race is our 'Big Game,' so everyone wants to drive. That's why you see pros from other types of racing and amateurs who never do anything else all year. Everyone wants to be part of it—and lots of teams add extra cars for it, like we've done."

Jack and the co-owner of the team, Ed Swift, had branched out for this race, fielding a third car for a talented group of three amateur drivers and the pro they'd hired to partner and coach them. That pro was Ian Davenport, a twenty-five-year-old from the IndyCar series and the son of Greg Davenport, Holly's former boss at Western Racing.

As the cars passed the pits again, starting their third lap, Ian nudged Leon out of the way and stood next to me. "We're both in for the third shift."

"What did you have in mind?"

He grinned. "Slowest lap buys the kettle corn. Fastest picks the stands for midnight viewing."

Driving together for the first time this week, Ian and I had discovered two points of remarkable similarity: nearly identical lap times in all driving conditions and massive sweet tooths. We'd stolen a golf cart Thursday afternoon to scout out good race-viewing spots around the track and had agreed to watch a bit of the night action together.

"Have your money ready, big shot," I responded.

"That's Rookie Big Shot of the Year to you." He stuck his nose in the air and flicked imaginary dust from his shoulders.

I couldn't help a chuckle. Ian was the current hot, young thing in the American open-wheel world, taking rookie of the year honors the previous year and even leading the Indy 500 on his first attempt.

Christine—or Chris—Syfert, one of the amateurs driving the 30 car and one of his coaching students, spoke up from his other side. "I wouldn't bet against the woman, Ian. You never know how far we'll go to win a challenge."

"You don't think I've taught you all my tricks, do you?" Ian winked at her.

I turned to the monitors again, picking out the three Sandham Swift Corvettes. The number 28 was a new Corvette Stingray, the C7.R, competing in the GT Le Mans class, for sportscars that adhered to specifications for the 24 Hours of Le Mans. GTLMs were mostly piloted by professional drivers.

In a dramatic upset, Mike had qualified our number 28 second in GTLM behind the pole sitter, a BMW Z4. The shock was our scrappy privateer team, the only privateer running a brand-new Stingray—due to the benevolence of General Motors—out-qualifying the better-equipped and better-funded factory team. Come race time, they wouldn't be behind us for long, but we'd savored the qualifying result.

Sandham Swift's 29 and 30 cars were previous-generation Corvettes, the C6.R, competing in the GT Daytona class. GTDs were run to similar car specifications, for a mix of amateur and pro drivers. Lars Pierson, a regular co-driver of my sister car, the number 29, had qualified that car eighth. Thomas Kendall, the rock-star-turned-racecar-driver and owner of the number 30, had qualified his car fifteenth.

On screen, I noticed the 30 sandwiched by matching silver and purple cars from Arena Motorsports, the mega-team up the way.

I elbowed Ian. "Weren't you having issues with their cars?"

"The 45 and 54 stuck like magnets to ours all week—always around in practice, quali, even tech inspection."

"And now they're ahead and behind you. Coincidence?"

He shrugged. "Seemed like they were there too regularly for that. Then again, there are so many of those team cars, one of them has to be nearby, right? Thomas has been warned to be extra careful of any car with those colors on it."

"I hope he can keep his cool."

"Copy that, Reilly. But I figure, if he can face down fifty thousand screaming fans in a concert, he can stay calm on track, too." Ian scrunched up his face and played an air guitar riff.

I smiled. "You look ridiculous."

"Thomas is giving me lessons, babe. I'm going to be a rock star if this driving gig doesn't pan out."

In his other life, Thomas Kendall was "Tommy Fantastic," the lead guitarist for a multi-platinum rock band. But what Thomas really wanted to do was race, and he did so every time he wasn't on tour. Between Thomas and Miles, Sandham Swift cornered the market on glamour at Daytona.

"Don't quit your day job." I patted Ian on the shoulder.

He shook his head. "Not today, at any rate. Here we go."

Everyone in the pits held their breath. The field of cars formed into pairs around the last turn and headed for the green flag.

Chapter Four

"Green, green, green! We are green for the 24 Hours of Daytona!"

All eyes in Daytona International Speedway focused on the sixty-eight racecars sweeping under the green flag. They crossed the start/finish line as the official clock began its twenty-four hour countdown.

Every one of the hundred-plus people packed into the Sandham Swift tent strained to monitor each twitch and bobble of our Corvettes as they negotiated the melee. I exhaled, my release of tension echoed up and down pit lane. The field got through the narrow, tricky Turn 1 with no accidents.

Holly grabbed my arm. Someone else pointed at the camera feed showing two prototypes shoving each other through Turn 2—only two cars ahead of Mike.

The cars slid off-track driver's left at the approach to Turn 3, the right-handed International Horseshoe. Mike and the rest of the sportscars checked up but weren't impeded. We breathed again.

Mike fought for position. Still second in class. Dogging the back of the BMW on the GTLM pole.

"Easy," I muttered. "It's only the first lap."

As if he'd heard me, the half a car length between Corvette and BMW widened as both cars powered through the Kink,

Turn 4, a flat-out, left-hand bend in the track's inner loop or infield section.

Through the West Horseshoe, Turn 5. One of the prototypes forced off two turns prior sliced through the GTs on his way back to the front. The prototype dove under our 29 Corvette, and a mechanic next to me growled, "Careful there, you sumbitch."

I laughed, provoking a sheepish grin from the mechanic. Daytona was big enough that unless the cars were all on the front stretch, or a car was directly in front of us making a pit stop, we could carry on conversations—and sometimes hear under-the-breath mutterings.

Someone leaned over me to point at one of the screens. The lead BMW had bobbled under braking. Distracted? Missed a shift? Whatever the cause, he drifted wide approaching Turn 6, the left-hander that transitioned from the inner loop to the banked oval track. I tensed as Mike pounced, slipping under him and scooting away into the lead.

"Woohoo!" We all cheered. I high-fived everyone around me. Regardless of what happened in the next twenty-four hours, we'd made a small mark on the race. Heavy emotion settled back on my shoulders, and I felt a flash of guilt for being happy while Stuart was hurt. I focused on the monitors.

Mike had clear road in front of him and the BMW on his tail as he hurtled through the thirty-one degree banking of NASCAR Turns 1 and 2, the oval part of the famed pavement that hosts the Daytona 500. Clean through the Bus Stop—the left-right-right-left wiggle two-thirds of the way down the backstretch, designed to slow us before we reached the other end of the NASCAR oval. Then Mike swung back onto the banking of NASCAR Turns 3 and 4.

He shot past a prototype slowed by a sagging rear tire. The BMW remained tucked up close behind Mike as the pavement leveled out to an eighteen-degree tilt in the tri-oval, the pointy bit in the middle of the front straight. Corvette and BMW flashed under the starter's stand. They barreled down to Turn 1 to start the second lap.

My heart pounded as I watched. Counting down to the braking point in my head, downshifting with Mike. Clear off the oval track banking and into the infield through Turn 1. Turn 2. BMW still behind him but not able to make a move. Turn 3.

I rolled my shoulders. Looked at the clock: 23:58 hours left. *Relax, Kate. Another six or seven hundred laps to go.*

By the fourth lap, the cluster of people in front of the monitors began to break up. Some of the adrenaline dissipated, and crew members wandered off. They prepped for the first round of pit stops, straightened or coiled hoses, and tidied "hospitality world," the three folding tables laden with food in the corner. Holly moved to stand in the entryway of the tent where she had a little breathing room—she wasn't a fan of crowds—and could still keep an eye on the action. Mike continued to lead, fending off the BMW and a Porsche that appeared within another lap to join the fight at the front.

I kept watching the monitors, but I no longer saw the cars. I reviewed memories of Stuart instead. Our post-race dates in different cities. Time spent at his house in Suwanee, Georgia, last October, after the season ended. New Year's Eve together. His frustration yesterday when I told him I needed to be alone for dinner. I was the racecar driver, but he'd moved at top speed in our relationship, leaving me struggling to keep pace. I wondered if I'd have the chance now.

I turned abruptly and blundered through the handful of guests between me and the walkway behind the tent. I needed air. Though open to the cars' pit spaces at the front and to the pit walkway at the rear, the enormous walled tent covering the Sandham Swift setup got stuffy. Or maybe the constant press of people made me feel I couldn't breathe. I felt a drop and tilted my head to the sky. Gray and cloudy overhead. Rain forecast. Plop. Another drop, right on my nose. I closed my eyes and let the sparse blobs of rain soothe my cheeks and eyelids.

Someone hurt Stuart. Don't let them win by damaging you also.

A minute or two later, Holly tapped my arm and handed me a bottle of water.

"Thanks. Having a moment," I said.

"One step at a time."

I downed half the water and turned my face to the sky again. I took deep breaths. Imagined I could feel the air and water flowing through my body, replenishing me. I pulled my cell phone out of my pocket to make sure I hadn't missed any updates. Nothing.

Logically, I knew I couldn't do anything at the hospital. But I still wondered if I should be there. I typed a quick text message to Polly, the Series person at the hospital, begging her to pass along any information.

I'd just hit send when Holly nudged me again and looked up the walkway. "Lookie there, sugar, sidewinders."

"Where? What? Snakes?" I glanced along the endless row of identical, white, canvas pit tents. Crew and guests milled outside the team next door, WiseGuy Racing, fielding a single GTD Mazda.

I turned back to Holly. "Why is Nik Reyes wearing jeans and talking to the guys next door? Shouldn't he be down with his Porsche team?"

"You didn't hear? He lost his ride when the revised driver rankings came out this week and had him ranked too high for his car. But he's not the point. Farther."

I looked again, up pit lane to the sprinkling of people outside the enormous Arena Motorsports tent. One of a pair of tall, handsome, and polished young men turned and caught me watching. He smiled widely and blew me a kiss. His cousin saw his gesture, looked my way, and glowered. I thought I might throw up.

"Snakes," Holly repeated.

"That's what we needed. My vile, good-for-nothing cousins."

"You knew it was possible your uncle—"

"Please. My father's younger brother."

"That he might be racing here. It must be true. And with Team Colossus, no less."

"I don't want to—can't—deal with them. Too much else to focus on." I turned back to our tent. I couldn't make out specific cars on the monitors, but the lack of tension in those watching meant the race was going smoothly for the moment.

"Another friend of yours up there?" Holly asked.

I followed her gaze and saw someone else in the entryway of the Arena tent staring at me. A woman, small and curvy in a fitted, purple, team button-down shirt. She had the kind of full, wavy brunette hair I'd always wanted. A former beauty queen, maybe, since every race paddock was full of those. Her looks were marred by the glare she gave me—like I was dog doo on the bottom of her favorite shoes. "Never seen her before."

"I wonder…" Holly pulled out her phone and looked something up. "That's her, all right."

I glanced over to see the Racing's Ringer site, a blog that covered all people, events, and gossip to do with racing. Run by a racing world-insider, it was known for being accurate and anonymous—to most people.

I knew who the Ringer was, and when I saw him, I was likely to punch him for posting the photos I hadn't wanted to see: shots of a curvy brunette kissing a guy in a bar. My guy.

I snapped my eyes back to the woman up the lane. *That's the bitch who kissed my boyfriend.*

Chapter Five

I'd run into Stuart that morning, not long after I arrived at the track. I'd been in our garage, one of the twenty-two spaces forming the back half of Daytona's main garage, a large V-shaped building.

I'd looked the 28 Corvette over and said good morning to the crew, then headed back to our team lounge. Stuart was walking toward me. We stopped, but didn't touch. I think that irritated him, but I wasn't into public displays of affection yet. If ever.

"Good morning, Kate." His smile was more closed-off than usual. I read affection, annoyance, and something else I couldn't identify.

"Morning." I took a deep breath. "Look, sorry again about last night. I'm nervous about the race."

He watched me silently for a moment before we were interrupted by a team owner stopping to shake Stuart's hand. Stuart turned back to me when the man was gone. "Presumably you had to eat."

He's going to be difficult. "You know the race is my focus, and you know I don't want to make a public statement right before a big race."

"I'm starting to think everyone wants something another person can't give—I want from you, others want from me." He rubbed his eyes behind his tortoiseshell glasses. "This isn't a good time or place for this conversation—especially when we won't cover ground we didn't cover the other twenty-seven times." He looked into the distance down the garage lane and ran a hand through his hair, dislodging locks onto his forehead.

"But I need to tell you two things," he continued. "One, your reluctance to be seen with me outside the racetrack by anyone in the racing fraternity—or to be seen looking anything more than business-like with me at any time—makes me question how much you care about this relationship."

I tensed, feeling heat in my neck and face. Anger? Shame? I wasn't sure.

He searched my face before speaking again. "Two, you're going to find photos online of another woman and me kissing at the restaurant last night."

Anger, that was it. "What?" I'd yelled.

Stuart looked speculative, not guilty.

"What the hell are you telling me, Stuart?"

"There was…an incident last night. And a camera caught it."

"An incident?" I yelled that too, then lowered my voice. "You're cheating on me with someone else, and you call it 'an incident?'"

He reared back as if surprised, then recovered. "I didn't initiate it, and I stopped it immediately. I didn't want it. But it happened."

Did he lead her on? Did he flirt? Was it retaliation for me canceling? "Why would you tell me like that? Like you did want it?"

He pulled his phone out and glanced at it. He raised an eyebrow. "Maybe I wanted to know if you'd care."

As I gaped at him, my ears getting hot, he reached out a hand to another passerby who'd veered his direction. "Vinny, I meant to tell you earlier, I'm glad to see you're making connections in the paddock."

The trim, dark-haired man shaking Stuart's hand looked confused. "Sorry?"

Stuart smiled. "I saw you and Richard Arena talking last night outside the Chart House restaurant. You couldn't find a better resource for understanding how to operate a world-class racing team here."

The other guy smiled and nodded, glancing at me quickly, then looking back to Stuart. He uttered some kind of pleasantry and took off down the paddock. I didn't pay attention because I was still steaming over Stuart's news. And how he'd chosen to deliver it.

Stuart slipped his phone back in his pocket and finally met my eyes again. "Sorry, Kate, I'm late to meet someone who actually wants something from me. Have a good race."

Before I could form words, much less come up with more questions or a comeback, he was gone.

I'd scurried into the team lounge and huddled with Holly, telling her about the interaction and deliberately not searching for the photos online. She made all the right noises until I'd calmed down. Then she burst my bubble.

"He does have a point, you know."

I gasped. "Whose side are you on?"

"Yours, of course. But it's not surprising he'd wonder how committed you are, if you won't be open about dating him."

I couldn't argue with that. "But kissing someone else, Holly?"

"I'm not saying that's right—but neither did he, from what you tell me."

"That's what he *said.*"

"Given he's not a habitual liar, believe him. Who knows what happened? You know how racing groupies are, they'll take any chance to get close to someone with power, money, or fame."

I'd felt better after Holly's words. I'd resolved to put the matter out of my head to focus on the race. But now I stood in the pit walkway, the race in full swing, confronted by the woman in question. A gorgeous woman who looked like no desperate race groupie I'd ever seen. She looked confident, in charge, and scornful. Of me.

I felt like I'd taken a knife to the gut. *Maybe he preferred her to me. Maybe he didn't want to deal with me anymore.*

I shook my head and looked away from her, back to Holly. "The world makes no sense today. First Stuart's hurt and now *she's* mad at *me*?" I threw my empty water bottle in the trash barrel next to us. "I'm taking a walk over to the real bathrooms."

"I'll go with you, then run up and see Greg at Western Racing."

After our stop at the restroom building above Victory Lane— an improvement over the port-a-potties that were closer and more convenient to the pits—I followed Holly up to the top end of pit lane, the pit-in end, to her old team. She'd worked for Western for the past five years as the team's hospitality coordinator or "team mom," keeping the paddock and pit areas stocked with food and drinks for crew, drivers, and guests. Keeping everything working. Aunt Tee played the same role for Sandham Swift.

But a change in fortunes for both Western and me had prompted Holly to switch jobs. Western's owner, Greg Davenport, had lost a key sponsor in the economic downturn, and he'd had trouble making a commitment to go racing this year—a fact not helped by the merger of what used to be two separate racing series, which created a shortage of spaces on racing grids. Greg made it here to Daytona, but he'd had to downsize—from two cars to one, from more staff to less.

At the same time, I'd gotten busier, with commitments to the Sandham Swift team and sponsors, but also to my personal sponsor, the Beauté cosmetics company, and the charity they supported, the Breast Cancer Research Foundation. I needed help, and Holly and I agreed to try her out as a combination personal assistant, manager, and public relations person. So far, so good, but I knew she missed her family at Western Racing. That they missed her was evident from the hugs all around when she appeared in their pit space.

After greeting Holly, Greg gave me a gentler version of his bear hug and expressed gruff condolences about Stuart. He reminded me of my grandfather: short and stocky, with a full head of white hair. But where Gramps was usually jovial, more like a goofy leprechaun, Greg Davenport was morose, taciturn. Not without reason.

The loss of one of his two main sponsors was the latest straw in a terrible decade for him—the only bright spots being the success his son Ian was having as a pro driver and the blossoming career of his daughter, Jennifer, as a race engineer. Greg had lost his wife to a season-long bout with cancer four years ago and had struggled through the intervening years in the ALMS, where the landscape got more complex every year. New teams, new cars, tougher competitors—all had conspired to produce only marginal results for a team that once won a GT championship. Then the Series merger, and sponsor, supplier, and entry problems.

I remembered Greg when he was cheerful, ebullient. It had been a long time. At this race, even his pit space looked depressed and disheveled. Tires were stacked neatly near the pit wall, but other equipment was scattered here and there without obvious organization. It was a far cry from the polished, professional opulence of the Arena Motorsports setup—or even Sandham Swift's mismatching but complete set of tools and supplies.

Reduced circumstances notwithstanding, Greg was warm and friendly, at least until his attention returned to the racetrack. Then his animated face settled into a sneer.

"How's the car running, Greg?" Holly asked.

He shrugged. "Not as fast as some. But we're fighting."

"You have consistency and reliability," I said.

He gestured toward the pile of body parts in the corner of the pit space. "But no hope on speed while running last year's car. There was no laying my hands on new cars, not with moneybags buying them all."

Holly raised an eyebrow. "Arena?"

"Buying his way into everything—the series, the paddock, the race."

"He's bringing lots of cars and sponsors, right?" I asked. "Isn't that good for the series? For racing?"

"Sure, if you want him to shut out the teams like me. Those of us who do it because we love the sport but can't come up with a seven-car battalion for this race." Greg shook his head.

"If that's what the Series wants, I won't be around long. And they'll be sorry when I'm gone. Especially if one of their rich, fumbling amateurs runs me out."

Holly put her hand on his arm. "They haven't told you they want you out, have they? They can't want to lose you and the others who've been so loyal to the ALMS and Grand-Am over the years."

Greg glanced at me. "No one's said it to my face, but actions speak louder than words." He patted Holly's hand and grinned, the old mischievous twinkle in his eye turning fierce. "But I promise you, if I go, I won't go quietly. They'll know how I feel."

Holly laughed. "I'll bring the popcorn."

"I'm not kidding." His smile faded. "I'm starting to question why I'm doing this. Why all this effort and expense? Ian and Jennifer have their own careers launched now. I'm asking myself if this is fun anymore. I'm not sure I've got the answers yet."

I thought if he was asking those questions, he shouldn't be in the game anymore. But Greg had to come to that decision on his own.

Once outside the Western Racing pits, Holly agreed with me. "I've never seen him so down on racing. Even after his wife died, he still felt like racing was his family." She looked worried. "I'm afraid for him if he feels like he's lost this, too."

Chapter Six

We wandered back down the pit walkway under a spattering of raindrops toward Sandham Swift, peeking into other team setups where we could, and keeping out of the way of crew members on the run. One driver nearly ran us over from behind. He was tall and graying-blond, a fifty-something businessman convinced of his own self-importance based on the way he paid no attention to anyone around him. He brushed roughly between us, charging down the walkway from garage to pits—sporting an Arena Motorsports firesuit.

I spoke close to Holly's ear. "Are they all complete jerks under that team tent?"

"So far, yes."

Without planning, as we passed Arena's pits we slowed our pace, watching, but trying to not look like we were staring. From their enormous chunk of pit lane, Arena fielded two GTLM Porsches with all-pro driver lineups and five GTD Porsches piloted by a mix of pros and amateurs—emphasis on the gentlemen drivers who'd paid to race.

A team effort that large seemed excessive—like flaunting one's wealth. Particularly when there were teams, or so the rumor mill ran, that couldn't secure sponsors, a competitive car, or an entry to the race. On the other hand, I had to admire the business savvy that could make a success of racing on that scale. The logistics alone were staggering, considering each car required four to five drivers and eight to ten crew members, not to mention car chiefs, engineers, and hospitality workers for the team as a whole. Arena had more drivers than many one- and two-car teams had on their entire staff.

It wasn't the size and scope of the Arena empire that made the rest of us in the paddock wary. No, that resulted from the personality of the team: closed off, uncommunicative, and downright unfriendly. Not to mention more than your run-of-the-mill racing arrogance unleavened by humor or kind words for anyone else.

But they took care of their own. The whole team had the very best and newest equipment, all painted silvery gray with purple accents. Multiple pit carts, two full sets of monitors displaying every track camera feed, and team-logoed cloth director's chairs. Everything clean and unblemished. Sparkling. They also used every inch of possible space—even filling the pit walkway with carts and spreading tables and equipment out under the stands behind the tent.

"Are they using space belonging to the team next door?" I gestured to the area under the VIP stands.

Holly shrugged. "Typical."

"Isn't that inappropriate?"

"Everyone who's ever next to them complains about how the Arena team encroaches on their space. Greg measured their tent one time, and it was six inches wider than the regulation. That's why everyone next to them always feels squeezed."

"Why bother for that little space?"

"If what's important is being bigger, newer, and flashier, no effort is too great."

I frowned. "Doesn't anyone complain?"

"Plenty have tried. Never goes anywhere. In fact, it's likely to boomerang on you—like when Greg was next to them at the Mid-Ohio race last year," she explained in a low voice. "They'd pushed the trash cans over in front of Greg's team, like usual, and Greg had no space to pull a golf cart in front of his tent without blocking the exit for his cars. So he centered the trash cans on the line dividing his space from Arena's. To do that, he moved two of Arena's folding chairs out of the way about a foot."

"Seems reasonable."

She laughed. "You'd think. A woman on the team named Monica—who, now I think about it, must be your Miss Precious over there—threw a hissy fit, calling the Series in, pointing to a broken chair, and claiming Greg had damaged their property."

"A folding chair."

"Not only had he damaged their property," Holly went on, "but Monica claimed he was also trying to intimidate and bully them. Greg says she kept spouting off about knowing her rights and going to the Series, rulebook in hand, because it wasn't fair for one team or owner to harass others. She wasn't going to stand for the team being discriminated against."

"Discriminated against? Because she's a woman?" I shook my head. "They're careful about that. I should know."

"I'm not sure. Maybe because she's female? Maybe it's Arena's ethnicity—or hers? Maybe he's gay, I don't know."

"If you don't, does anyone?"

Holly shrugged.

"How could someone be discriminated against for something people aren't aware of?" I wondered.

"Sugar, I'm not saying it makes sense."

"And how can she possibly claim harassment or bullying when they're going over the boundaries of their own space and pushing trash cans around?"

"No one's proven those actions, we simply all *know*. Plus, all it takes is nerve to claim to be the victim of the same thing you do to others. Nerve and blindness to your own hypocrisy."

"Or not caring you're a hypocrite."

Before we reached the end of the Arena tent, a golf cart barreled toward us down the walkway. We pressed ourselves back against the fence, still observing the team. Every single person under the Arena tent wore team colors—whether firesuits, polo shirts, button-downs, or long parkas. One car's crew hurried around, prepping for a pit stop.

I shook my head. "I guess it's good Greg's not next to them this weekend."

At one end of the giant tent, I spied my cousins talking with a nondescript, clean-cut guy in a green shirt and two beefy guys in sport coats, jeans, and expensive-looking western boots. As I watched, Tug Brehan approached the group, shook hands, and visibly preened in response to a comment from the guy in green. I looked away quickly, hoping they didn't see me.

"Time to get out of enemy territory," I muttered.

Holly glanced at the Arena pit cart nearest us. "Isn't that your new best friend?"

Monica, the home-wrecker—if Holly had her name right—sat at one end of the pit cart next to four men, all facing the track with their backs to us. Three of the men hunched over laptop monitors. The man next to her sat tall and straight, watching the monitors hanging above his head. Given his "I'm the boss" aura, I assumed he was Richard Arena.

"Think she has an actual role with the team?" I nudged Holly to move along.

"She's not here as someone's girlfriend if last night she was—" Holly stopped when I glared at her. "Not saying it doesn't make it go away, Kate."

I didn't want to think about the woman kissing Stuart. I didn't want to think about Stuart in the hospital. I wanted to think about him well and healthy. I refused to imagine the alternative—I couldn't, not while I was in the middle of the artificial, manufactured world of the twenty-four-hour race day. I pulled out my phone and typed another plea for information to Polly at the hospital.

Between the Arena expanse and our smaller Sandham Swift tent was a one-car team space similar to Western Racing. The WiseGuy Racing Mazda was out on track, and a small crew gathered around four monitors set up on a folding table behind a smallish pit cart. It was another modest, but stalwart, operation and a team name I recognized as having participated in Grand-Am for many years. I hoped their story was more positive than Greg's. I wondered if we'd see them the rest of the season.

We finally reached Sandham Swift again and nodded hellos to the crew. Holly made a beeline for the disheveled food table and started tidying and refilling supplies from coolers and boxes under the cloth drape. I headed for the far end of the pit space, where I saw Colby sitting, balaclava and helmet in front of her, on one of the smaller pit boxes.

A step later, I tripped over Cooper Whiteside, clad in black and bent over a tub of equipment. Cooper was one of the two spotters on the 28 car who would spend the entire race at the top of the Daytona Speedway tower building, keeping us updated on traffic.

He shook his head at my apology, his hands full of radios and headsets. "No harm done. I'm not usually underfoot once the race starts. The 29 car's spotters are having radio issues, so I offered to run over for extras. Millie and I—" he referred to his wife and spotter-partner for our car "—will be ready to swap units if something goes wrong with the primary."

I was impressed with the planning and forethought that went into every aspect of the race team. We had contingency plans for the driver not hearing radio communications or the pits not hearing the driver. Now we had a backup plan if spotters were unable to communicate. "Good idea. Talk to you later, Coop."

"I'll be on when you get in."

I made it to the far end of the pit and climbed up next to Colby. I waited for a racecar that putted down pit lane, then turned to her. "Any word from Mike on the car?"

"He says the car's still good, and the traffic is crazy," Colby reported. "Track's already messy at the exit to the Bus Stop. Dampness forming offline."

"He's staying on slicks, right?" Those were the dry-weather tires, with a slick, smooth surface and no treads. We also had the option of intermediate tires, or "inters," with a few grooves cut in them for something between wet and dry track. Rain tires, or "wets," had lots of grooves for channeling away water on the surface of the track. I hadn't felt enough rain in pit lane to require either inters or wets.

Colby nodded. "Still dry on the racing line. Jack's radar says we'll get rain at some point, though. Hopefully not in my stint."

I grinned. I was driving the car after her. "Leave the rain to me." I'd come to terms with racing in the rain over the past year—having done it just enough in the Corvette to build confidence in my ability to feel the car's grip.

"I like rain, but you've had this car out in it before." The pit cart rocked, and Colby looked at the man climbing two steps and settling down next to me. "Right, Miles?" She shouted to him, to be heard over the noise of a prototype passing us in pit lane. "We'll leave the rain to Kate?"

Miles snickered. "As long as I'm not out there at the same time."

My introduction to Miles had involved the rain, multiple impacts, and broken cars during a race in Wisconsin last year. We'd both tried to take the same line through Road America's notorious Kink at about 120 miles per hour, which hadn't turned out well for either of us. I'd fared better than Miles, at least physically. He'd broken a collarbone and lost out on a chance at NASCAR's season championship. I'd spent two weeks as the most hated woman in America—or that's how it felt at the time. It hadn't helped that later the same day as the accident, I'd found an old friend dead.

The story had a happy ending—mostly. I'd solved two murders, Miles had recovered and won the last two races of his season, and once Racing's Ringer stopped hounding me, the rest of the blogosphere and NASCAR Nation slowly let go of their "Kate hate." To my surprise, Miles and I became friends, which led to him joining Sandham Swift for this race.

An even bigger surprise was Miles and Holly ending up more than friends. I still wasn't used to my best friend dating a guy who'd been named *People* magazine's most eligible bachelor—twice.

He'd treated her well so far, I admitted, as she climbed up the side of the pit box and Miles hauled her onto his lap. But I had personal experience that proved one shouldn't trust drivers who reached celebrity heights.

I saw movement in my peripheral vision and discovered the reason for my mistrust standing in the Sandham Swift tent opening. He surveyed the scene and caught sight of me, then smiled and started forward.

Cornered. Nowhere to run or hide. I'd avoided him successfully for the past three days, but no longer.

Sam Remington, NASCAR rock-star. My ex-boyfriend, ex-love, ex-almost-fiancé.

Chapter Seven

I slid past Colby and climbed down from the pit box. *Why the hell did you have to descend from NASCAR mountain to run this race, Sam? This is my turf now, and you can't make me feel inadequate here. Not ever again.* I felt a flare of frustration. *Besides, who cares about your ego when Stuart's facing real problems?*

I pasted a smile on my face and moved forward to meet Sam. He was as handsome as ever, with blue eyes that seemed to smile on their own and a way of focusing as if you were the only person who mattered in the world. Curly dark hair you wanted to run your fingers through. A charming, disarming grin. A total package that made women swoon for no single, identifiable reason other than "handsome and approachable."

I stopped two feet away and stuck out my hand. I wasn't going the hug-and-kiss route. "Hi, Sam."

He looked from my eyes to my hand, surprised. Then he shook, wrapping my much smaller hand in both of his. He looked delighted. "Kate. It's so good to see you. I tried to find you the last couple days, but kept missing you."

That was my plan. I smiled and tucked my hand in my firesuit pocket, out of reach. "Good to see you, too. Congratulations on last year." He'd placed third in NASCAR's season championship. Not bad for only his fourth year in the big leagues.

He hung his head the way millions of women—minus me—found endearing. "Thanks. It was a hell of a run. Great team. I've been lucky." His face lit up. "But wow, you've been on a tear. I'm so happy for you. So proud of you—the team, race results, the sponsorship deal. Congratulations."

I hesitated. I could respond with: "How dare you be proud of me when you didn't think my career would be worth anything?" or "Why would you care when you're more interested in a woman who supports your dreams than a woman with her own?" I considered all the accusations and cutting remarks I'd practiced over the years when imagining this conversation.

I let them go. "It's been a good year for me, too. I guess you never know what the future will hold."

"You sure don't. Look, Kate, is there somewhere we could talk more privately? I wanted to…" he paused, wrung his hands, and finally finished with, "catch up a little."

Perhaps he'd meant to say "explain" or "apologize." Maybe "beg forgiveness" or "grovel." I didn't care. The action around us saved me. All three crews had been quietly prepping for pit stops for the last fifteen minutes, and now they stepped up the activity, pulling on helmets and uncoiling hoses. At the same time, Tug Brehan ducked into the tent and made a beeline for Jack on the central pit box. *Stuart?* My heart leapt into my throat.

I looked at Sam. "Now isn't a good time." If I had my way, there'd never be a good time.

Then Holly and Miles were next to me, Miles reaching out to shake hands with Sam.

"I'll catch up with you later then, Kate," Sam said. "I'm up with Carnegie Performance Group if you can stop by."

"Sure. See you on the track." I walked over to stand next to Colby near the pit box where Tug spoke with Jack.

Colby dragged her attention to me as I approached. "Wow, Sam Remington. Friend of yours?"

"My ex."

She glanced at Sam, who was still a few feet away, chatting with Miles and Holly. "You let *that* get away?"

"He's attractive."

"Are you kidding me? Try gorgeous and *hot*." She growled a little bit.

I laughed, probably for the first time all day. It felt good. "You're welcome to him, Colby. But I'll warn you, he wants a support system, not an equal partner. That's why he's my ex."

Her eyes narrowed. She looked from me to Sam again. Then back to me. "Much less hot now." She turned back to face the track.

I saw Tug finish with Jack and look around. He reached me just as the crew stepped onto the low wall between the hot and cold sides of the pits.

"Have you—Stuart?" That was all I could force out through my suddenly dry throat.

He shook his head. "No word yet, I'm sorry. I'll tell you personally or text the minute I know anything."

I swallowed, trying to force my heart rate to slow down.

"We did want to talk with you for a moment, Kate," Tug went on.

I finally realized he had a woman with him, who'd followed him through the tent and stood next to us.

I apologized to her and introduced myself.

"Elizabeth Rogers." She shook my hand with the grip of a limp fish. I wondered again why more people didn't value a good handshake the way they valued orthodontia or clear skin.

I saw our lollipop—the car number on a long stick waved out in the hot pit lane to orient the driver—start to move and knew we were seconds away from the car's arrival.

"After the pit stop?"

Tug and Elizabeth nodded, and I studied them as we waited.

Tug wore the most expensive brands, latest trends, and even regulation Series attire with a flair that made some men assume he was gay. Women knew better, recognizing the glint in his eye that signaled a deep appreciation of females as a species. His chatty, almost flowery conversational style didn't counteract the suspicions most men harbored about him. But it put women at ease.

Tug and Stuart had competed for the job Stuart eventually won. When the American Le Mans Series and Grand-American Road Racing officially merged into the United SportsCar Championship at the end of last season, there were two qualified people to fill every one new job. In the face-off between two heads of operations, Stuart had come out the winner with multiple years of vice presidential experience at the ALMS.

Tug Brehan, twenty-seven and new to the job in Grand-Am, had accepted the role as Stuart's second-in-command. Tug had been a friendly team-player the two times I'd met him, though the puffed-up, self-important vibe I got from watching him work pit lane was new. Or maybe I didn't know him very well.

I hadn't met Elizabeth before. She was decked out in a Series shirt and radio headset, so she had some role at the race. Compared to Tug, however, she was less everything. Less stylish, less outgoing, less warm. She wasn't unfriendly or unattractive, but she suffered in comparison to the charm and style Tug possessed. She was plain standing next to him, with her unpolished fingernails and shoulder-length straight blonde hair held back by a headband, of all things. Not to mention the neutral, unmoving expression on her face. Everything about her projected, "I am serious and focused."

I snapped out of my daze as the 28 car jerked to a stop in front of us, the 29 and 30 cars arriving behind it within seconds. All three crews leapt into motion, filling the cars with fuel and putting on fresh tires.

Jack's strategy was to dive right into double stints for each driver—each stint representing anywhere from thirty to sixty minutes, which was the most we could do on a full tank of fuel. The exact time was dependent on yellow flags, because if caution flew past the halfway point of a fuel load, we'd pit under yellow. Each driver would do triple stints or more later in the race, especially in the late-night and early-morning hours, but to get our feet wet, we started with about two hours of driving time, give or take those yellow flags.

Thirty seconds later, Mike had pulled out of the pits, the 29 and 30 cars following shortly after.

An SGTV pit reporter appeared in their wake, speaking into the microphone. The reporter turned, zeroing in on Jack leaning off the side of the pit box to talk to a crew member. I narrowed my eyes at the reporter. *Hello, Scott Brooklyn. We will talk later.*

But first, I gestured Tug and Elizabeth out to the walkway behind the tent, to be out of the way of crew members recoiling hoses and refilling fuel tanks. I grabbed a bottle of water on the way and waited for them to tell me what they wanted.

Tug opened his mouth to speak, but reached for his phone instead. He looked at me. "News from the hospital."

Chapter Eight

3:10 P.M. | 23:00 HOURS REMAINING

I grabbed Tug's arm. "How is he?"

Holly was next to me in an instant. Tug glanced around, making sure only the three of us could hear him. "The first part of the surgery is done, to relieve pressure on his brain." He typed something into his phone.

"The first part?" Holly repeated. "How many more will there be?"

Tug shook his head. "Not sure."

"And he's—still…" I fumbled.

He looked at me. "He's still alive. They're not guaranteeing anything, but making it through the first surgery is a good sign." He checked his phone again. "There will be other surgeries to fix his broken bones. They might need to induce a coma to give the brain more time to heal."

Cars buzzed around the track as I tried to imagine Stuart lying still in a quiet, sterile hospital room, fighting for his life. The comparison was almost obscene. I covered my face with both hands and breathed deeply.

I felt my cell phone vibrate in my pocket, a message from Polly assuring me she'd send word and repeating the same news Tug had delivered.

Tug spoke again. "His parents are on their way down from

Boston to be at the hospital—though it'll be a while before he can have any visitors, depending on how things go."

What am I doing here? I should be there. Shouldn't I?

Tug must have read the confusion on my face. "At this point, no one can see him. Then it will be family only. I can let you know if that changes."

I felt numb. Elizabeth stood there with her arms at her sides, a look of mild curiosity on her face. That irritated me.

I drew in a breath, squaring my shoulders. "What can I do for you, Elizabeth? Tug?"

They glanced at each other, and Tug spoke, smiling. "Our point was to make sure you knew how to contact us and to make you aware of the current situation at the hospital. I'm glad we had up-to-the-minute news for you. I was able to call in Elizabeth to help me this weekend in Stuart's absence—since she worked for me at last year at Grand-Am, she's familiar with most of the players. She will also have all updates on Stuart, so if you can't find me for some reason, you can reach out to her."

She handed me an old Grand-Am business card with a cell number circled and finally spoke. "We're touching base with each team to make sure they know who to contact if they need anything."

The two of them work fast. Stuart isn't—don't go there, Kate.

Holly smiled at Elizabeth. "How convenient you were able to take the last-minute call today."

"Lucky for all of us," Tug put in.

Holly made a "hmm" sound. "Everything going well so far?"

Elizabeth smiled, and I was surprised by the change in her appearance. She lit up. "We're keeping all the plates spinning. Solving the little problems, keeping everyone happy."

Tug clasped his hands together. "Excellent. We'll—"

He was interrupted by two men charging toward us. Charging toward *me*. I flinched, moving behind Holly for protection—scant, as we were the same size—then saw everyone else smiling at them.

"A photo, please!" The two men waved cameras.

"It is Calamity Kate!"

"The boo-tiful Calamity Kate, with the makeup!"

Seriously? I'm not done with that yet? In the middle of his hate-campaign, Racing's Ringer had bestowed the nickname on me. I couldn't argue the nickname wasn't appropriate at the time, but it didn't originate in humor or goodwill.

The men in front of me, however, found it hilarious. They were in their late-twenties, round-faced, beefy, and Russian. They'd have been the perfect caricatures of young Slavic thugs, except for their ear-to-ear grins, cameras, and boisterous good spirits. I still wasn't sure I'd want to meet them in a dark alley, but that had more to do with having spotted them with my cousins under the Arena tent.

"Please, a photo, so we send to our mother and sister," the first one said.

"They reading about you and say why we never meet you," added the second one. He had a squarer face and thinner hair. Otherwise, they were superficially the same: medium height, solid muscle, close-trimmed brown hair, brown eyes. Plus huge grins and bad teeth.

The first one spoke again. "I am Pyotr—spelled with y-o-t. This is Vladimir. We Twitter this."

Of course they were and of course they would. I looked a question at Holly.

"Harmless. Mostly," she murmured, as the brothers turned to Tug and Elizabeth and enthusiastically greeted them.

Tug took the opportunity to extricate himself. "Let me know if there's anything at all you need."

I thanked him and returned Elizabeth's half smile and wave as they left.

Then I turned to the brothers. "How did your mother and sister hear about me?"

Vladimir kept smiling. "Our sister Sofia, she is racecar driver. Our mother is manager. Go with Sofia, in Russia. They read on Racing's Ringer." He pronounced the Rs way back in his throat. It sounded more sinister that way.

Holly chuckled as she took their cameras and aimed them at the three of us, the look in her eye telling me I wouldn't live this down. The Ringer had a lot to answer for. Again.

A brown-haired guy wearing a friendly, open expression and a green Benchmark Racing polo shirt hustled down the walkway. He walked the same way teenage boys and Tom, our media guy, did: rolling up onto the balls of his feet at every step, as if he had springs under his heels.

Once the photos were done, he offered his hand to me. "Vinny Cruise, nice to meet you. I hope these two—" he hooked a thumb in the Russians' direction "—aren't taking too much of your time, after they gave me the slip." He grinned, softening the accusation.

I introduced myself and Holly, assuring him all was well. I remembered seeing Vinny that morning while I was talking to Stuart. My stomach clenched. *Stuart's hanging in there, Kate, keep it together.*

"We do not bother these lovely ladies," Pyotr protested. "We only take photos to send home."

Vinny laughed. "More photos. But you shouldn't miss your car's next pit stop, which will be very soon."

"*Hola, Vicente,*" a passing driver called out. "Don't you know your space is at the other end of pit lane?"

Vinny grinned and did the part-handshake, part-embrace, all-back-slapping thing guys did. "Hey, *amigo*. I'm only here for a visit." He turned to the rest of us. "Have you all met Raul?"

I hadn't met Raul, but I'd seen him. I figured him for late twenties, with the standard driver's height and build. Not much else was ordinary. His lush, black hair curled onto his collar, and his black eyes held laughter and secrets. Add to that an expressive, friendly face and dimples, and Raul Salas was hard to miss. Honestly, he made me a little shivery inside, especially when he took my hand and looked into my eyes to tell me how delighted he was to meet me.

You have no business feeling shivery with a race to run and a boyfriend in the hospital, Kate.

I pulled myself together and gently retrieved my hand. "Nice to meet you, too, Raul. Who are you driving with?"

"Redemption Racing, also at the other end of pit lane. I'm down here to see a friend in a Porsche team." He smiled, and the dimples made my insides flutter. "I look forward to chatting more in the future."

I made a noncommittal response and Mr. Temptation took himself off down the walkway.

Pyotr and Vladimir stepped forward to give me loud, smacking kisses on both cheeks. "We see you in pits, Kate Calamity! But please, you try not to hit our car." They left, laughing uproariously as they loped up the walkway.

Vinny followed, chuckling and waving good-bye. I had a vision of a terrier trying to keep two bull moose in line.

I turned to Holly. "Filthy rich team owners and their minder?"

She dabbed at her eyes from laughing so hard. "Vinny's the guy running that team, but you pegged the brothers."

After a tire cart went past us, loaded with worn, gunked-up rubber fresh off a racecar, Holly and I crossed back to our tent to watch the monitors. Mike was maintaining second in class—though the two factory Corvettes crept ever closer. The race was still green into the second hour.

A crew member pointed me to the pit wall, and I walked around the front side of the command center to find Scott Brooklyn waiting. I paused, then approached him. I got close enough no one else could hear. "Am I talking to the SGTV pit reporter or…?"

"I'm on the clock for SGTV. But what I do off the clock with what I hear on the clock?" He shrugged.

"I'm warning you, I'm not a fan today. What do you want?" I shouldn't have been so abrupt or unfriendly with a member of the television crew that covered the race, but Scott and I had history. I didn't completely trust him. I hoped he knew better than to try to cause me trouble.

A hurt look flickered across his face. "Regardless, I'm here because the word's out about Stuart's accident. The bosses want me to ask if you'd talk about it on camera."

"No." I barely let him finish.

"I don't blame you. I told them you'd say that." He saw the look on my face. "Really. They told me to ask, so I asked. You said no. End of story."

I turned to go.

"But Kate?"

He had a smirk on his face when I looked back.

"If you do want to say anything—on camera or anonymously—let me know." He winked. "I'm your guy."

I rolled my eyes and returned to stand next to Holly at the monitors. My cell phone buzzed in my pocket again, and my breath hitched. *More news from surgery, already?*

I was unprepared for what I saw when I looked at my phone. My knees dissolved, and I collapsed onto a nearby chair.

A text message from Stuart.

Chapter Nine

Holly plucked the phone from my numb hands. Her jaw dropped. "For heaven's sake." She tapped the screen and read the message. "Someone's got his phone. It's not Stuart. Someone else."

I read the message. I'm a friend of Stuart's. I need to tell you what happened, and I need your help.

Are you kidding me? I typed in response. Who are you and why do you have his phone?

A minute later. Friend. Reporter. I saw Stuart get hit. His phone landed near me. I took it and ran.

I gasped and typed back. You RAN?? You didn't call for help or go help him? How dare you?

Hang on.

I stared at the phone, waiting for more and shaking with anger.

Another message. I called for help, so did a bunch of others. People were helping him. I ran because I didn't want to be another target.

What do you mean…My typing was interrupted by a fresh response.

I ran because someone tried to kill me last night. Like they tried to kill Stuart this morning. It wasn't an accident.

Holly sat down next to me, and I handed her the phone. She shook her head. "I hope he told this to the cops."

I took the phone back and typed that message.

Whoever was on the other end replied. Not yet. I will, but I need to finish my article first. Other people saw what happened better than I did. I might know some of why, but I need to put it all together first. I'll talk to the cops tomorrow.

My thumbs flew. I'm telling them, if you won't. What's so important it's worth not catching the person who did this? I grew more furious with every response from the jackass on the other end.

Tell them. I'll talk to them tomorrow. One day won't make a difference. Especially when I expose the fraud and illegal activities going on in Richard Arena's businesses.

It was too much. What does exposing that team have to do with finding a hit-and-run driver? I typed. Are you saying Arena did this to Stuart? And why are you messaging me?

"Seriously," I muttered. "Why me? Why now, when I've got to drive soon?"

Someone in that organization had to have been responsible, he responded. You because I hear you're the only trustworthy person in the paddock. Plus you're dating Stuart. You deserve to know this was attempted murder, not an accident. You can help me get the bastards responsible.

I blinked and typed. Who are you?

His explanation continued. I need your help seeing who's there at the race with the team. Connections between Arena and other organizations or companies. Someone in the Arena team thinks Stuart knows something. I want to figure out what that is and prove who tried to kill him. I can't get close. They know me. Afraid they'll try to kill me also. Again.

My head spun, and I typed back. This is a joke, right? You're pranking me?

No prank, for real. Turning off now, will text later.

I texted again. TELL ME YOUR NAME OR I WON'T HELP YOU. I shook my head. "Unbelievable."

I stared at the monitors for a few minutes, not really seeing the cars, trying to process the text conversation.

Colby walked over and stood in front of the bank of screens. She was suited up, helmet on, and ready for her turn behind the wheel. The on-deck driver was supposed to be in the pits as soon as the previous driver got in the car, so there was always a backup in case the person in the car had a problem. Past the midway point of a sixty-minute stint, we could be called on to get in the car at any moment. When we were on-deck, we were suited up in our fire-retardant head socks, or balaclavas, and helmets by thirty minutes into the other driver's stint.

A variety of questions crowded into my brain. I turned to Holly. "Do we tell the police about this?"

"He doesn't care."

"But without a name or any proof, why would they believe us? 'Hello, Mr. Police Officer, someone who says he's a reporter—who stole the phone of a hit-and-run victim—says that fine, upstanding businessman over there is a crook.'"

"CYA, sugar. Cover you-know-what. Tell the cops. Better they think you're crazy than you get in trouble later for withholding information. I'll contact Detective Latham and see if we can talk to him before your stint."

I pondered while she typed the message. I spoke again when she looked up. "Help me figure out what I need to ask this guy."

She opened a notepad app on her phone. "Fire away."

"What happened last night when he says someone tried to kill him? Who told him I'm the only trustworthy one here? What does he mean he wants my help seeing who's here with that team? Am I supposed to give him names of who I see in their tent? I don't know people. Besides, how does helping him with his article find the person who hurt Stuart."

I paused to let her catch up. "Most of all, I want to know how he's connected to Stuart. And why he cares."

"That's the big question."

"What makes him sure it wasn't an accident? Why does he think he'd be next? How did he see it happen? How did he know to contact me from Stuart's phone? How did he know we were dating?"

She looked up. "Basically, tell us why we should help him."

Colby jerked into motion, moving toward the front of the pit space and pulling on her gloves. I spotted the problem on the monitors: a Viper nosed into the tire wall at Turn 6. As I watched, the car rolled backward a few feet, then rocked forward and stopped. Thirty seconds later, when it became clear the Viper couldn't get going on its own, the race went yellow—our first full-course caution. Our crew scrambled to ready more tires and prep fuel lines.

Two laps later, as the racecars were finally collected into a line behind the safety car, Holly nudged me. "Detective Latham can't get to the pits right now, but he wants to know what's going on—now he's calling." She answered her phone and mouthed "I'll tell him" at me.

I nodded my thanks and stepped around the central pit cart to have a direct view of the 28 car's pit box. Prototypes went past us, exiting pit lane after their stops. The lollipop waved, ready for our car. I focused on Colby, standing on the low pit wall next to Bubs, our driver-change assistant. I imagined breathing with her. I rehearsed the driver change sequence in my mind, as I knew she did.

Mike pulled the 28 car in and quickly climbed out. Colby was buckled up within ten seconds, and twenty-some seconds later, she was on her way. The crew gave each other high-fives and started cleaning up. I was diverted out to the walkway by a wave from Holly. She grimaced and handed me the phone.

"Detective Latham?" I asked.

"Ms. Reilly, you need to listen to me," he bellowed. "*Do not engage.* Do you hear me? Do not engage with this person messaging you. Is that understood?"

"I understand you, Detective. We will contact you the moment we hear anything back from him—if we do. Okay?"

"That's not quite—"

The noise from a Porsche exiting a nearby pit space obliterated whatever else Latham was going to say.

"We'll be careful," I promised. "And we'll contact you immediately. Now I have to deal with my car." I shook my head and handed the phone back to Holly. *He thinks I need protection from text messages?*

I crossed back to our tent, heading to the pit cart. I was one step below Mike as he climbed up the side to report to Jack and Bruce Kunze, our car chief for the 28 Corvette.

"How is it out there?" Bruce asked him.

Mike shook his head. "The traffic never ends—always something, someone, somewhere. It's a nightmare—but I tell you, I bet the fans love it."

"Let's hope it doesn't turn into the wrong kind of show," Jack muttered.

Chapter Ten

Colby had a quiet first stint—escaping danger by inches when a prototype behind her went into the braking zone for Turn 1 too hot and spun into the runoff area.

I spent the hour with thankfully few interruptions, which gave me time to process the day. I started by checking in with Polly at the hospital—no news on Stuart. I tried to replace the fear and worry I felt for him with visualizations of his successful recovery. Then I mulled over the questions Detective Latham had asked after he broke the news, specifically, who had a grudge against Stuart.

I'd interpreted the question as "who'd want to kill Stuart?" I couldn't answer that. But "who might be mad at him?" could be easier to consider, starting with anyone angry about not having a role in the new, combined series—whether that was a team owner, a driver, or a member of Series staff.

I sat down next to Holly on a cooler near the food. "I'm thinking about Grand-Am or ALMS people who didn't make it to the new series and who might blame Stuart for it, since he was so involved in assigning new roles for USCC. Whatever happened to that Shane guy? I haven't seen him around."

"He's here. Went to work for Wicked Oils, which mostly does support race stuff. When I saw him yesterday, he looked great. Said moving to a supplier was the best thing that ever happened to him."

That's one off the list. "What about…who was the guy in charge of sponsor stuff from the ALMS?"

"Jonathan Charles. I didn't tell you about him. There was some last meeting of staff from both series, and—to hear Jonathan tell it—the guy who'd gotten Jonathan's job gloated nonstop. Got in Jonathan's face. Taunted him so much, Jonathan hauled off and punched him, then walked off the job then and there."

"The merger of the two series was more contentious than I thought. Where's Jonathan now?"

"No idea. You think he could be here?"

"Make a list of names for Latham, would you? Starting with his."

She pulled out her phone. "We haven't thought about sponsors or manufacturers."

"I haven't heard complaints, have you?"

"Other than the high-level manufacturer politics, nothing but small supplier wins and losses. Except the guy from Elias Tires has been stomping around mad he can't run his tires this year."

"He could in GTLM." That was the only class where teams could choose their own tire supplier. All other classes ran a specified brand.

"He can't find a partner there like he did in the ALMS GTC class last year."

"That's a technical decision, not anything Stuart did."

Holly shrugged. "You asked. That's all I've heard."

"Back to staff, any idea how Tug accepted working for Stuart?"

"I don't know, but he came up with his own assistant in record time."

"Who is she?"

"She was Tug's junior staffer in Grand-Am Operations last year, doing the grunt work. When Stuart got the big job, our showy friend Tug was demoted down to grunt, and Elizabeth was out of a job."

I blinked at Holly. "She was on the spot to step in today. It's been three or four hours since Stuart was hurt?"

"Guess she was still in town. Not that she looked excited to be back." She paused. "Tug looked plenty pleased to step into Stuart's shoes."

"If he can."

Holly snorted. "He thinks he can, that's for sure. Speaking of capable…what do you think about Raul?"

I grinned at her. "What's his story?"

"Seems like I'd better find out." She pulled out her phone.

By the time Colby came in for a smooth, green-flag pit stop, collecting new tires and a full load of fuel, I was ready to focus on the car. The "real" world of angry people and violent acts seemed much more unreal than the race in front of me. I handed my phone to Holly and spent half an hour watching Colby's view out the windscreen via the in-car camera feed.

On my return from a run to the port-a-potty, my father, James Hightower Reilly III, was waiting for me at the entrance to our team tent. Our relationship was still tentative. It wasn't something I wanted to deal with on race day.

Raised by my maternal grandparents after my mother died within days of my birth, I'd only met my father three years ago. We'd only become friendly in the last year. He was the twenty-years-older male version of me: short and slight, with black hair, blue eyes, and a pointy chin. But while my uniform was a firesuit, his was a suit and tie.

I spoke before my father could. "I'm in the stop window. I've got to get ready."

"I know. I heard about Stuart, and I wanted to see how you were doing." As the chairman and CEO of Frame Savings, James represented a major sponsor of the new United SportsCar Championship, and as such, he was up and down pit lane, in and out of team tents all race long.

He followed me to the back corner of the Sandham Swift tent, opposite the food tables, where Holly waited next to some open, plastic shelving. Mike and I usually had small lockers in one of the pit carts, but for this race, all drivers used temporary shelves for our gear, partly because Sandham Swift was fielding a dozen drivers, up from its regular four. In addition, the extra equipment required to service three Corvettes for twenty-four hours straight meant our crew needed a lot more tools and car parts on hand. Those occupied all the locker space in all three carts.

I took the bottle of water Holly had waiting for me and slugged down half of it in one go. I could lose as many as five pounds in sweat during a single stint. Overhydration was vital before I got in the car.

My father studied my face. "How are you handling Stuart's situation, Kate?"

The concern in his eyes and voice made me feel like weeping for the first time in a couple hours. "Fine. I have to think about the car." I sounded curt, bordering on rude, but I couldn't afford to get emotional, not with my shift in the car coming up. I drank the rest of the water and set the empty bottle on my shelf, then inserted my earplugs and put tape over my ears to hold them in.

"If there's anything I can do, please tell me," James said.

I nodded at him, before pulling on my fire-retardant balaclava and tucking it into the neck of my firesuit. Despite my own statement, all I could think about was Stuart as I zipped up my firesuit and pressed the Velcro collar closed.

Holly took my head and neck system, or HANS, from me and slid it onto my shoulders. I paused with my helmet above my head. "James, you could find out what's going on with Stuart. And if anyone knows why. Tell Holly. Please."

"I'll find out whatever I can." He wished me well and left the tent.

I turned to Holly as I fastened my chinstrap. "Don't tell me anything about Stuart while I'm out there."

She knew what I meant. "Don't think about it. It's all going to be okay."

Five minutes later, Holly interrupted my visualizations of the driver-change and the track by pointing to the monitors. The track feed showed a prototype high-centered on curbing at the outside of Turn 5. If the prototype couldn't get off the curb, Race Control would throw a yellow flag to retrieve him.

As I grabbed my gloves, the double-yellow flew in the twilight, bringing out a full-course caution. I hurried across the pit space to Jack for last-minute instructions. Three steps up the side of the command center, and I was eye-to-eye with him.

Jack raised his eyebrows. "You ready to drive?"

"Ready to do my job."

He looked back at the array of monitors above his head. "Not sure if it's going to really rain or not."

"You giving me slicks?"

"Slicks are ready. Racing line's still dry. Be careful if you move offline."

I stepped back down to the floor of the pit space and went around to the other side to check with Bruce, our car chief. He assured me the Corvette's handling hadn't changed much—only what I might have expected from a couple hours of running and a track growing cooler and damp. "But the traffic is brutal," he added.

"How'd the prototype go off?"

"Someone must have laid down fluid, because four different cars slid off the road in the infield, but continued. The fifth got stuck."

"Fluid, not rain?"

He shrugged. "Colby says not rain."

Our crew was perched on the pit wall, tools and tires in hand. I pulled on my gloves as I hurried to join them. Bubs helped me step up on the adjacent metal bench and then onto the wall in the center of the crew lineup. He handed me my custom-molded seat insert. I took a deep breath then let it out slowly. Cleared my mind of everything but the Corvette C7.R and Daytona International Speedway. Visualized the driver-change process. Breathed deeply again.

The lollipop swung down, and I knew the car was coming down pit lane. I ran through the steps of our driver-change over and over, focusing on the car. Ready to leap into action.

It's all going to be okay.

Holly had better be right.

Chapter Eleven

Colby stopped the car smoothly, turning off the engine and tilting the steering column up to give us space to get in and out. The car was already up on its jacks and fuel was flowing. She released her belts and hauled herself through the doorway Bubs had already opened. The near tire-changers finished their job as she pulled her seat insert clear of the car. They moved to the right side of the car, and I settled my own insert and climbed inside.

Bubs leaned in to help me fasten my five-point safety harness and plug in my radio cable and helmet air-conditioning hose. I lowered the steering column back into place. The car bounced down onto its tires—tire change done. Waiting on fuel.

Bubs snapped the window net in place and slammed the door shut. I heard Bruce's voice. "Five more seconds."

I tightened my belts quickly, ready with both feet on the pedals. Though Series regulations allow teams to keep cars running during pit stops, for safety reasons, we chose to turn off our Corvettes while fuel flows and sparks fly from tire changes. My finger rested on the ignition button.

A tug at the back of the car. The crew member at the front waved me on.

"Clear. Go, go, go."

I was in motion as Bruce spoke. Push the button. Car starting. Throttle down, steer right out of the pit box. Check mirrors for other cars. Be sure the pit lane speed limiter was engaged. Tighten belts more.

Bruce's voice in my ear again. "Radio check, Kate."

I pushed the radio button on the steering wheel with my left thumb as I approached the end of pit lane. "Copy."

"Great. Easy out of the pits. Remember that exit's tricky, and you've got new tires on damp track."

We'd seen plenty of drivers be overly ambitious on cold tires and run into the wall of the pit lane exit. I had the possibility of wet pavement on top of that. I was cautious.

Once out on track and in the lineup behind the pace car, I found the drink tube and inserted it into the front of my helmet. Pressed the button to make sure it worked. Pressed the radio button again. "Who ended up around me?"

"Ferrari jumped us in the pits," Bruce reported. "BMW is P1, four cars in front of you." I could see the BMW ahead, a couple prototypes between us. "That Ferrari in front of you is P2. You're P3. Two prototypes behind you. The Porsche-Corvette-Porsche sandwich after them are P4 through P6."

"Lap times?" I asked, as I turned left through Turn 6 and swung up onto the banking of the oval part of the track.

"Hard to tell for sure with so much traffic, but Ferraris seem to have the speed by a couple tenths, though the Porsches and factory Corvettes have shown flashes. We're in there. Mike and Colby held their own."

"Copy, thanks." I usually knew our competition's lap times even before I got in the car, but I didn't get to those today. Not with Stuart in the hospital fighting for his life and text messages from strangers.

Stop it! Nothing but the car! I yelled at myself inside my helmet.

I wove in and out of the Bus Stop. Keyed the mic. "It's the most damp on the backstretch, but I wouldn't call it wet."

A new voice on the radio. Male. "Kate, your spotter here. To confirm, you want ten lengths' warning of overtaking cars?"

"Yes, please, Cooper."

"And you want 'inside' and 'outside' as indicators, rather than 'right' and 'left,' correct?"

"You are correct, Spotter. Thanks."

Cooper and Millie had spoken with all of the 28 car's drivers earlier in the weekend to understand what each of us wanted in terms of warning about other activity on the track. A couple teams had started using a new radar system that integrated with our rearview camera displays to warn drivers of overtaking cars. Though Jack had investigated it, he hadn't sprung for the new system yet. We were using the original, low-tech spotting method: humans with binoculars, stationed up high.

"Copy that, be careful out there," Cooper returned. I knew he was standing on top of the ten-story building in the cool air and mist—or even rain—with no cover. It wasn't only the drivers who worked hard in a twenty-four hour endurance race.

We'd cross our fingers for clear skies and sun tomorrow morning, but first we had a dozen or more hours of cool, and possibly wet, night ahead of us. The stadium lights had been turned on an hour ago and were already helping illuminate the pavement all the way around the track.

Bruce radioed. "Race Control says going green in two laps."

"I'm ready." I pulled my belts tighter. "Who's in the prototypes near me?" I knew the drivers in the Ferrari, BMW, Corvette, and at least one of the Porsches were professionals, but I wasn't sure about the faster prototypes.

"The two ahead are a pro and an amateur—Andy Padden in front and Roger Lee behind. Roger's pretty good."

Sportscar racing was a mix of pros and amateurs—the gentlemen drivers, who paid their own way to race cars. They had to qualify for a racing license with training or seat time in lower-level races, but those guidelines still allowed for a wide range of skill level. It was the rare amateur who had the hours of experience a pro had—and mostly it was seat time that was crucial. Given a set of on-track conditions, from weather to other cars, I knew how a pro would react. An amateur wasn't as predictable, which could easily make him, or her, dangerous.

Bruce came back on the radio. "Right behind you is a NASCAR guy, Sam Remington, and behind him is a rookie amateur, Francis Schmidt. Careful of him. That's the red car."

Has to be Sam behind me. I shook off the distraction and focused on the guy in the red prototype. He was sure to want to pass me in the first lap, as would Sam. The difference was the amateur might not know how to do it well.

We rolled under the starter's stand in our orderly line. I glanced left, found our pits. Noted a Porsche with its hood up in the massive pit complex two spaces up from us.

"Lights out on the pace car," Bruce said. "Green next time by."

I spent the last yellow lap thinking about braking points, turn-in points, apexes, and moisture on painted areas. Watching the rain, looking for puddles. Time to go to work.

The green flew as I exited NASCAR 4. I got on the throttle as much as I could, given the traffic ahead. The Ferrari right in front of me was sluggish, but I wouldn't do anything rash to get around. Not yet.

As expected, Sam was past me by the start/finish line. The red prototype—with the amateur, Schmidt, at the wheel—didn't start as quickly, but zoomed up as we curved down toward Turn 1.

"Prototype moving inside. Inside," Cooper said in my ear.

As Cooper warned, Schmidt pulled to my left, coming even with my rear wheels—then ahead of them. Making a very late move.

"Ready for you, jackass," I muttered. I braked early and wide, giving him space to shoot by. Which he did, carrying too much speed into the corner and breaking his rear tires loose. He saved the slide, wobbled dramatically, and continued.

If I'd taken my normal line, he'd have punted me straight into the tire wall. I shook my head. I focused on getting my tires up to pressure and catching the Ferrari in front of me.

From the left edge of the track, I braked for Turn 3 at the end of the pit exit blend line. Late apex through that 180-degree turn, unwinding the wheel on exit, tracking all the way to the left edge of the track.

Cross back to the right side of the track before the Kink. Where the white stripe in the road turns right onto an access road, I turn left to the Kink's apex. Lift slightly at apex—only this lap, only because of cold tires. No braking, no lifting there usually. Brush the apex curbing with left-side tires. Check mirrors. Track out to the right side of the track.

Ready for Turn 5, the West Horseshoe, a long right-hander. Braking. Wide entry. Turning tighter, tighter. Brush the curb late in the corner. Throttle out of the corner. Look ahead.

Closer to the Ferrari in front of me. I must be faster through there than he is.

Accelerating to Turn 6, staying right on track. Mirrors. Braking, turning as early as possible. Getting back to the throttle as early as possible. Stay to the left of the black line of asphalt sealer—leave the outside for the faster cars coming up behind.

"Two prototypes outside. Outside on the banking," Cooper told me. Then, as the first one passed, "One more prototype outside. Now clear."

Onto the banking. On the throttle, set my hands. Stay low.

I took a breath. Took a moment to enjoy the sweep of the banked track—even the weird, early dusk caused by overcast and mist. Around the curve, the track flattened out. I drifted right. Brake hard starting at the "2" marker for the Bus Stop. Onto the left curbing at apex. Feed throttle on. Curbing on the right. Build speed slowly. Second curbing on the right. More speed. Point the car at the banking, over the curbing on the left. Out of the Bus Stop, back to banking. Full throttle. Around NASCAR 3 and 4. Cooper in my ear, prototypes flashing past. Ready for the dip in the track over NASCAR 4 that makes the car wiggle. Through the tri-oval, passing a GTD car, flashing over the checkers on the pavement.

I stayed low on the approach to Turn 1, touching the left side of the track by the patch of grass near pit lane exit. Braking, then turning left, touching the inside of the turn at the stack of tires. Curving through the narrow Turn 2. Mist lighter here, less damp offline. I radioed that information to Bruce. Then I focused on chipping away at the two car-lengths between me and the Ferrari.

In the next fifteen laps, I used every bit of skill I could muster, pushing my limits in damp corners, weaving through traffic, trusting my tires, trusting the car. Two-thirds of the way through my hour-long stint, I was up on the Ferrari's back bumper, itching to get past him, when a yellow sent us back to the pits for service.

Not long into my second stint, I got through the traffic and took the battle to the Ferrari again. Ten laps of precision driving later—from both of us—I was grinning under my helmet.

"Who is this guy?" I radioed to Bruce.

"Raul Salas, new guy out of open-wheel, going to run for Redemption all year."

Well, Raul, you're good. And this is fun.

I managed a pass four laps later, only to have him return the favor on the next go-round. I was working on my next opening when I suddenly had a front-row seat to all hell breaking loose.

Chapter Twelve

Raul and I had just swung onto the back straight out of NASCAR 2 when I noticed the wrong kind of motion in the distance. I saw cars entering the Bus Stop chicane, arrowing through the turns instead of swinging side-to-side through them. Going way too fast.

I kept pushing, pressing the Ferrari ahead, but I was ready for cars off-track, debris, or a flag. I wasn't ready for racecar carnage. For flames.

Over the next minutes and hours, I pieced together what I saw from a combination of split-second glances as I passed, and from video replays they showed briefly on SGTV.

My sister car, the number 30 Sandham Swift Corvette with Ian Davenport behind the wheel, had come out of the track's inner loop onto the banking of NASCAR 1 behind one of the all amateur-driven Benchmark Racing Porsches, the 77. Though the driver of the 77 tried to make his Porsche three lanes wide, he couldn't keep Ian behind him in the Corvette. As the track flattened out onto the back straight, Ian had passed the Porsche and begun to pull a gap.

Then came the Bus Stop.

Ian braked and turned in for the first, left-hand bend of the four-turn complex. The Porsche behind him slowed enough to make the first turn—barely. Then everything went wrong. The Porsche slammed into the left rear corner of the Corvette, which propelled both cars across pavement and grass, straight into the wall. Hard.

Neither driver could change the trajectory of the two-car missile—turning and braking were useless efforts when tires no longer had grip on the track—and the recent drizzle of rain meant the slick grass of the runoff area offered more help than resistance. Ian was fortunate to make impact with the right-front corner of the car first, so there was more car to absorb energy from the impact. But it was a huge hit.

Nearly every wall in the Speedway was lined with steel and foam energy reduction, or SAFER, barriers, designed to absorb and dissipate the forces in an accident. That action reduced deceleration forces on a driver and vehicle and hurt drivers less. In addition, in high-impact areas, walls were lined with stacks of tires that absorbed even more impact and energy. But tires and foam can only do so much.

Somehow Ian's Corvette swung around at the last second before impact, so the car slammed into the tire wall broadside at something north of 150 mph, burying the passenger side of the Corvette in the stacks of rubber.

The bit of turning by the Corvette opened up the driver's side to bear the full impact of the Porsche—which also managed to pivot. The end result was the worst possible: the Porsche's engine swung like a pendulum and smacked into the driver's door of the Corvette. The heaviest piece of the Porsche hit the Corvette at its point of least crumple zone for the driver.

Most of this was visible to me in the moment only as a vague sense of movement and plumes of dirt, mud, and grass kicked into the air. Plus an explosion of foam in the air as the cars hit the wall. As I followed the Ferrari down the back stretch, I didn't even know which cars were involved.

I braked on my mark. Glanced left again, looking for my line and trying to gather information on the accident—how bad it was, who it involved, and if it would bring out a caution.

First glance. Only two cars. Green Porsche limping away from the wall. Turn in to the left-hander. Sighting my line for the two right-handers.

Second glance. Dark car gleaming under the lights. Black Corvette against the wall. *One of ours?!* My breath caught in my throat.

Right-hand turn. Sight the right-left turn combination to get back onto the banking. Next to the incident now. Green Porsche on the grass verge three hundred feet away. Turning my head away from the track more than really safe. Having to know.

Third glance. Our 30 car. With a cockpit full of flames.

Time elongates for drivers in a race, as we process large quantities of information at an extremely rapid speed. But time did one better for me at that moment in the Bus Stop, as I watched my sister car burn. Time nearly stood still, along with my breath and my heart.

Stop! I've got to stop. I've got to help. Now! I need to stop.

It took envisioning the steps—getting my car slowed down and parked on the shoulder of the track, unbuckling and extracting myself, and running a hundred yards back to the 30 Corvette—to realize I'd never make it there before the safety crew. Plus I'd have no tools or gear to put out flames or care for the driver. And I'd be in danger of getting hit by other cars.

Corner workers and safety crews were trained for these situations. I knew the nearest corner workers would be there in seconds with handheld fire extinguishers. A full crew in a truck with fire-fighting equipment could be there in a minute or two.

You're driving, Kate, you can't stop! I shouted to myself as I bounced over the curbing of the second right-hander at 95 mph. I dragged my attention back to my car before I bobbled the left-turn exit to the Bus Stop. Focused on accelerating and breathing.

Ohmygod, ohmygod, ohmygod that was bad. Is he okay? Ohmygod, ohmygod.

It took all of my training and will to dam up the worry I felt and focus on my line and my car.

Once I was settled on the banking of NASCAR 3, trembling foot on the floor, I keyed the radio. "That's Ian in the wall.

Hard." I choked up and released the button. I swallowed. Hit the button again. "Where's the damn yellow?!"

The lights blinked on, garish against the dark sky beyond the Speedway. I lifted my foot from the throttle.

"Full-course caution now, Kate, slow it down." Bruce sounded calm, which both reassured and infuriated me. *Why isn't he worried or upset?*

Jack's voice on the radio. "What did you see, Kate?"

I took a deep breath. *Be a pro.* "Green Porsche and 30 car straight after turn-in to the Bus Stop. Straight into the wall. The Corvette is right side to the wall, driver's side to the track. Porsche moved off slowly after impact. Flames in the cabin of the Corvette." I swallowed again. "Is he okay?"

Jack was back on quickly. "Ian doused the flames from inside the car."

That meant Ian was conscious and able to hit the button to activate the fire extinguisher mounted in every car for exactly this possibility. My arms shook with the force of my relief.

Cooper, my spotter, radioed instructions about where the pace car would pick up the field in relation to my current location. Bruce repeated the information from Race Control that the whole field would take the Bus Stop bypass, staying on the oval track, instead of going through the turns. I followed their instructions and thought about what I'd seen.

Foam flying wasn't good, because it meant an impact heavy enough to break up the barrier. The Porsche being able to move off again after impact could be good—maybe that suggested the damage to our car wouldn't be that great. But flames in the cabin meant something important had broken. I wondered if Sandham Swift would be able to repair the car. If they could get it back out to finish the race.

Of course, the big question was if Ian was injured—but he'd been conscious. Maybe he was hurt—a broken bone. He'd been awake.

I followed the line of cars down the back straight and through the Bus Stop bypass. I looked left to the accident site and couldn't see the 30 car for the cluster of trucks with light bars flashing. The view was unchanged on my second time by. I called in to the pits.

"Is Ian out of the car yet?"

"Negative." Jack's voice.

"You said he was conscious, right?"

"He activated the fire bottle. He's not out yet. That's all we know."

I bit my lip, wanting more. Wanting reassurance.

Bruce spoke next. "I'm sure they're being careful. Safety crews are staffed by experts."

I knew he was right. Expert doctors, firefighters, and safety crew worked races for a pittance to be involved in a sport they loved, and as a result, they were highly skilled teams. Knowing it didn't ease my concern over Ian.

Bruce went on in his smooth voice. "How are you doing, Kate? How's the car?"

What do you mean, how's the car? How's Ian?! How's Stuart, for fuck's sake?!

I drew a breath and pressed the radio button to transmit those sentiments. Then I released the button and took another deep breath. The answer to Bruce's question? I was more than a little freaked out.

I breathed deeply twice more and put everything and everyone outside of the car. Only room for me in there. I pressed the radio button again and made sure I spoke calmly. "I'm worried about Ian. I didn't like seeing the fire."

I really didn't like the fire. I never liked fire. Truth was, fire scared me more than anything. Spiders, snakes, bad guys in dark alleys, amateurs on track with me…I could cope with those. Fire gave me nightmares. I wasn't proud of it.

I focused on the car and spoke to Bruce and the team, describing changes over the ninety-plus minutes I'd been driving. "Any indication if something broke in the 30 car to cause his accident, Bruce?"

He heard my unspoken question. "Nothing to be worried

about in your car, Kate. We think he was an innocent victim of something going wrong in the Porsche."

"Other than incompetence?"

"Easy," Jack put in. "We don't know anything yet."

I knew Race Control and anyone with a scanner—including other teams—could be listening to our conversation. But I'd exhausted my small store of calm, and I didn't care. "All I'm saying is some of the amateur drivers in this race have been a menace."

My hands tightened on the Corvette's steering wheel. "And they're going to need to watch out if Ian and the 30 car end up paying the price for their mistakes."

Chapter Thirteen

"Enough, Kate. Not on the radio." Jack sounded angry.

"I'm not saying anything everyone else doesn't know. Some-one needs to stand up for those of us getting run over out here!" I stopped, finally hearing the shrill quality in my voice that must have been apparent to everyone else listening. I was short of breath and my heart raced. Those symptoms weren't unusual while I was in the car, but not while I was in the car under cau-tion for the fourth lap.

"Kate, no more." Jack's voice was lower and more formal than usual. "I repeat. No. More." He paused. "Pits are open, and you will pit with GTs in two laps. You will change to Miles. Do not transmit anything that is not about the car. Do you copy?"

I felt embarrassed and suddenly exhausted—though anger and fear overrode those emotions. "I copy. Pitting in two laps, driver-change."

I spent those laps fretting and straining to see something of the 30 car in the scrum of emergency vehicles. Seeing nothing only ratcheted up my anxiety. The second time by, when three ambulances still waited next to the four emergency trucks, I realized my whole body was trembling. I hit myself on the side of the helmet and called myself a few bad names, which got me steady and focused on the procedure for our pit stop.

Once I was out of the car and over the wall, Miles roaring off with a full tank of gas on fresh rubber, my knees gave way. I collapsed into a plastic chair in our pit space. Disgusted with myself, I yanked my gloves off and pulled at my helmet's chin strap. Aunt Tee helped pull my helmet and HANS off and offered me a clean, wet towel once I'd peeled off my sweaty balaclava.

I wiped my neck and face with the towel, then tilted my head up, draped the towel over my face, and breathed for a minute. No more shaking or weakness. Bad things happen on the street or in a race, but they're unusual. I wasn't going to live my life in fear.

I looked around. The 30 car crew milled about their portion of the pit space, each person expressing tension their own way—one pacing, a couple obsessively cleaning and organizing tool drawers, another biting his nails. Chris Syfert, the music agent and amateur driver who should have been climbing into the 30 car at this stop, stood square behind the pit cart, helmet still on, eyes on the monitor, arms folded. Her rock-star cousin, client, and racing partner Thomas Kendall stood next to her, also staring at the monitor. In the other two-thirds of the Sandham Swift tent, the 28 and 29 car crew and drivers cleaned up after pit stops.

On the central pit box, the command center, Jack ran the whole show. He turned my way, studied me a moment, then beckoned me over.

Aunt Tee handed me a bottle of water and my cell phone. "Holly left this with me, when she went to see Ian and Greg."

I clutched Aunt Tee's arm. "Stuart?"

"Nothing more yet."

I closed my eyes and breathed again, then drank half the water down before I climbed up to sit next to Jack.

He spoke before I could. "We don't know anything yet. They're not showing that part of the track on the feeds." He paused, and I heard what he didn't need to say out loud, *Which isn't a good sign.*

Broadcasters of auto racing were quick to replay footage of accidents and their aftermath over and over to fill the yellow-flag period—and to satisfy viewers' lust for wreckage—unless there was any concern about the well-being of the driver. Then they kept cameras pointed away.

The butterflies I'd momentarily calmed sprang to life again in my gut.

Jack went on. "As soon as there's status, Holly will let us know."

"Did they show a replay of the accident?"

"A couple times right after it happened. Nothing tells me what the hell happened to that other car. But Ian was an innocent bystander taken along for the ride. Nothing wrong with our car then. Plenty wrong now."

"And it's that car's fault." I pointed to the monitor showing the Benchmark Racing team working on the 77 Porsche. Near us, I saw two members of the 30-car crew make furious gestures at the screen.

"It may be," Jack said, "but you need to calm down and keep your mouth shut. No one goes vigilante on them. We'll let Race Control respond."

"Did they get a penalty?"

"The incident is under review. We don't know yet if it was driver error or mechanical failure." The former would be assessed a penalty by Race Control, but the latter wouldn't.

"I hope it's mechanical, because that kind of driver mistake is so unacceptable it's criminal."

Jack raised an eyebrow at me.

"Who was the driver, anyway?" I asked.

"Some rich kid. Ricky Amick, I think. He may have made it back here in that car, but they sent him off to the medical center also. He didn't look steady."

I shrugged. I'd give the driver a wide berth if he got back out on track.

"Can you keep your cool, or do we need to keep you away from video cameras and microphones?" Jack's tone was dry, but I heard the force behind the question. He was reminding me that part of my job was to represent the team in a classy, appropriate way—something I'd slipped up on, memorably, in the past.

I stiffened. "I'll be appropriate in public."

Jack pointed a finger at his radio headset. After listening a minute, he leaned over to glance at the 30 car's chief, who nodded at Jack and gave instructions to the car's crew. Within seconds, the 30 car team departed at a run, presumably for the garage. Chris—still helmeted—and Thomas followed them more slowly.

Jack confirmed it. "They've got Ian out, over to the infield care center, and they're loading the car up to bring it back to the garage. Repairs are going to be extensive."

"But—"

Jack shook his head. "Still no word on his condition."

We were silent as the field passed on the front straight, still behind the safety car, still full-course caution. The live camera feed showed the Bus Stop area again, starting with a shot of our Corvette leaving on a flatbed, a huge blue tarp covering it, front to rear. Then the camera swung back to focus on track workers and forklifts repairing the damaged track wall.

The combination of the wall damage and the blue tarp on the car made my stomach jump around more.

Bruce leaned over and spoke in Jack's ear. They turned to me.

"We need a straight answer, Kate," Jack began. "Are you all right?"

"I'm a little cold, but I'm fine."

Bruce shook his head, and Jack spoke again. "Emotionally. First Stuart, then seeing this accident—maybe it's too much. You were upset in the car and shaky after…are you going to be all right when you get back in the car?"

The fog in my head cleared. I understood what they were asking. Finally understood what everyone's concern would be. Was I emotionally stable enough to drive?

I could almost hear Gramps in my head: *Figure out if you're all right, and let people know. Don't malinger, because it doesn't help anyone.*

I definitely heard Zeke's voice: *Stop feeling sorry for yourself, Kate. Suck it up and pull it together.*

I sat up straighter and looked each man in the eye. "I have a thing about fire—it's the only thing that freaks me out. But it happened, Ian put out the flames, it's fine. I'm good. That's why I was rattled in the car." I paused, embarrassed. "I'll be fine in the car again. I'm fine now. My concern over Stuart has nothing to do with my ability to race. I'm upset about the 30 car being damaged—and Ian possibly being hurt by an idiot driver—but I'll be extra careful. I'll make sure it doesn't happen to me."

Jack and Bruce shared a glance.

I looked from one to the other. "Are you asking this of everyone? Or only me, the female? You don't need to coddle me."

Jack held up a hand. "Easy, tiger. I asked Miles and the others if they had any concerns. You're the only one who saw the accident close-up. And you're the one with a significant other in the hospital." He quirked a corner of his mouth up. "Trust me, if anything, I think you and Colby are tougher than most men."

I tried for a smile. "Thanks."

Jack flicked his eyes to the ceiling and pointed to his headset again. Message coming in. He turned to me. "Car's pulling up. I'm heading over. You may as well ride with me, so you can get to the motorhome and clean up."

I followed him out of the pits to the golf cart parked outside the nearest pit lane entrance. I realized the rain had finally stopped as Jack whisked us back through the paddock and around the garage building to the back row containing our three spaces. The 30 car was on the flatbed in front of its space, but hadn't yet been unloaded. Jack parked the cart and walked toward the four Series officials gathered around the back of the rig.

I followed more slowly, not sure if I wanted to hear the outcome of the discussion or excuse myself to the motorhome where I could get clean and dry.

Another golf cart pulled up with a flash of headlights, Tug at the wheel with Holly in the passenger seat. She looked shattered. My heart leapt into my throat, and I couldn't hear the roar of cars on track over the hammering of my pulse in my ears.

Holly and Tug approached Jack, and I followed. Holly reached out and clutched my hand as if I were the only thing saving her from drowning. She looked from Jack to me and took a deep breath. Then finally spoke.

"Ian's dead."

Chapter Fourteen

I couldn't process the words. Couldn't form a response. Stood there looking from Holly to Tug to Jack, waiting for what she'd communicated to make sense. To seem reasonable. For anything in the world to seem fair.

Jack drew a sharp breath and moved away from everyone into the center of the paddock lane. He stood, hands on his hips, face to the sky.

Tug stepped aside to speak quietly to the senior Series official standing at the rear of the flatbed.

I realized I was clenching Holly's hand, and I forced myself to let go. "Holly." It came out in a whisper. "What happened? Wasn't he conscious?"

"They're not completely sure yet what—why…he was awake when they got to the car—spoke to the first responder. But he fell unconscious pretty quickly after that. They were working on him, trying to figure out where he was injured, but he…died. Minutes ago. They couldn't save him." Her eyes swam with tears.

I hugged her and let my own tears fall.

She sobbed the words. "It's not right. I can't believe it."

"Kate? What's the news?" Mike stood next to us, looking like he already knew the answer.

I shook my head as more tears welled.

Holly spoke through her tears. "Ian died, Mike."

Mike flinched, as if he'd been punched in the gut. "Shit, shit, shit," he muttered. He put an arm around each of us and leaned his head on mine.

My thoughts were stuck in a repeat loop of snapshots of Ian in the days leading up to the race and my final vision of his helmet silhouetted in the car against a backdrop of flames.

A couple minutes later, Jack finished his solitary communion and walked back to us. In the light from the garage, I could see his eyes were red and damp. "Holly, how's Greg handling this? I can't imagine what losing a son might do to someone."

She pulled away from us and exhaled, shaking her head. "Not well. He's angry at everyone, from the track staff right on up to God."

Mike wiped his eyes and looked at Jack. "Do we stop or keep racing, Boss?"

I hadn't considered what this meant to the rest of the team.

"Do you want to go on?" Jack asked us.

"Yes," my answer was out of my mouth before my brain even engaged. Mike agreed.

Holly pressed a tissue to her eyes. "Greg said he wanted Sandham Swift to keep racing, as a tribute." She smiled, the smallest upturn in the corners of her mouth, "He expressed with some force to 'not let those fuckers win.'"

Jack looked grim. "I'm going to assume that means the Benchmark team—and specifically the 77 car."

I waited for a lesson on turning the other cheek, Jack's typical response to any on-track conflict. But he surprised me.

"Let's be clear." He leveled sharp looks at me and Mike. "There will be no retaliation. But beating that team fair and square on the track is a goal I can get behind. Something I want more than any winner's watch. You both with me?"

"Absolutely. Let's kick some butt on track," Mike said. "For Ian."

I nodded, not trusting myself to speak.

Jack rubbed his hands together. "Mike, take time to deal with this and get to the pits when you're ready—Miles can stay in for a triple if we need it. Kate, get cleaned up and dry so you don't get sick. Both of you, grieve as you need to. But when you come back to the pits, be focused and ready to do this. I want a hundred and twenty percent effort."

He straightened his shoulders and looked past us to the car. "Now I'm going to handle everything."

After a short exchange with Tug and other Series officials, Jack moved to speak to the Sandham Swift crew members stationed in the garage. Holly, Mike, and I stood close together, touching, needing the physical connection.

Tug looked strange as he approached us, his natural exuberance subdued. "I'm so sorry for you all. I'm not sure what else to say. If there's anything the Series can do, please call on me personally."

Mike lifted his chin. "Are they going to bench the 77 car driver? Arrest him for homicide?"

"Easy now." Tug held up his hands. "I can confirm they assessed a penalty on the 77 car for avoidable contact."

We waited for more.

Tug's eyes widened. "Surely you don't think this was anything but a tragic accident? The team reports the throttle on the 77 car stuck. The driver tried to brake, but couldn't override the wide-open throttle. At that point, he was a passenger. The team asked us to pass along their condolences to Sandham Swift and Ian's family."

"A young man with a brilliant future ahead of him loses his life," Mike's voice cracked, and he paused. "And the guy who caused it says, 'Gee, sorry' and gets a—what? A stop-plus-seventy-five?" Mike referred to the usual penalty for avoidable contact: a stop in the penalty box plus being held for seventy-five seconds, which totaled the equivalent of a single lap.

"I understand your frustration," Tug responded.

Holly snorted.

Tug raised an eyebrow at her. "It hurts us all to lose a member of our community, especially in the middle of this iconic race."

He'd feel less terrible about it if Ian's death happened during practice?

"But this is racing," Tug concluded. "As safe as we try to make it, it can be a very dangerous sport. And dreadful, horrible accidents sometimes happen."

Mike frowned. Holly crossed her arms over her chest.

Tug hurried on. "As I said, the 77 car has been assessed a penalty. They are back running on-track, but they're some thirty laps down. I can also tell you the driver involved was sent to the infield care center and diagnosed with a concussion. He will no longer be participating in the race—though, to be clear, it's for medical reasons, not through Series action."

I shook my head. "At least I won't have to worry he'll run *me* off the road also."

Tug looked as if he smelled something bad. "I understand you're upset. But may I suggest—or perhaps, request—you keep those comments to yourself and don't share them with the media?"

My sad turned to mad pretty fast. Tug must have seen the change on my face, because he held up both hands again and spoke quickly. "You have every right to say whatever you want. I'm asking you as a favor—and I expect it's what Stuart might ask of you, were he standing here."

I closed my eyes. *Low blow, Tug. Are you fighting to stay alive, Stuart? We all need you back here, because you'd handle things better than this over-promoted peacock.*

Mike's hand tightened on my shoulder. "I'm sure there will be a team statement. We will let that—and our on-track perfor- mance—speak for us. I'm sure you realize we're speaking from the emotion of the moment—and we trust you won't repeat anything indiscreet. Personally, I don't see a need to badmouth that car or driver. His actions speak louder than any words we could say."

Tug looked self-satisfied. "Very wise. Of course, I won't repeat anything you've said. Again, please let me know if there's any- thing I can do for you." He nearly bowed as he took his leave.

"That guy." Mike shook his head.

I felt shaky and anxious from grief, cold, and lack of food, as well as a vague sense I'd missed something.

Holly must have felt me shudder. "Let's get you cleaned up."

Mike gave us one last squeeze. "I'll pull myself together and get to the pits to relieve Miles. You hang in there and get ready to kick some serious ass."

"Have a good stint," I told him. "I'll see you in a bit."

As we moved away, the flatbed carrying the 30 car rumbled to life and moved off down the lane, headed for a secure impound location. Holly and I stopped to watch.

The inside of that car might have been the last thing Ian saw. I bit the inside of my cheek in a futile attempt to stop my eyes from welling up.

"I'm sure the technical inspectors will go over it with a fine-tooth comb." Holly drew in a ragged breath. "I just—my God. I can't imagine Ian not here."

"Holly, if you need to be with Greg, go ahead. I can take care of myself."

She shook her head. "He's got his daughter and friends there. I can't do anything now. Trying to get back to sort-of normal is a better idea."

We both caught sight of a reporter and cameraman rounding the corner of the paddock lane, headed for Jack and the Sandham Swift garage area. We glanced at each other and made for the garage exit on the double.

I wondered if we'd ever feel "normal" again.

Chapter Fifteen

Holly and I crossed the speedway road behind the garages, waved our credentials at a lone security guard watching the entrance, and entered the dark and deserted team motorhome lot. Our goal was a quintet of rigs in the back, right corner.

Typically for a twenty-four hour race, Sandham Swift would have one motorhome per car, and the four drivers who shared a car would also share the rig for rest periods, showers, and food. But a couple drivers had come to this race with their own equipment. Thomas Kendall had the motorhome he traveled in to rock concerts, and he'd shared with Ian. Miles also had his own coach and shared it with Mike to give Colby and me some privacy. In turn, we'd invited amateur driver Chris Syfert to join us in the "ladies' RV."

The only person in our motorhome when we arrived was Aunt Tee—officially Tina Nichols, but an honorary aunt to everyone in the paddock. Since Aunt Tee had gone straight from the pits to the motorhome, Holly had to break the news about Ian. I headed for the shower, as desperate to get out of my wet clothes as I was to have some time alone. A few minutes later, I emerged dry, warmer, and dressed in a clean firesuit. I'd shed more tears in the shower—for both Ian and Stuart—and though I still felt off-kilter, I was better.

Aunt Tee gave me a big hug before she dished up the double-portion of food Holly had collected for me from Linda's Catering Services. Usually, Aunt Tee cooked or provided whatever meal we needed for a race. But with three times the number of drivers and crew to feed for a full twenty-four hours, we'd signed up with one of the two catering services that fed teams and staff out of big, mess hall-like tents. Holly had collected the food while I showered.

"Holly's also getting Gina for you," Aunt Tee told me. She pointed to the frozen hunks of chocolate-chip cookie dough she was arranging on a baking tray. "I thought we all needed a little comfort."

I agreed with her and dug back into my heaping plate of spaghetti and meatballs. Holly returned with Gina as I was wiping my plate clean with a roll and finishing my fourth bottle of water.

Gina was a volunteer for the Sandham Swift team, an amateur racer who liked attending races, but wanted to feel useful while she was doing it. We welcomed her into the team because she was smart and friendly, but also because she was a chiropractor. She happily gave drivers and crew members mild adjustments and a bit of massage or physiotherapy anytime we needed it. I liked a tune-up after every stint.

Gina set up her portable table in the middle of the main area. While she worked on me, Aunt Tee changed cookie trays and Holly worked her phone.

After the shower, meal, and Gina's tune-up, I finally felt able to cope. Gina waved off my thanks and left with a hug. Aunt Tee departed with her, taking half the baked cookies and leaving Holly in charge of taking the last tray out of the oven.

I sat down next to Holly on the couch and eyed her phone. "What's the news?"

She frowned. "You ready to deal with this?" At my nod, she continued. "Stuart's still hanging in there, but they've only gotten through some of the surgery. I'm not sure if you want details."

I waved her on and bit into the cookie Aunt Tee had left me.

"The biggest issue was a skull fracture and blood causing pressure on his brain, so they had to make a hole to get the blood out—but they've done that successfully."

"That means drilling a hole into his skull?"

At her confirmation, I put my half-eaten cookie down and took a deep breath. "That's only the first part?"

"Next they're going after internal bleeding in his abdomen. After that, they'll address his broken bones."

I stared at the floor, stunned by how tragic this day had been for so many close to me.

"He's fighting, sugar." Holly put a hand on mine. "I think he's going to make it."

I sighed. "The alternative doesn't bear thinking about."

"It sure doesn't."

I picked up my cookie again. "All right, he'll make it. Any other news from Sandham Swift? About Ian's accident? How Greg is doing?"

She shook her head. "But you've gotten a few texts and emails."

"I forgot about the anonymous reporter."

"He hasn't responded yet."

I picked up my cell phone and read my recent messages. Zeke, up in the SGTV broadcast booth, was worried about me and wanted to meet once he went off the air around midnight. I typed a quick text response telling him I was surviving and that he could find me in the pits before my early-morning stint.

My grandfather's email was short and to the point: Call us.

He picked up on the second ring. "Katie, my dear. Are you all right?" I'd rarely heard him so subdued.

"You heard?"

He sighed down the line. "Where to start? A friend called to tell me about Stuart. We're upset for you—for him, of course. We like him."

I blinked back tears at the memory of Stuart's visit to Albuquerque four weeks ago over New Year's. He'd been there two days, staying at a nearby hotel—spending part of one day in business meetings I was sure didn't need to be face-to-face. But he'd come out to meet my grandparents and see where I grew up and still lived. It had been an important step in our relationship.

I sniffed. "It sucks, Gramps. I'm coping, and he's hanging in there through the first surgeries—we got that update recently. It helped to get in the car—at first, anyway. You also heard about Ian?"

"I had heard, yes, and they recently announced it on the television coverage." Gramps had a network of racing cronies from his decades in the industry as a wiring harness supplier. He often got news at home before I heard it at the track. "I knew that accident was bad from the start. And there you were, passing right by."

His words set off a replay of the accident in my mind and a roiling in my gut.

Gramps kept talking. "Poor Ian, and his poor father and sister. I feel so badly for them and your whole team. But listen to me, Katie, you need to take care of yourself. Don't neglect yourself because you're upset—don't allow yourself to get careless. Get some rest and good meals, and don't ignore your body's needs."

I promised him I'd stay focused, which calmed him down, until I told him about the exchange with the anonymous reporter.

"Do the police think Stuart was hit deliberately?" He sounded agitated again. "Or is that only the nameless reporter's opinion?"

"I don't—"

"This reporter has no proof of his accusations, but he wants you to spy on people who might be dangerous? Katie, do *not* put yourself in danger. Do you hear me?"

I waited a moment, to be sure he'd stopped. "I hear you, Gramps. I promise to be careful. Holly and I are only keeping our eyes open. I'm also talking to the police. I'm not hiding anything from them."

"Please put Holly on the line for a moment."

Surprised, I gestured to Holly and handed her the phone.

"Yes," she said. Then, "I agree. Don't worry, I will." She smiled. "Yes, sir, that's a promise." She returned the phone, the smile still on her face. "I'm to keep you in line."

I rolled my eyes at her. "Feel better, Gramps?"

"Not much, but as you're an adult, I'll have to trust you."

I started to protest, but he cut me off. "I have a very bad feeling in my bones about you out there. Please, Katie, for me, stay focused on the race and be careful."

He'd never sounded that concerned for me before—not in my entire career as a racecar driver. "I swear, Gramps. I'll be extra cautious."

Short of crawling down the phone line, there was nothing else he could do. I told him I loved him and would call him in the morning after I woke up.

I looked at Holly as I disconnected. "I've never heard him so worried."

"Maybe he's got reason. We don't know what the hell's going on. We have to be careful not to stick our necks in a bear trap."

"That's a good goal."

Holly stood up. "Are you ready to go deal with the rest of the world again?"

I considered. Imagined being asked for status on Stuart. Pictured receiving condolences for Ian. I was steadier on the first topic than the second. But I knew, ready or not, it was time.

"One question first." I hesitated. "Ian—the cause. I mean… did the fire have anything to do with it?"

I saw concern and maybe pity on her face. I rushed to explain. "It's not about the fire—or not totally. I have two images I can't stop seeing. One is his car full of flames. The other is seeing the 77 dive-bombing him." I frowned. "I'm not sure why I'm holding onto only those images."

Holly blinked back tears. "He wasn't burned. What I was told—" she paused to swallow. "The issue was the impact."

"Thanks." I hoped the information would dispel some of my uneasiness. Then again, I knew witnessing the fatal accident of a teammate would always stay with me.

With a sigh, I checked the race time. "It's been six hours and change since the start of the race. Still more than seventeen hours of racing to go."

"All I can say is, they'd better not be as eventful as the first ones." Holly wiped her eyes. "I don't think we can take much more of this."

Chapter Sixteen

We'd heard the constant din of circulating cars from the motorhome—there was no escaping the sound until you were three blocks away from the Speedway. But back in the paddock, we were surrounded by the bustle and the drama of racing, from the noise of a car putt-putting to its garage for a lengthy fix, to the sight of a crew member running to the pits with a forgotten part, the light strapped to his forehead bobbing with every step. I felt more connected to the race—and my world—by being closer to the action.

The loss of Ian and the danger to Stuart were twin weights dragging me down. But surrounded by other teams and the other members of my own team, I remembered what made racing fun. My spirits lightened a fraction.

Inside the team lounge, Tom Albright sat in a chair typing furiously on a laptop computer. He looked up at our entrance. "Good, Kate and Holly. Let me update you."

I sat in the empty chair next to him, and Holly perched on its wide arm. "You dealing with the media?" I asked.

"Sending out a standard release and responding to a few select outlets." He eyed us. "You two okay?"

Holly and I both nodded. I wondered how soon we'd get tired of that question.

"Good," he went on. "We've issued a team statement asking the media to respect our privacy and not intrude on our drivers or crew. That's especially you, Kate. I assume that's fine?"

"I have no desire to speak to the media."

"SGTV or the track announcers may still interview you in the pits, but they'll restrict questions to the car and race."

"Sure." I got up and crossed to the coffeepot to pour myself a small cup. I raised my eyebrows at Holly, and at her nod, poured another. My plan had been to take a short nap after my first stint, since I'd be awake and driving until the wee hours of the morning. But a nap wasn't in the cards now. Caffeine would get me through.

Holly addressed Tom as I added cream to my cup. "Did you hear anything from the crew about damage to the car?"

He clicked something on his computer. "The fire in the 30 car was caused by a fluke, the fuel line coming loose. A one in a thousand thing." He looked at me. "The mechanics guarantee it's nothing to worry about. Plus they'll double-check the 28 and the 29 cars."

"Thanks." I handed Holly her coffee and sat back down.

"Also, one of our guys went to talk to the Benchmark Racing crew," Tom reported. "They said something broke in the throttle system—it stuck wide open and braking didn't do any good."

Holly and I absorbed that news in silence. Tom went back to rapid typing. I didn't know if the explanation of mechanical failure seemed wrong, or if I simply wouldn't ever find an explanation acceptable given the result.

My cell phone buzzed in my pocket, and I pulled it out. Another message from "Stuart," aka, the mystery reporter. I raised my eyebrows at Holly.

"Excuse us, Tom," Holly said. "We've got to discuss something."

He flapped a hand in the air without taking his eyes from his screen. We moved to the other side of the small room to sit at the meeting table.

I set the phone down between us so we could both read the messages, as a barrage of loud booms sounded, making us both jump. We looked up at the TV feed to see the fireworks being set off along Lake Lloyd in the Daytona Speedway infield.

Holly checked the time. "Nine o'clock, on the nose."

We turned back to the text message: My name is Foster Calhoun. Freelance investigative journalist, mostly big stories for major print papers, but also online media outlets now. Look me up. I'm legit.

Holly typed his name into an Internet browser on her phone.

I asked my first question. How did you know to contact me?

Stuart raved about you, came the response.

That surprised me, and I elbowed Holly to look.

"When and how'd he come to be speaking with Stuart?" she asked. I typed those questions.

He'd mentioned you a couple times, especially how clever you were. Then a second response: We were college roommates. Hadn't talked in a bunch of years, until recently.

"Stuart reconnecting with an old friend has gone about as well for him as it went for me to reconnect with my old friends last year," I commented to Holly.

"Which is to say, not so well," she returned.

"Right." I focused again and typed, Why do you think it wasn't an accident?

Holly held her phone out, displaying a page about Foster Calhoun, multiple Pulitzer Prize-winning journalist and graduate of the same university Stuart attended. "I guess he's for real," I muttered.

The text response came back. I don't think, I KNOW it wasn't an accident. Someone saw Stuart meeting with me last night. Tried to run my car off the road. Then tried to take Stuart out today. Someone from the Arena team.

I texted back: Did you tell the cops about last night? How do you know it was someone from Arena?

No cops. Looked like the driver wore a purple shirt. Car had a race parking tag hanging from the rearview mirror.

I gasped and typed. What kind of car? Why haven't you told the police yet?

White Chevy rental, no back plate. Writing story. Now, what can you tell me?

NO, I typed back. The cops need to know so they can catch who did this to him!

He replied: Six other witnesses had cell phones out. Cops have info. I owe it to everyone, especially Stuart now, to publish this story and prove who the villains are in the paddock. Talk to the cops if you want. I'm finishing the story first. Do you have any info for me?

I shook my head, trying to clear it, then typed again. What do you mean, you were meeting with Stuart?

We had a beer last night at a bar, then we were supposed to meet for coffee across from the track this morning. He was hit walking there. Can you tell me who you've seen in Arena's race paddock? Who their sponsors are?

I turned to Holly. "That's a weird set of ethics. He knows this and hasn't told the police."

"You want to tell them?" she asked.

"Hell, yes."

"I'll get them over here." She tapped on her phone.

I typed a message telling Calhoun the sponsors I knew of on the Arena Motorsports cars and names of any individuals I knew associated with them. It was a short list. I threw in names of supplier representatives also, and told him we'd look around, plus I'd ask other trusted contacts.

That's it? he replied.

Take it or leave it, I returned, furious. I haven't had much time since being in the car for two stints and watching a teammate be killed on track.

I sat there, shaking, until he responded. Shit, sorry. Didn't know. Send me whatever you can, asap. I'm writing all night. Turning off now.

I wished I could throw my phone across the room without doing damage.

Holly leaned over and read the last couple exchanges. "What a jerk. Latham's right around the corner. I told him to come in here."

I tried to calm down by watching the race feed. Miles was still in the car, trading second, third, and fourth positions in class back and forth between our car, one of the pro-driven Arena Motorsports Porsches, and the Ferrari I'd trailed earlier.

Latham entered the lounge and joined us at the table. "I thought I told you not to engage, Ms. Reilly?"

"What if he really knows Stuart and really saw what happened?" I paused and finally let go of something that had gnawed at me for a while. "If this wasn't a random attack, if it was someone related to the race, how are you going to investigate once the race is over?"

Latham crossed his arms over his chest and stared at me, stony-faced.

I pressed on. "How are you going to question people when we all pack up and leave? You're on a countdown clock like the race is. You need all the help you can get to figure this out *now*."

Chapter Seventeen

"I won't deny it'd be easier to get this wrapped up before everyone involved with the race leaves town," Detective Latham conceded. "But that doesn't mean putting you in danger. One person in critical condition is enough."

He held out a hand, and I gave him my cell phone, the text messages on screen.

"Foster Calhoun," read Latham. "I've heard that name before."

Holly had the information ready. "He's won two Pulitzers in the last decade, for stories on the proliferation of identity theft in the United States and how the Mob's money laundering operations touch all levels of society."

Latham scrolled up and down a couple times, reading the messages more than once. "You don't know who it *really* is on the other end. He could be lying to you about someone going after him. About all of it."

"Why would he say it's okay to talk to you if he was lying?" I took the phone back.

He frowned. "I'm going to need to hold on to that."

I was shaking my head before Detective Latham finished the sentence. "Not a chance. Mine." I slipped it into the pocket of my firesuit, in case he had grabby intentions.

Holly spoke up from across the table. "You need her to keep talking to him, in case he's for real."

His frown turned into a scowl. "You've got to keep me informed of every interaction you have with him. Try to get him to talk to us directly."

"We're here now, aren't we?" I crossed my arms over my chest. "You've got Stuart's phone number, can't you track the cell phone or something? Triangulate the coordinates?"

Latham rolled his eyes. "We're trying to get help with that, but this isn't a TV show. It's not that straightforward."

"Sorry." I briefly felt foolish instead of angry.

"We get it a lot."

I lowered my voice, making sure no one else could hear me. "Will you investigate Arena Motorsports? Question everyone on the team who has a parking pass?"

He didn't react.

"You already are," I concluded. "Did someone else tell you about the parking tag? Did anyone else get a look at the driver? The reporter says it was a white Chevrolet rental car with no back plate—are you searching for the car?"

"I'll only tell you this much." Latham looked exasperated. "The report of the driver in question wearing a purple shirt is new—and conflicts with other reports. We'd heard about a parking pass—which only limits the suspects to any race participant with infield parking. Yes, we're searching for the car. We will investigate all allegations, but I'm not prepared to share any other information we may or may not have about the vehicle or driver."

I snapped my fingers. "That woman who kissed Stuart is part of the Arena team. Maybe you can check her out. She's got to be up to something."

He raised an eyebrow at me. "Could Stuart have been cheating on you?"

I winced. "I don't think so." *He might have been disappointed in me, but he'd break it off with me before turning to someone else.*

"Stuart would never do that," Holly put in. "He's a Southern gentleman enough to be polite, no matter how forward or poor someone else's behavior was."

"She's part of this suspicious team—" I began.

"Says someone who may or may not really be a reporter," Latham interjected.

"She's acting aggressive," I went on. "She keeps giving me dirty looks for no reason."

Latham looked blank. "In that case, I'll be sure to check her out. Can't have dirty looks."

"Don't make fun of me." I dropped my head in my hands, tired of the whole day.

Holly shoved her chair back and stepped around the table to face him. Her fists were balled on her hips. "Don't patronize either one of us. Would you prefer we don't tell you about any of this? Because that was on the table."

I studied them: the tall, gun-toting detective facing off against a petite, flaming-redhead. I had to go with Holly.

"I apologize, you're right. I was out of line." He looked chagrined as he rubbed the top of his bald head. "Let me write down the messages—and I'd like screenshots of them also. I won't take your phone. But make sure you tell me about anything else you get—and don't go digging on your own. I'll take you seriously if you let us do the investigating."

"Deal." I handed my phone back to him so he could read and make notes. Five minutes and a few more warnings about not getting ourselves into trouble later, he left.

Holly ran her fingers through her short, corkscrew curls. "You gonna listen to him? Leave all the investigating to the po-lice?" She drawled out the final word.

"Are you crazy? I'm going to figure out if this reporter is for real and if he's right. Because I want to know who hurt Stuart—" I faltered, but kept going. "To make sure they get what they deserve." I eyed her. "You in?"

"Call me Dr. Watson, Sherlock."

I smiled and followed her out of the lounge into the garage area. She went to check in with the folks in the Western Racing team garage. I aimed for the Tommys: Thomas Kendall, our rock-star gentleman driver, and Tom Albright, our media guy. The two of them—who we'd agreed to call Thomas and Tom to avoid confusion—stood talking in front of the 30 car's closed garage door.

Thomas tossed an arm around my shoulders while Tom finished scribbling in a small notepad.

"You taking off, Thomas?"

"You kidding me?" He shook his head. "I'm part of this team, and I'm here to the end. I'm gonna soak it all in to be ready for next year—plus cheer the rest of you on."

"What happened today hasn't ruined racing for you?"

He ran a hand through his hair. "I won't tell you it's been a great experience. It's also been an expensive one—but I can't consider money when we think about poor Ian." He paused, and scrunched his nose, looking down the paddock. "I know racing is about taking the ups with the downs. I figure this place owes me some ups after starting with the downs." He shrugged. "Bottom line, I love racing."

I smiled at him. "I'm not going to argue with you."

He chuckled, then looked down the paddock. "*There's* someone I'd like to meet. Guy who made it from sportscars up into NASCAR."

My stomach lurched as I realized he meant Sam Remington. Tom turned to me. "You know Sam, right?"

I did my best not to grimace. "Sure, I'll introduce you sometime." *How about not right now?*

But there was no avoiding it. Sam was coming our way, a beauty queen tucked under his arm. I took a deep breath.

Sam greeted me and nodded at the two Tommys. "I'm so sorry about Ian. My condolences to all of you."

Hearing this has to get easier, right? "Sam, do you know Tom and Thomas? Tom Albright, our team media and logistics guy. And Thomas Kendall, owner of the 30 car."

Sam shook hands with Tom and then with Thomas. When he gave Thomas a confused look, I added, "You probably know him as Tommy Fantastic."

"Of course!" Sam gushed. "I'm a fan. So sorry about your race."

"I'm a fan of yours, too," Thomas replied. "I hope this will be your year in Cup."

The woman wrapped around Sam's elbow cleared her throat, and we all turned to her. She was inches taller than Sam and gorgeous—slim, blond, and perfectly proportioned. She was decked out in skintight clothing and wedge heels that made her legs look like they should be insured. I was shocked the men had ignored her this long.

"Sorry," Sam said. "Tommy—Thomas—and Tom, this is Paula Quinn."

She smiled, displaying perfect white teeth. "Sam's fiancée. Lovely to meet you."

I waited a beat, then reached out a hand to her, since no one else was making the introductions. "Hi Paula, I'm Kate Reilly."

I got a quarter-wattage version of the smile and a handshake with only the tips of her fingers, as if she didn't want to touch me at all. "Of course, Kate."

She knows about my history with Sam. I felt better than I had all day.

She saw my smile and smoothed her thick, straight hair over her shoulder with her left hand, flashing her enormous diamond engagement ring. As the three men traded compliments, Paula leaned over to me. Keeping her right hand locked around Sam's arm, she pasted a fake smile on her face and said quietly, so only I could hear, "Keep away from my man, bitch."

Chapter Eighteen

I laughed out loud, unable to help myself. When the guys all turned to us, I gave them a genuine smile and pointed to Paula.

She fluttered her eyelashes at them. "Girl talk."

Don't make me puke.

Sam patted her hand and turned back to Thomas. Paula glared at me. "I will *hurt* you if you get in my way."

I spoke quietly. "You're always welcome to my leftovers, Paula." I leaned around her to speak to Tom and Thomas. "I've got to go. Catch you all later."

I set off back to our team lounge. I hadn't paid much attention to who occupied the other rooms in the small building, but as I approached our door, Raul Salas exited the room to the left of ours.

He broke into a smile and threw both arms in the air when he saw me. "My racing partner!"

I couldn't help smiling back. "That was fun, wasn't it?" I held out a hand.

He raised an eyebrow and shook my hand. "Very much fun, Kate. You are quite talented."

"As are you." I gave an experimental tug, but he held onto my hand with both of his. He started caressing it with one of his thumbs. The sensation drove all thoughts from my mind. I stared at our hands, then looked up at his face.

He ducked his head an inch or two to look me in the eye. "You are a compelling woman, Kate Reilly," he whispered.

His eyes, his focus on me, and his voice were all mesmerizing. I don't know how long I stood there staring at him.

What the hell are you doing, Kate?

I took a deep breath and pulled my hand free. "Same goes. See you later." I fled back into our team lounge.

I spent the next ten minutes inside, watching the live race feed and coming to a few conclusions. First of all, Raul Salas was dangerous. But a hell of a driver. Second, Paula was crazy, and so, by extension, was Sam. Third, I was a horrible person because while I wanted Stuart recovered and back at the racetrack more than anything, I was glad for a break from his disappointment in me about our relationship.

Fourth, I was angry at Foster Calhoun, who I figured bore at least some responsibility for Stuart being hurt. Fifth and last, I wanted whoever had run down Stuart to pay—whether that person was from the Arena team or not.

Calhoun believed an Arena team member was responsible, but it would take more than the word of a stranger to convince me. That meant I needed intelligence on the people in and around the Arena Motorsports megaplex in the pits. When Holly arrived in the team lounge, I was wrapping up messages to my father and grandfather asking for anything they knew about the team owner, Richard Arena, as well as his partners and supporters in racing—and swearing them to secrecy.

Holly laughed hysterically when I quoted Sam's fiancée. "Was Sam always so controlling, Holly?" I asked, reflecting on his comments earlier in the pits.

"He's always been friendly, gorgeous, humble, but still somehow in charge. Always the one offering praise or comfort. You needed a boss or mentor. Someone to help talk through decisions. Maybe that's controlling, maybe it's guidance. But you sure need it less now than you did back then."

"I don't want it."

"It appears he found someone who does. I hope they'll be very happy together." She ignored my eye rolling and waggled her cell phone at me. "Different topic, back to Calhoun. I found something you should see."

I read the headline of the article displayed: *Journalist Jailed for Assault on Potential Source.* The journalist in question was Foster Calhoun.

"It was eight years ago," Holly said. "But he did punch a guy who promised him a scoop and didn't follow through."

I looked at her. "You think he attacked Stuart because Stuart wouldn't give him information?" I supposed it was possible Calhoun had become irate at Stuart refusing to help him with his article, and then Calhoun had run Stuart down.

Possible, but not likely?

Holly sighed. "I'm not sure what I think, but I found the article."

"It's hard to know what to believe or who to trust, isn't it?"

"You're not kidding, sugar."

I changed the subject by asking how Greg and the others down at Western Racing were coping with the news about Ian.

She shook her head. "Greg wasn't there, but everyone else is shaken up—upset, angry. The car's still running sixth, but they're all unsettled because they're not sure what Greg's going to want to do, if and when he reappears. I can't blame them—or him."

I looked at the clock on the wall then pointed to our long, water- and wind-proof jackets with Sandham Swift, Beauté, and BCRF logos embroidered on them. "Time to bundle up and get back to the pits."

The fastest route there was through the Fan Zone, an extensive area that offered everything from viewing windows into the garages—this was a NASCAR track, after all, and fans couldn't be allowed to overrun the garages; they had to watch through windows—to a stage, gift shop, and concession stand. Plus the real bathrooms I was so fond of. The zone extended from the interior of the V-shaped garage buildings to the Daytona 500 Club that loomed above Victory Lane, opposite the track's start/finish line.

At the Daytona 500 weekend, the Fan Zone would be packed, and any driver who dared show their face inside would be mobbed. But during the 24 Hours of Daytona, drivers, teams, and fans mingled everywhere. The real rock stars—of racing and music—were still surrounded by small crowds when they ventured into the public-access space, but drivers like me typically wandered everywhere unrecognized and unmolested. That level of acceptance or anonymity suited me fine. I didn't need the insane fan worship Miles had, for instance.

This time through the Fan Zone, we ran into Zeke Andrews, a former driver, on-air commentator for SGTV, and my friend and mentor. I was surprised to see him in the infield of the track, because this race was his first in his new role of reporting from the booth instead of running up and down pit lane all race.

"You couldn't stay away?" I asked as he enveloped me in a hug.

He laughed, releasing me and turning to hug Holly. "Did my opening stint, didn't I? Now I get a break for dinner like a good lad." Zeke was born in South Africa, grew up in Australia, raced for many years in Britain, and currently lived in North Carolina. His accent and expressions were all over the map, depending on who he'd spent time with recently.

He turned back to me. "Plus I hoped to catch you now rather than later tonight. Are you doing all right, Katie-Q?"

"I'll be okay." I was already tired of the question, though I appreciated those, like Zeke, who asked and really meant it.

"And yourself, Miss Holly?" he asked.

"Coping."

Zeke nodded. "Best that can be hoped for. You tell me when you need anything at all. A shoulder for your weeping, a drinking buddy, someone to help you face down the bullies. Either of you, say the word."

I smiled at my burly, big-hearted surrogate big brother. "You can help us with one thing."

"Anything, luv."

I looked around to be sure no one was within earshot. "Tell us what you know about Arena Motorsports and Richard Arena."

"Tell me first how you'll use it."

"Nothing public," Holly assured him. "No publication, no spreading stories around."

He raised an eyebrow. "Then, why?"

I explained about the accusations made by Foster Calhoun. "In fact, maybe you can find out more about Calhoun, too. From your journalism sources or something."

"If it's his investigation, his story, and his arse in danger, why are you asking questions?"

"To find out stuff the police can't. I swear, we're in the cops' back pocket with this, Zeke." I took a breath and looked across the Fan Zone. "But I need to do everything I can to make sure whoever hurt Stuart is caught. And punished."

Zeke hugged me again.

"Dammit, I'm not crying, Zeke," I said against his shoulder. "I'm pissed off!"

He chuckled and released me, then thought a moment. "What I know is the Arena team raced in Grand-Am for half a dozen years, getting better and bigger each season. This is the first year they've had such a presence." He shook his head. "The logistics of that many cars, trucks, and people is amazing."

Holly twirled a finger in the air.

"I'm getting to your point, luv. The money comes from Richard Arena, who's made several fortunes in a few different businesses. He drives. He's gone from being a raw amateur to quite good and respected—for his driving skill, at least. He's especially good at capitalizing on other drivers' mistakes on track—keep that in mind when you're out there, Kate." At my nod, he continued. "On a personal level, most people find him withdrawn and aloof—particularly the media, who can't get an interview. Ever. His official bio says he grew up poor in Los Angeles, the oldest of five kids."

"I know about the olive oil business—that's one of his, right?" I asked. "What else?"

"A national chain of Laundromats and a home security

company. And now the racing team, which must bring in some money, the way he's got a dozen or twenty guys paying for a ride."

Holly looked between me and Zeke. "None of that sounds like something to have a reporter on the run, afraid for his life."

Zeke rubbed his chin. "There's also the federal investigation."

Chapter Nineteen

"The what?" Holly and I chorused the words.

"No one I know will talk about the details," Zeke said. "The media knows multiple federal agencies spoke with the Series and some of the team's partners. No charges yet, but we're all assuming it's a matter of time."

I sputtered. "If he's doing something illegal—"

"Is he?" Zeke looked at our shocked faces and glanced around. "No one has proof of anything. I suspect the racing world is making as much money as they can from him before he goes down. Or goes away."

Holly lifted a shoulder. "I've seen that happen before. Out-and-out crooks racing until the day before they're carted off to jail. Racing takes all types."

I put some pieces together. "Calhoun must know more of Richard Arena's story." Another thought occurred to me, and I swallowed my distaste. "Zeke, what do you know about the brunette woman associated with the team?"

His eyes brightened. "Yeah, *her*. Wowzer."

My insides clenched. Holly hit Zeke on the shoulder. "Cut it out."

"What?" When he got nothing but stern looks from us, he sobered. "All I know is she works for the team—or for the boss in general, not sure. Her name's Monica. She's gorgeous but unfriendly."

Holly shook her head. "Or she's only friendly to the *right* people?"

"Which doesn't include me, more's the pity." Zeke shrugged, then waved at someone approaching behind us.

I turned to see a guy I recognized from the former ALMS, Perry Jameson, who'd had something to do with media or marketing.

Perry turned when Zeke asked if he knew us.

"Of course, good to see you. How's the race going for you?" He shook our hands.

"Our car's—"

Yet another man in a firesuit walked past and darted over to shake hands with Zeke.

Perry turned and then looked my way again. "I'm good, thanks. Working freelance now for a few teams."

I saw the same mystification on Holly's face. I cleared my throat. "The merger turned out all right for you?"

His expression soured. "For me it's been great. I can't say the same for everyone, can you? The teams don't know whether they're coming or going with regulations, drivers don't know their rankings—it's no way to run a series." He sighed. "But the *geniuses* in the front office aren't asking me, so I'll withhold comment."

That's what you were doing.

Zeke said good-bye to the other guy and rejoined us. "I've got to be off to my dinner. Perry, which way are you going?"

"I'll walk with you toward Linda's."

Zeke gave Holly and me each a quick hug. "I'll pass the word if I hear anything else. Tell me what I can do for you." He headed off with a jaunty wave, Perry at his side.

I looked at Holly, my eyes wide. "What was *that*?"

She shook her head. "Self-absorption at its finest. Also an example of how even someone who's better off after the merger still has strong feelings about it."

"I expect Stuart is one of his 'geniuses in the front office.'"

"Seems likely. Let's keep moving."

Holly and I finished crossing through the Fan Zone and entered pit lane at the opening nearest the garages. A Chevrolet-powered prototype went by, making a loud, uneven, popping sound. We stuck our fingers in our ears until it passed.

Western Racing was the fifth team along, and we stopped briefly, not expecting any news, but unable to walk by without comment. Holly was right: emotions ranged from grief to despair to anger, usually in the same person, in the same two minutes. The team might be reduced in numbers, but everyone who remained had been with Greg for a decade or more and had watched Ian grow up. They were hurting.

I worked hard to keep the tears at bay as I exchanged condolences or hugs with half a dozen people. I was determined to hold it together while I was in the pits. The motorhome, and if need be, the team lounge, were my safe zones for excess emotion. The pits were where I focused.

We set off again down the walkway behind team pit spaces. Lights blazed in every active pit setup, and we peeked into them as we walked. We saw every approach to equipment and configuration: big, small, ornate, sparse, and everything in between. Carnegie Performance Group, or CPG, had some of the nicest gear and pit boxes, which wasn't surprising, since that team primarily ran NASCAR—a series second only to Formula 1 in terms of the opulence of team equipment. As we passed CPG, I was glad I knew Sam to be safely back in the garage area, so I didn't have to worry about being ambushed.

Holly nudged me. "You going to let the boy have his say this weekend?"

"Sam? There's nothing I want to hear. There's no point."

We'd been following the on-track race action from one set of team monitors to another, and as we pulled even with the Benchmark Racing tent, the race went yellow for debris. We stopped, along with a handful of other non-Benchmark people who were in the area, to watch the replay of an incident between a prototype and a Ferrari.

The two cars had tangled after successfully navigating through the infield and exiting Turn 6 onto the NASCAR banking. Typically the slower car stayed low on the oval and left the high line to the faster car, but the Ferrari swung wide to avoid a Porsche nursing a deflating tire—and swung into the prototype. The impact sent both cars into the outside wall, then back down the banking onto the flat, grassy shoulder area, where the Ferrari narrowly missed also taking out the wounded Porsche. The prototype's left front tire was immediately cut down. Half a lap later, it tore open and started whipping apart the car's bodywork. Debris from the car's carbon-fiber panels littered the back straight, which brought out the full-course caution.

We stood near the entryway to the Benchmark pits watching the incident replay, the flying car parts, and the eventual decision by the affected car's driver to stop and wait for a tow. I checked the crawl at the top of the screen. Mike was still in third place.

Someone in a team shirt I didn't recognize asked Holly a question. As she answered, I looked around the pit space. It was triple-wide, to support their three cars—all Porsches, the numbers 72, 73, and 77. My stomach plummeted to my feet.

Of course, the 77 car. Benchmark Racing. The car that took Ian out.

I looked at the people in the tent and saw subdued expressions, bowed heads, and no smiles. Granted, that might be the case for many teams up and down pit lane. I couldn't be sure I wasn't imprinting on them what I expected to see. But everything about the team felt muted, except for one crew member in a green Benchmark team shirt who sat on a drinks cooler staring at the ground in front of him, arms wrapped around himself, his whole body shaking from the jittering of his right leg up and down.

I stepped back into the walkway to wait for Holly, feeling like I was prying by staring at the team that had caused Ian's death. A man on top of the big pit box turned around to look for someone, caught sight of me, and waved exuberantly. It was Vladimir—or Pyotr, I wasn't sure—one of the Russian brothers.

I saw the other brother and Vinny, their minder, sitting next to them.

I felt someone watching me, and I glanced around, catching sight of a young woman on the next pit box over. Slim and blond, with familiar blue eyes. She raised a hand when she saw recognition on my face, and I returned the gesture. She looked intrigued. I hoped I looked blank—instead of dismayed at the thought of having to interact with more members of my father's family.

"Isn't that…?" Holly spoke at my elbow.

"My half-sister, Lara. I wonder what she's doing here."

"At the race or in these pits?"

"Either. Both." I lowered my voice still further and changed the topic. "It's hard to accept the 77 car is still running."

She sighed as we resumed our trek down the pit lane. "Racing can break your heart."

"Ladies," said a lovely British baritone right next to us.

We'd only gotten twenty feet, but that had brought us to the next team tent, this one for the LinkTime Corvette team, our competitors in the GTLM class. Our rivals for Corvette glory. And, let's face it, our superiors in all but determination, given the might and wallet of GM behind them.

Duncan Forsythe, one of the Corvette factory drivers, leaned against the chain-link fence opposite his tent, a hand raised.

His gesture seemed more "stop" than "hello," so I moved out of the middle of the lane toward him. "How's the race going for you, Duncan?"

He shrugged. "Fine so far. Early hours yet. I wanted—all of us did, really—" he gestured to the tent, indicating the rest of the team "—to express our condolences and support." He paused. "Bloody dreadful, that was."

"Thank you," I managed.

"If you need anything at all, let us know," he continued. "I mean that, Kate. You've got friends here in the paddock—all of you at Sandham Swift do. We may compete out there, but we'll back you up, should you ever need it."

I studied him, considering. We were both professional drivers, Corvette drivers, and part of well-respected teams that had been with the former American Le Mans Series for the majority of its fifteen-year duration. The message felt like a welcome to a more exclusive club. "You sound like you're offering to hold someone down if I need to beat him up."

He smiled. "Perhaps I am."

"Do we get a secret handshake with that, sugar?" Holly drawled.

"If you like." Duncan went from chuckling to serious. "I don't care for what I've seen around the paddock at this race. I don't want the good teams and people," he gestured at us, "to be drummed out by those who lack good sportsmanship."

"By those with more dollars than sense?" Holly suggested.

"Just so."

I lowered my voice. "We're talking about Arena?"

Duncan frowned. "I suppose so—the team, at least. The man himself seems to have some class. I was thinking more of Benchmark next to us. There's a secretive feel to the team that's very strange."

"Why do you say that? Is it the Russian guys? They were nice and so was Vinny. Then again, I'll never forgive the people with the 77 car."

Duncan pushed off from the fence, looking to his pit where someone waved at him. "The Kulik brothers seem all right—aside from an occasional violent streak. But maybe you expect that from blokes who sell alcohol and live in Las Vegas. And Vinny Cruise seems nice also—I don't know for sure. They all *seem* nice. It's a feeling."

"How have the Kulik brothers been violent?" I asked.

"Saw one of them nearly get run over by a crew member from their own team," Duncan explained. "Before you could blink, he had the guy by the neck up against the chain-link fence. His brother had to calm him down."

"That seems extreme," Holly said.

"Indeed it does, though it seems to have been an isolated incident."

"Since you offered help," I said. "Keep your eyes open and tell us if you see anything that backs up your feeling."

"I'll do that," he replied. "You all take care. Kate, I'll see you out on track." He crossed the pit lane back into his tent.

Holly and I started walking again in silence.

"How does that connect to anything else?" she asked, a few pit spaces later.

"I'm not sure. Maybe it doesn't. Maybe Duncan doesn't know what he's talking about. But I'll mention it to the reporter, in case."

"What about the cops?"

I shook my head. "Latham didn't like my speculation about Monica, so I'll hold on to this, unless Duncan finds evidence."

We'd reached the first opening in the long Arena pit tent, finally nearing our Sandham Swift pits, when we were nearly run over by two men who only looked where they wanted to go, not where anyone else might be. One of them bumped into Holly, knocking her into me. He turned to help catch her before she took a nose dive.

We all froze, recognizing each other. Holly recovered first, finding her footing and slapping the man's hands away. I heard her mutter, "Snakes."

I flashed back to the previous October and the threats these two men had made after being introduced to me as family. The menace they radiated in my direction wasn't dimmed by time. My heart rate picked up, from equal parts trepidation and anger.

As usual, Holden Sherain glowered at me. This time he also glared at Holly, no doubt blaming her for the collision he'd caused.

Billy Reilly-Stinson grinned, also as usual. "We meet again."

Chapter Twenty

I waved a hand up the walkway. "Don't let us stop you from rushing away. Please, carry on." *Out of my sight. Out of my life.*

Holden, the dark, brooding one of the duo, took a step before realizing Billy wasn't moving. A gaggle of cars went by on the front straight, momentarily stopping all communication. I itched to be in one of them so I didn't have to deal with my irritating pseudo-family members.

Billy was planted, arms crossed over his chest. I wondered if others saw malice in his smile. "We've got a moment to visit with *family*. How have you been, Kate?"

I played along. "I've had better days. Yourself?"

"Fine, thank you. How's the race been for your car?"

Why are you here and what do you want? "We're holding our own so far. Are you here with your father?" I'd known of the possibility my father's brother Edward would drive in this race. But I hadn't seen his name on the official driver roster, which had relieved me. Disappointment was a mild word for what I felt as I faced my cousins.

Billy glanced at Holden, who still hadn't said a word—this too, according to script. "Here with my father," Billy confirmed. Maybe his father was here but not driving.

Billy lifted his nose higher in the air. "We're also here as official representatives of the bank, which is sponsoring two cars, as well as the entire United SportsCar Championship."

As if I hadn't noticed? I looked at Holly, who seemed content to observe the farce playing out in front of her. I turned back to Billy and fake-smiled. I didn't speak, merely looked at him and his cousin.

"Billy, come *on*." Holden finally opened his mouth.

I raised my eyebrows at them. "Don't let us keep you from whatever deals you need to make. People to see, all that."

Billy followed Holden down the walkway, with a look back over his shoulder at us. "We'll talk more later. See you, Kate."

"Not if I can help it," I replied, for Holly's ears only.

"It's too bad they're such jerks, because they're damn fine-looking."

"What do you suppose that was about?"

"Clear as the day is long. They want something—at least Billy does."

"I'm not giving them anything. This is not the day to mess with me. I've had enough already." I pulled my phone out—no new information about Stuart.

We started walking again. As we passed the big tent, I was dismayed to observe my father inside talking to Monica and three men: the man I assumed was Richard Arena, along with the fifty-ish, gray-blond man who'd nearly run us over earlier in the evening—who I suspected was my father's brother—and Raul Salas.

My stomach churned as I considered the timing. Not thirty minutes ago, I'd sent my father a request for information on Richard Arena. The next thing I knew, he was talking to the man himself.

Is my father ratting me out? Should I feel guilty wondering that about him?

Yes, he was my father, but I didn't know him very well. Didn't know who or what came first in his loyalties. I assumed he'd help me and keep my secrets, but was I sure?

Calm the hell down, Kate.

I forced myself to breathe deeply as Holly and I finished traversing the length of the Arena pits and arrived at Sandham Swift. I waved her into the tent and moved to the fence side of the walkway. I took three more breaths of race-scented air, thinking about why I'd leapt so quickly to assume betrayal.

I heard Grandmother's voice in my head. *Betrayal's all you can expect from that family.*

I didn't know for sure what had happened at the time of my birth between my grandmother and my father's family—or even who had been involved besides my father and his father. All I knew was my parents had met, fallen in love, gotten pregnant, and gotten married while attending Boston University. My mother had died in the hospital two days after I was born, and my maternal grandparents had raised me in Albuquerque, New Mexico. I'd met my father for the first time three years ago, only because the racing world had brought us together.

My grandparents' side of the story—via Gramps, because Grandmother refused to discuss it—was my father and his family hadn't cared about me, didn't want me, and didn't have the decency to see me in the hospital. I had photographic evidence the latter wasn't true, as well as my father's word he and his father had cared.

A cautious relationship with my father was one thing, trust was another. While I had two years of my father offering support and affection—at arm's length, by my own choice—I had a lifetime of *knowing* the only people I could count on were myself and my grandparents.

I'd grown to trust Holly and Zeke. But I'd also trusted Sam, and he'd let me down. Was it too soon to be sure of my father? He'd given me no reason to distrust him—except for his continued association with my scheming cousins. Could I blame him for his family?

And what was Raul doing mixed up with those guys? He'd seemed like a good guy, but maybe he wasn't to be trusted either. Or maybe he was as big a flirt with everyone as he'd been with me, and he was trying to get close to Monica. *Which shouldn't be hard, right?*

I'm turning into a hypocrite.

I saw members of our pit crew stand up, stretch, and start to move to hoses and other equipment. I shook off my gloomy thoughts. Time would make my father's actions clear. Until then, I had better topics to focus on. Like the race. Or Stuart. Or trying to figure out who hurt him.

I pulled out my phone. Still no news. I texted Polly again for an update and got a prompt reply of no change in Stuart's condition. I moved across to our tent to think about my job.

Colby shifted to make room as I joined her in front of the monitors. I quickly located Mike in our 28 car coming through the tri-oval. I ducked down to look at the small section of track we could see and spotted him as he passed.

I spoke to Colby. "We're still on schedule? You'll be in after Mike does a triple?" My next turn in the rotation, a planned triple stint, would come after Colby did a triple—probably somewhere between one and two in the morning.

"That's the plan." She paused. "Kate?"

I transferred my gaze from the monitors to her, and she continued. "I know we're all trying to deal with what happened to Ian, but you've got extra to deal with. You're clearly coping. I know you'll be as tough as you need to be to finish this race. But let me know if I can do anything."

I smiled, feeling pleasure in Colby as a friend and a fellow warrior. She knew exactly what it was to be a woman in the male-dominated racing world. To be tougher than many men, but still feminine. To bury emotion. To always have something to prove.

I hugged her. "I've got your back too, whenever you need it."

We stood together watching the monitors for the next fifteen minutes, until Mike brought our car in for a green-flag stop—our ninth of the race. The crew, including our Michelin tire representative, inspected the tires carefully, but didn't change them. They filled the car with fuel, cleaned the windscreen, and sent him away again.

After the stop, I climbed onto the pit cart to get an update on the car from Jack and Bruce. Their verdict: everything working fine so far, brake wear within expected levels, and double-stinting tires now that the track was dry and cool. We were still on schedule—which I took to mean something would go wrong soon, simply because nothing ever went according to plan in a race as long as this one.

Not two minutes later, another team's plans stuttered to a halt at the side of the racetrack as Race Control threw a double-yellow to retrieve a stalled car. The Mazda of our next-door neighbor, WiseGuy Racing, had no "go." I knew their crew would hustle out of the pits, up the lane, and back to the garage to meet and fix the car. Tough break.

"Full-course caution, Mike," Bruce radioed. "Stopped car driver's right between the International Horseshoe and the Kink. You'll stay out, since we just pitted."

I gave Bruce and Jack a thumbs-up and climbed down from the cart. I could have kicked myself for moving when I did. When I reached the ground, there was Sam Remington again.

Chapter Twenty-one

Sam was as focused on me as he'd been the last time he walked into my team's pit space, but he wasn't likely to start a conversation I wanted to avoid. This time he had his fiancée and an older gentleman with him.

"Kate." Sam put a hand on my shoulder. "Let me introduce you to Mr. Jimmy Baker. Mr. Baker, Kate Reilly."

I smiled with real pleasure as I offered a hand to the trim, smiling gentleman in front of me. He was taller than me—taller than Sam and Paula also—sporting salt-and-pepper hair and a blue-and-yellow striped bow tie.

"A pleasure, Mr. Baker." I pegged him as five or eight years younger than Gramps, but possessed of the same cheerful, feisty spirit. It was the twinkle in the eye that gave him away.

Paula stood to the side looking as if she'd eaten a lemon. The other two didn't notice, and I chose to ignore her.

"Call me Jimmy, please, Kate. Lovely to meet you as well."

Sam patted me with the hand still resting on my shoulder. "Jimmy's here with one of my sponsors—Belcher's Supply."

I was familiar with the supplier of everything necessary to build, wire, or control a physical object. The brand featured prominently in my grandfather's creations. After early days in sales and then as a race-shop apprentice, Gramps made a career out of weaving wiring harnesses for racecars, work he continued to the present day. More than one of his products circled the track at Daytona, including in my own car.

"He especially wanted to meet you," Sam went on.

Jimmy smiled even wider. "I've been working for Belcher's for thirty years, and I've handled your grandfather's orders for twenty-five of them."

"You go way back with Gramps. Come to think of it, he's talked about a Jimmy plenty of times."

He chuckled. "That's likely me. We go back to when you'd just arrived on the scene. I've hoped to run into you on the circuit someday, and here we are, finally."

We chatted briefly about how often he got to races and what the track was like. Sam chimed in, obviously familiar with Jimmy from sponsor activities throughout the full racing season. Paula continued to stand aside and scowl at me.

I walked the three of them to the tent opening to continue their tour and encouraged Jimmy to return to our pits or visit our driver lounge. They set off up pit lane, but almost immediately, Jimmy returned and tapped my shoulder.

He spoke in a low voice. "Your grandfather put the call out to his network a couple hours ago for us to watch out for you."

To his network? Good grief. "I don't—"

"You probably *do* need watching out for." Jimmy smiled. "Besides, I'll thank you to humor a couple old men who'd like to pretend they're being helpful."

I laughed. "Fair enough."

"Call or get word to me if you need anything at all." He pressed a card in my hand. "Information, assistance—anything."

A new voice caught our attention, and we turned to see Tug fawning over Sam and Paula. Jimmy heard my sigh.

"I've had my doubts about that Tug Brehan," he muttered.

"Why's that?"

Jimmy shook his head. "I suppose I should judge on the present, not the past, but I've been skeptical of his character since I saw him manipulate and backstab his way into a higher position—at the expense of someone else's career."

It was all I could do not to turn and stare at Tug. "Where was that?"

"In his early days with Grand-Am—six years ago now. Mind you, he's never done anything like it again, not that I was aware of. But as a stand-in for your grandfather, I suggest you be careful placing your trust in him, Kate."

I assured Jimmy I would and sent him away again with a kiss on the cheek. To my relief, Tug continued up pit lane with them. The list of people I could trust was dwindling.

The GT class cars pitted, including the 29 car, which came in for a driver change. The cars in first and second place in the GTLM class stayed out with Mike, who was still in third. I watched the 29 car's stop from an out-of-the-way corner of the tent. Then I returned to the monitors to watch the rest of the stops taking place up and down pit lane—including the Arena mega-team servicing six of their seven cars at once.

Four laps later, the field was collected again, and we went back to green. Sadly, we proved the old saying "cautions breed cautions" true once again.

This time, it was two GT cars in Turn 3, the International Horseshoe. The result was one damaged Porsche trailing a bumper, but continuing around the track back to the pits under its own power. The BMW it tangled with, however, was off-track driver's left, stuffed into the tires. The live SGTV feed replayed the accident. Anyone who hadn't caught it the first time reacted with winces and gasps.

The Porsche, one of the Arena fleet, had completely and obviously misjudged the braking zone. It had barreled out of control through the turn, slamming into the BMW and sending it spinning into the tires—not unlike Ian's accident. SGTV focused on the wounded Porsche entering the pits, identifying the car as one of the pro/am combinations and the driver as an amateur, Ed Grant. Which figured.

Grant had been involved in two different incidents this year already, both resulting in multiple damaged cars. The accident at the winter test days, three weeks before this race, was clearly

Grant's fault, but no one was too outraged because we all knew amateurs made mistakes. Especially in the first practice session, when dozens of newcomers had only excitement to draw on, rather than experience.

But then Grant got mixed up with a prototype during practice on Thursday before the race. That mistake sent the prototype into the wall of the tri-oval at nearly 200 mph. The extremely charitable might have called it a racing incident. The rest of us began to suspect that particular driver was a menace.

"Not him again." Bubs stood with me, watching the mess. "He's a one-man wrecking ball."

Lars Pierson arrived for his on-deck shift in the 29 car and asked what happened. I pointed to the replay.

Bubs jerked his thumb in the direction of the Arena pits, where we heard engine noise. "Back for repairs already."

Lars narrowed his eyes at the screen. "They should stand that driver down. He should no longer be allowed to race. He is a plague."

Leon Browning, fresh from the 29 car, walked over from a debrief with his crew chief and overheard Lars. "You're right on that front."

"Weren't you right there for this one, Leon?" I asked.

"Aye, what a stupid git," Leon bit out. "Totally Grant's fault. You could see it coming yards away. I'm with Lars, Grant ought to be stood down."

"Have either of you ever seen that happen?" I hadn't witnessed a series pulling a driver from a race because of poor skills—that problem usually took care of itself, with accidents that damaged cars beyond repair. But Leon and Lars both raced in Europe—Leon nearly full-time, only moonlighting in the States.

Leon shook his head.

Lars lifted a shoulder. "I know they can do it. I think the ACO—" he meant the Automobile Club de l'Ouest, the organizer of the 24 Hours of Le Mans "—pulled someone out a few years ago at Le Mans."

"I guess he's bringing big money for the ride—extra, since

he has to keep buying more car parts," I offered. "The suppliers can't hate that."

Leon snorted. "I don't care how much he's pouring into coffers. When he's taking other cars out and endangering everyone on the track around him? Money can't make up for someone who's incapable of racing at this level."

I agreed, though I thought half a dozen amateurs had escaped the same fate as Grant only through sheer good luck. Dozens of amateurs competed in the 24 Hours of Daytona—and their skill level varied dramatically. But that's what this race was all about.

In silence, we watched the cars circle behind the pace car for three more laps. Leon shook his head, rousing himself. "I'll be off to clean up. You two are in next?"

"After Paulo's double-stint," Lars agreed.

"One more stint for Mike, Colby for a triple. Then me. Maybe around one." I did some rough calculations. "You'll be back in around four or five tomorrow morning?"

"Aye, something like that. I'm away now for a wee bit of a meal and sleep." Leon waved and set off up pit lane.

Lars went to talk to his crew chief. I moved forward to the pit wall to take a look at the damaged Arena car. The biggest problem was the torn-up radiator, which had leaked fluid all the way from the point of impact and now bled onto pit lane.

The team opted to push the car back to the garage to make the repair—which shouldn't take more than a few minutes, assuming no other damage. Back on track a few laps down didn't seem like justice, not when the BMW might be out of the race through no fault of its own. But justice wasn't up to me. Besides, I should know life was hardly fair these days.

Grant had climbed out of the car. As I watched, he stripped off his gloves and unfastened his helmet, all the while talking with a member of his crew. He waved off an SGTV pit reporter and turned to observe the crew rolling away the car he'd wrecked. Then Grant pulled his helmet and balaclava off and accepted a towel from a young, blond man, clapping a hand to the towel-delivery guy's shoulder.

I sat down hard on the wall. The two men were carbon copies of each other, separated by twenty or thirty years.

The younger man was my cousin, Billy. Which made Ed Grant, the scourge of the paddock, my uncle.

Chapter Twenty-two

I caught Holly's eye back in the hospitality corner of the tent and waved her over, whispering my discovery in her ear. We watched my uncle turn away from the car being repaired and disappear into his tent—snubbing the SGTV reporter once again.

"I would not have guessed that," she said. "Ed Grant and Edward Reilly-Stinson. Maybe Grant's his middle name?"

"Must be. At least I don't have to deal with jokes or questions about being related."

"Your racing talent clearly came from your mother's side."

We headed out to the walkway again, the better to observe comings and goings at the Arena team. I caught sight of movement in the pit space next door, but my brief hope we'd see their car pull up faded quickly. It was activity of the wrong kind: WiseGuy Racing packing up its gear. I returned to our crew at the monitors and asked what they'd heard.

"Electrical," reported one of the tire changers. "Something fatal. No replacement parts."

I shook my head, sorry for everyone on the WiseGuy team who'd spent immense amounts of time and money to get a car to the track and ready to race, but who'd go home with nothing to show for it—not even the badge of honor of taking the checkered flag. In a race like this, the ultimate glory was a podium finish—with winning being nearer a miracle. Simply to be running at the end was a monumental achievement. Teams that folded up early would get a better and warmer night's sleep tonight than any of us at the track. But no one welcomed that rest. Everyone wanted to be here.

Stuart should be here, dammit. I pulled my phone out of my pocket, sure it was time for news from the hospital or for more information from Foster Calhoun.

"Anything?" Holly asked.

"Nothing. From anyone." I texted Polly at the hospital. Then I texted again apologizing for so many messages.

"Do we know anything we can tell Calhoun?" Holly continued.

I shook my head. "Do we know anything at all?" I felt tired and emotionally wrung out, overwhelmed with the enormity of it all. Worse, I had no idea who to believe or how to figure out who the culprit was. Foster Calhoun was pointing us at Arena, but did I agree with him? Did I have a better idea? Did I have the stamina to answer those questions while also trying to make sense of the senseless—Ian's death? While also facing fifteen and a half more hours of racing?

Holly put both hands on my shoulders and turned me toward the hospitality area. "Sugar, you need a pick-me-up."

"I'm not—"

"Coffee and a snack. Then we'll sit down."

She collected a banana, some peanut butter, and a Styrofoam cup of coffee with sugar and cream. We took seats on the 30 car's empty pit box. The field continued to circle the track behind the safety car, while the last track vehicle pulled away from Turn 3, cleanup complete. I estimated they'd go back to green in another three laps.

"What's going on in that head?" Holly prepared to make notes.

I spoke quietly. "Do we believe Calhoun about Stuart's accident? That someone from the Arena team did it?"

Holly pursed her lips. "Look at it this way. Stuart was hit. The person didn't stop. That makes it a crime, and the driver ought to be punished."

"True."

"Maybe it's a simple accident, but the driver didn't stop. Or maybe it was a deliberate hit. Either way, we want to know who did it."

"But if we do what Calhoun wants and focus on Arena, are we investigating Stuart's accident or investigating the team?" I could hear the frustration in my own voice.

She pointed to the banana. "Eat. How did you figure out who killed Wade Becker? Or Ellie?"

I swallowed the bite of food and sipped some coffee. "Dumb luck?"

She rolled her eyes at me. "Try again."

"I talked to people. Asked questions. Put two and two together." I took another bite and considered. "I see your point. Let's funnel Calhoun the details he wants. On top of that, you and I will become the biggest gossips this race has ever seen— at least you will. Everyone talks to you. I can't leave the pits much—though you never know who will come to me. Then we'll see how the information we collect adds up."

"Sounds like a plan." Holly took my phone and accessed the message thread with Calhoun. "Starting with telling the reporter who we see connected with the Arena team."

"I'm not sure where to start with 'connected.' Is that known associates? Anyone we see in the tent? Random visitors might not be connected to the team at all." I shook my head. "Hell, he can make sense of it all. Calhoun wants names, we give him names."

"What about the cops? What do we tell them?"

"Everything they're willing to hear."

The safety car went by on the front straight, sixty-some cars in its wake. The noise made speech pointless for a moment.

Holly stopped thumb-typing. "Calhoun wanted us to tell him about sponsors and anyone associating with the team."

"We gave him sponsors—unless you noticed any other tiny stickers on the car?" For the privilege of logos on a racecar and official team uniforms, sponsors paid varying amounts of money—from small all the way up to enormous, corresponding to size and frequency of the logo.

"I haven't seen anything new. What about people?"

"Aside from sponsor reps and team members, we've seen the technician and head guy from Michelin."

Holly typed names.

I kept thinking. "They'd have to have a Porsche rep—*that* was a face I recognized. A woman, Sabine Bauer. But I'm not coming up with other suppliers."

"Forget suppliers. Think about walking past the tent and tell me who you saw."

I closed my eyes, trying to picture the scene any of the times we'd passed. I frowned. "My father. My cousins—but I don't know if they count as sponsor representatives."

"Doesn't matter. Tell me people."

"Pyotr and Vladimir. What's their last name?"

"Kulik."

I opened my eyes. "What are they, anyway? Russian mafia?"

"We don't ask those things, Kate." Holly raised her eyebrows. "They're representing Kulik Vodka."

"The vodka car, of course." I murmured. "Their minder Vinny was with them, too."

I looked to the monitors. The safety car's flashing lights were turned off, which meant they'd go green the next time past us. "We didn't see Tug in there, but he must have stopped, because he went to every other tent, right?"

"And Elizabeth with him, I'd guess."

"Elizabeth. She's so…"

"Forgettable?"

"I was going to say unmemorable, compared to Tug."

Holly snorted. "That boy does have charisma."

"Do we count reporters? Scott Brooklyn was there."

She shrugged. "I'll give it all to Calhoun."

The noise increased as the cars powered through the tri-oval to take the green. We stopped talking to watch the monitors.

Mike held station in third place, fighting off a challenge from a factory Corvette behind him.

I heard a shout from the pits behind us even before I saw the action on-screen. More overeager drivers, more contact. This time in the West Horseshoe, in the infield. Two cars banging, brushing sides. An impatient prototype diving inside a Viper and paying the price. Both cars continued, but the prototype's left front fender broke loose and started shredding, sending bits of bodywork flying.

Carbon fiber shards worked on tires like knives worked on soft butter. All of the cars past the injured prototype were sitting ducks for debris. Which included Mike.

The 28 Corvette dodged hard left, both left-side tires cut down.

Chapter Twenty-three

The yellow flag flew for debris. Mike steered down onto the flat apron of the track, planning to enter the closed pits—which would incur a minor penalty. The alternative was to ride around on track until the pits opened, but since the tires wouldn't last even a full lap, there was no choice. Our crew scrambled for their tools.

By Series regulation, a car that couldn't safely continue on track—due to a flat tire, not enough fuel, or another issue—was allowed to come in for service on the problem item only, even if the pits were closed. However, it had to rejoin the field on-track and return to the pits during regular pit stops for full servicing. Mike arrived within seconds. Our crew changed the two cut tires but didn't do anything else, and Mike went back out.

We'd lost positions, but it could have been much worse. The rapidly disintegrating prototype had slowed its pace to a crawl, still depositing debris around the track. It was only now entering pit lane. That car looked to have suspension damage in addition to the torn bodywork and disintegrated tire. The driver had paid a tough price for his lack of patience.

A few minutes later, Mike followed most of the GT field in for a full service of fuel and tires all around. The good news, though we'd lost positions on the field, was we were only one lap down to the leaders, in eighth place. Our Corvette had suffered no lasting damage to anything but the tires. With more than fifteen hours still to run, we had plenty of time to fight back.

Holly and I exhausted our memories of people we'd seen associating with Arena Motorsports, and I reviewed the list while she threw away the remains of my snack. A minute later, we stood at the monitors to watch the field go back to green—which stuck this time. As the cars settled into a rhythm, we did also, leaning against the chain-link fence in the pit walkway. We kept one eye on the monitors and the other on the comings and goings at the Arena setup.

I elbowed Holly, seeing two men walking down pit lane. "Isn't that the main SGTV guy there?"

"Yep, the one next to the head of Porsche Motorsport Worldwide."

I looked at her with raised eyebrows. "Who do you figure they're there to talk to?"

"Arena himself? Ed Grant? Look who's greeting them."

I turned to see the SGTV and Porsche representatives standing in the walkway with my father. "He's been in with that team this long?" I felt uneasy again about his loyalties.

Before the three men could exchange more than hellos, they moved into the tent to get out of the way of the WiseGuy crew removing the last of their equipment—the main pit cart, with folding tables lashed to the top—from pit lane.

Holly and I crossed to the pit wall in the now empty and dark space between Sandham Swift and Arena Motorsports. Across from us, behind the start/finish line, rose the tall grandstand. I squinted up at the tower building looming above the stands, trying to make out spotters on the roof, high above suites housing Race Control, broadcast and other media booths, and top-tier hospitality suites.

In the sudden quiet caused by no cars in front of us, we heard a voice from the tent next door. "Richard! Come meet—"

The rest was drowned out by a Porsche on-track. Holly and I looked at each other. We took three steps to the right, close to the canvas wall of the Arena Motorsports tent.

We heard a mixture of voices: "This year…cars…sponsors and drivers…funding…features…possible."

Then three sentences in another long lull between passing racecars: "I'm aware it takes money to make money. But it's better if you throw in a little more. I encourage you to be creative, gentlemen."

Then nothing but a sense of movement next door and one last phrase. "Protect my brother."

"Who's talking?" I hissed to Holly.

She shrugged and pointed to a gap where two canvas side panels overlapped. The rope that laced through the wide grommets of each panel had missed a set of holes, leaving an opening that flapped open and closed depending on wind or someone pushing on the canvas. I carefully positioned my hand to keep the flap on my side from blowing open and exposing me, then put my eye to the small opening. I jumped back immediately at the sight of Ed Grant's angry face.

I waved Holly off when I realized he couldn't have been looking at me. I peeped through the canvas again. Grant stood a few yards away, talking to someone. I shifted and saw Billy listening to him, with my father next to Billy, closer to the tent wall. Then Grant turned to his right as someone else spoke.

A gust of wind swept past us and sucked the other panel open. It was only a two-inch movement, but it felt like complete exposure. My instincts took over. I dropped straight down into a crouch below the opening and waved Holly out of the pit space. She scurried out to the walkway. I crab-walked a few feet before standing up and following her. Thirty seconds later, we were leaning against the chain-link fence behind our pits, half hidden behind a rack of tires, when Billy walked out of the Arena pit and around to the spot we'd vacated.

My heart pounded in my ears as we watched Billy stick a hand and then his head through the opening.

He withdrew and turned to leave. I pointed to something in the Sandham Swift pits, saying to Holly, "Look over there so he doesn't think we're watching him."

"That was close."

I laughed, too loud, releasing tension. I turned to her, glancing at the walkway. Billy watched us. "Too close. He's still looking this way. Come on."

We kept our attention on our own team area as we crossed the walkway and entered our pits.

I collected two bottles of water from a cooler and handed her one. "Grant, Billy, and my father were talking. There was at least one other person, but I couldn't see who."

"Could you ask your father?" She saw me squirm. "You did ask him for information already."

"He's been over there talking to them for so long. And that's his brother. I'm not sure who he's more loyal to."

"Speaking of brother, you think it was your father saying 'protect my brother' about Grant or Grant saying it about him?"

I thought back to the voice we'd heard and frowned. "I don't think it was my father's voice, but I'm not sure."

"Probably it was Richard Arena demanding people think creatively about making money."

"I wonder who he was talking to. My father? My uncle? The SGTV or Porsche guys?"

"Seems like a bold demand to make to the head of a network or a car company."

I raised an eyebrow. "Seven cars in his stable. 'Bold' is an understatement."

"The coast is clear, let's go back out to the walkway."

"No more peeping Tom. I'm not cut out for this spy stuff."

Chapter Twenty-four

I made it back to the chain-link fence in time to watch my father leave Arena Motorsports with the SGTV and Porsche representatives. He looked in my direction and lifted a hand. I nodded, not wanting attention called to my presence. He kept walking.

At the Arena tent, Monica reappeared. My stomach clenched. She stood with a different man with close-cropped dark hair and long sideburns.

"Who's that with her?" I asked Holly, my words swallowed by a prototype roaring out of the pits past us.

"The hatchet man."

"That's his title?"

She laughed. "Rumor is he does the dirty work for Arena in the team. Officially, he does a combination of computer setup and logistics. Nice guy, more friendly and open than some of the others around there."

"Except for maybe being a hatchet man."

"I think his name's Ryan. Ryan Johnston."

I glanced back and saw Ryan and the witch greet Tug Brehan and Elizabeth Rogers. I looked at Holly. "When did I start thinking of the Arena team as the evil empire?"

Holly pointed to the empty pit space between our teams—except it wasn't empty any longer. The wall panels between the

Arena space and the former WiseGuy space had been unlaced, and someone had rolled a tool chest into the opening to hold open one flap of the tent wall. "You did call him bold," she noted.

I drained the last of my water and walked to the garbage can near Arena's tent to toss the bottle. Two plastic chairs and a cooler were set up next to the pit wall in the WiseGuy space. A crew member ducked through the opening into the dark, empty pit space and lit up a cigarette. A second guy arrived a minute later, and the two held an animated conversation, judging by the red ends of their cigarettes being waved around.

"Taking full advantage of the space," I commented to Holly. "Is that allowed in the rules?"

"Doubtful."

I shook my head, pulled out my phone, and typed an update to Calhoun.

Holly glanced over. "Are you ratting them out to the Series?"

"Calhoun. Updating who else we've seen."

"Wrap it up, because someone's on his way to talk to you."

I caught sight of my father headed back down the walkway toward me.

"I'll leave you to it." Holly crossed to the tent.

He greeted me, taking Holly's spot. "How are you doing?"

I shrugged. "I'm coping. I've had better races. Better weekends. Did you—were you able to find anything out for me?"

"Not much more than you already know. The Series staff I spoke with said they're keeping you informed, and I could only press them for so much."

Keeping me informed? He's not talking about Arena, he's talking about Stuart. I pressed the heels of my hands to my eyes. Guilt washed over me. I hadn't forgotten about Stuart. But I was focusing more on the details of who'd done him wrong—at least I could have some impact on that.

"Kate, are you all right?"

I dropped my hands and tried to find a smile for James. "What did they tell you?" He hesitated, and I pressed him. "I'd rather hear it from you than through paddock gossip. You know it'll get out."

"And better you hear it from me than from someone excited about the details of someone they don't know."

I braced myself.

"The scuttlebutt concerns some of the more distressing details of the accident itself." He took a deep breath. "A witness says when Stuart was hit, he flew at least fifteen feet and bounced three times. Also his non–life threatening injuries are more severe than they've reported to you. Both arms and both legs are broken, along with a shoulder blade and an undetermined number of ribs."

My throat felt like it had seized up. I fought to drag a breath into my lungs.

My father put a hand on my shoulder. "I'm sorry. That's why I didn't want to tell you."

I felt numb, my whole being focused on a vision of Stuart being hit by a car. Almost killed. Maybe dying on an operating table. I surprised myself with a single sob, though my eyes were dry.

My father hesitantly reached out and pulled me into his arms, patting my back softly. It was the first time we'd hugged. I relaxed into him for three heartbeats before realizing I didn't want our relationship to make the rounds of gossip along with the details of Stuart's injuries.

"I'm all right." I pulled away, but gently, trying not to notice his disappointment.

He cleared his throat. "On another topic, did you see that your—my daughter, Lara, is here? With Benchmark Racing?"

"I saw her. What's she doing? Isn't she still in college?"

"She's majoring in math and wanted some experience running computational models on the raw data the cars transmit." He smiled, obviously proud. "I'm not sure of the details, but she's volunteering for them. Maybe you can stop in and say hello. She mentioned hoping to see you this weekend."

I hesitated. Thought of all the reasons why *not* to see her, primarily my reluctance to leap into the bosom of my father's family, as well as not wanting to broadcast the connection. I sighed. "I'll try."

My father looked around and lowered his voice. "What was it you were asking me about Richard Arena?"

"I need some information, and I can't exactly explain why. And I need you to not tell anyone. Please."

He regarded me solemnly for a moment, then spoke. "As long as it's not illegal or immoral—which I don't expect, mind you—I'll help you in any way I can."

Now I'm going to owe him, dammit. "Thank you. I don't think this is either. I'm looking for information about who is interacting with the Arena team. Who the team principals are—besides Richard Arena, of course. Who the partners and sponsors are, who the drivers are, especially the gentlemen drivers." I saw him start to frown. "I'm not asking for any information that's private—I don't want to know who's spending what or why. I'm looking for names. Even photos of the scene and people would be great."

"I don't—sorry. You can't say why." He paused. "Forgive me, I have to ask this. The information won't compromise the team or car—or bring harm to anyone?"

How do I answer that? "Not unless they deserve it."

"I can live with that."

He gave me a brief rundown on the corporate sponsors of each Arena team car, most of which had a company executive doing a rotation behind the wheel. "That includes my brother Edward, of course," he said. "You knew that."

"I didn't think he was here. I didn't see his name in the program."

"He goes by Ed Grant—his middle name—when he wants to downplay his relation to the bank."

"He's not the most popular driver in the paddock today, after mixing it up with the prototype."

My father looked momentarily troubled. Then he shrugged, an unusual gesture from him. "That's his situation to manage. Nothing I can do about it."

My father ran down the basic, public facts about Richard Arena, adding he'd been impressed with Arena's focus and business acumen, even through limited interaction. "To be so successful across multiple corporations—and racing teams—almost requires some amount of aggression or ruthlessness. I speculate that exists. I don't know it."

He paused again. "Let me think more about other individuals who may have a connection to him. I'll send a message with anything else."

"Thank you. Again, please don't tell anyone. Especially not Arena. Or your brother."

He went still. "My brother can take care of himself."

"I didn't know if you were concerned with…*protecting* him in some way."

"My brother doesn't need my protection—and I'm long past taking his advice, especially when the topic is y—my personal life."

I wondered if he'd started to say "when the topic is you." My insides twisted at the thought of his brother saying anything at all about me.

My father put a hand on my shoulder and spoke again. "Besides, Kate, this is what families do for each other—and you're family now. Finally."

I found it hard to breathe again. *That's what I was afraid of.*

Chapter Twenty-five

After my father left, I joined Holly at the side of the tent. We had a view of a pit stop by the Viper in the pit space on the other side of us—an unplanned stop, if the smoke coming from the engine was any indication. As we watched the mechanics work, I filled her in on what my father told me.

She studied my face. "Are you all right about Stuart? I'm sorry you had to hear that."

"Had *you* heard it?"

"No, but I knew something was making the rounds."

I felt visceral pain at the thought of how badly Stuart was hurt. "I'm dealing with it." Almost without thinking, I pulled my cell phone out of my pocket to check for messages. Nothing. I texted Polly to ask when the next surgery would take place.

"If your father's not interested in protecting his brother," Holly went on, "it wasn't him we heard in the Arena tent."

"We can't assume every stray comment we hear means something." I shrugged and handed her my father's list of names.

She raised her eyes from the list. "I didn't realize the Arena team was also sponsored by SunWise Oil."

"Isn't that a typical supplier deal where the team runs the sponsor logo in return for a discount price on the product?"

"I think there are only three teams using SunWise: Arena, Benchmark, and Western Racing."

"I'm not sure what that tells us."

"Hell, me either," she said on a laugh, turning back to the list. "Here's something interesting."

I looked at the name. "Willie, the Michelin rep?"

"Willie used to be married to Cecilia, down at Carnegie Performance Group."

Sam's team. "That's interesting?"

"Cecilia and Willie don't get along so well these days. Cecilia's brother Robert hates Willie with a passion. Robert is here driving with his Grand-Am team, Redemption Racing, which is owned by CPG—CPG is the parent company, only runs NASCAR, and Redemption is the sportscar racing offshoot. Here at this race, they're really one team sharing resources."

"Two teams associated like that is pretty standard. Didn't one of the main tech guys from the ALMS end up with Redemption? Plus Raul Salas is driving for them."

Holly smiled. "Mmmm, Raul. And you're right, Bob Something-long-and-Slavic wound up there after not being invited to join the new series. Plus Redemption is home to Joe Smith." She gave the name air quotes. "Robert's good friend and teammate here and in Grand-Am."

"What's with Joe Smith?"

"We all know it's an alias, we just don't know for what. Or who or why."

"Have you met him?"

"Seen him," she said. "Ordinary, late twenties, dark, sort of Latin looking. Decent driver—not a pro, but a good and improving amateur who must bring money."

"Is the alias to hide where the money's coming from?"

"We assume. Did I mention the reason Willie and Cecilia split was because Willie had an affair with a woman who works for Arena Motorsports?"

"No doubt who that is."

Holly agreed. "Also, Joe Smith used to race with Arena, until a heated fight in the paddock at this race last year. By mid-year, Redemption Racing appeared with Joe and Robert featured.

Rumor has it Stuart was involved in helping Redemption get connected, supplied, and approved in time to run half a season last year."

"To summarize: there's more than one person up at Redemption Racing, and the sister team of CPG, who's got it in for Arena Motorsports. Also the existence of Redemption Racing might be a reason for someone at the Arena team to be mad at Stuart."

"Bingo. And if you want pure gossip—"

"Why stop now?"

"There's the man Cecilia took up with right after she and Willie split—he was responsible for spreading the news that Willie and Monica were sneaking around." She nodded down pit lane.

Tug Brehan exited the Arena tent, shooting his cuffs and looking up and down the walkway. Elizabeth Rogers appeared a moment later, escorted by evil cousin number one, Holden Sherain. It was difficult not to stare at the group open-mouthed.

"That's quite a story," I muttered. "And that's quite a trio."

"I'm not sure of Tug's role, but the other two remind me of Little Red Riding Hood and the big, bad wolf."

"Elizabeth looks enamored." Every bit of body language, plus what I could see of her facial expression, said the blonde, bland Elizabeth was infatuated, flirting with Sherain. His body, in contrast, read as no more interested or less aloof than usual. But I couldn't see his face.

Holly shrugged. "Maybe he's into her."

"The soap opera you told me, Holly. As entertaining as it is, how does any of it relate to someone hurting Stuart? Or—" I glanced around and lowered my voice further "—to Arena being a crook?"

"I'm not sure. I'm curious why Joe Smith bailed out so fast on a good car. Plus I know there's still a lot of anger, at least on Redemption's side. I wonder if there are revenge or retribution plays in process."

"Maybe you can find out." I stopped there. Tug and Elizabeth were on approach.

"Are you both out here studying the stars?" Tug had a smile on his face. "Reading the zodiac to predict what will happen in the race?"

"Getting some air." I wasn't in a mood to be teased.

He sobered. "No more word yet, I'm sorry."

"How's everything going from your end?" Holly asked.

Tug shook his head, smiling again. "It hasn't been the easiest race. Terrible events to be dealing with. But I think we have things sufficiently in hand."

"And fortunately," Elizabeth put in, her voice low and firm, "It's not as if we were new to the job."

Holly turned to her. "You're now back to the jobs you held in Grand-Am last year?"

Tug let Elizabeth respond. "The same positions, yes, though the landscape has shifted significantly."

I studied their contrasting styles and personalities and understood the choice of Stuart over them. Stuart offered the whole package, while Tug and Elizabeth made a balanced team. For the first time I wondered exactly how difficult it had been for them to lose the jobs they'd had. To lose the influence they'd wielded—or a career, in Elizabeth's case. I wondered how hungry they were for power.

"I've heard the merging of two series into one hasn't always gone smoothly," Holly put in. "I know at least one person who was angry about not being given a position in the new Series. Felt undervalued for the work he'd done over the years. Threw around some pretty dramatic words."

Elizabeth looked as composed and impassive as ever.

"That's been straightened out." Tug waved his hands in denial. "He's quite happy now at Benchmark."

Holly agreed. "The other guy hasn't found a job yet, has he?"

Tug looked uncomfortable. "Not that I'm aware of, but you know, the new structure didn't suit everyone. Tough decisions had to be made."

Someone from a team farther down pit lane paused as he

walked past, asking Tug a question. While he responded, Elizabeth stepped closer to me and put a hand on my arm.

"I know you're concerned about Stuart, but believe me, the moment we hear anything, we'll let you know," she murmured.

I didn't like the thought of strangers as the conduit for news of my boyfriend's fate, but there was little I could do about it. "I appreciate it."

"I hope his situation isn't hampering your efforts in the race. I want to see a woman do well, so give 'em hell out there."

"That's my plan."

She smiled. "I also know Stuart wouldn't want his problems to get in the way of your racing."

I fought to keep my expression neutral. *She wasn't hired by the new Series. She never worked with him. How did she know him?*

Chapter Twenty-six

"It's clear he's a man of compassion and integrity." Elizabeth kept elaborating on Stuart's character. "And understanding. He appears to be wonderful as a mentor and a problem-solver."

I struggled for a response. "He's a great guy."

With a final pat on my arm, Elizabeth turned to Tug and asked him something about a meeting. She looked serene, a small smile on her lips.

In contrast, she'd left me unsettled. I wondered how she had any idea what Stuart was like. How she presumed to know what he'd think or say. *Had he tried to hire her? Made her any promises?* I needed to get a grip and stop overreacting. Stop assuming betrayal.

Tom Albright crossed the walkway from our pits and greeted everyone.

"How're the cars running, Tom?" Tug asked.

"The two we have left are running well. How's everything on the Series level?"

I easily read the expressions that flashed over Tug's face. He started to respond with enthusiasm, remembered Stuart's accident, Ian's death, and his audience, then reconsidered his level of exuberance. He belatedly struck a balance between confidence and regret. "We're getting everything taken care of."

A little more poker face, and he might be a worthy successor to Stuart.

The man I thought was Richard Arena exited his pit space and looked at our group. He strode quickly in our direction, calling Tug's name from some paces away.

Tug turned around. "Richard, what can I do for you?"

Arena reached us and glanced around, greeting Elizabeth and studying me for a long moment. I pegged him as mid-forties, tall and slender, but muscled. He had pale, pock-marked skin, short brown hair, and brown eyes. Up close I could see he exuded confidence and power, mostly via the expression on his face that suggested he was prepared for the rest of the world to disgust or disappoint him. Arrogance of that sort annoyed me.

I held his gaze until he stepped forward, offering his hand. "Richard Arena."

"Kate Reilly." I shook, making sure to return a strong grip. "This is Tom Albright, with Sandham Swift, and Holly Wilson, my manager."

He nodded at them, but didn't offer his hand. He looked speculatively again at me before cracking a very small smile. Then he turned to Tug. "Can you or Elizabeth provide us assistance with something?"

Tug glanced at Elizabeth, who stepped forward instantly. "Anything we can do, Mr. Arena," she replied.

"Richard, please."

Tug addressed the rest of us. "Please excuse us. We'll check back with you all later. Kate, we'll be in touch the minute there's anything to tell."

"My apologies," Arena said, as he led Tug and Elizabeth away.

"I'm not sure what I think about him." Tom sounded thoughtful. "Kate, Jack wanted to update you on the car when you've got a minute."

"Be there shortly," I promised

Before I followed Tom back to the tent, I turned to Holly. "You never told me the stories about Series people who lost their jobs in the merger. How'd you hear?"

She looked smug. "All fishing."

"You made that up?"

"You bet. Now we've got someone to talk to."

"I suppose there's only one former Series employee working at Benchmark Racing?"

"Their new Team Manager, Keith Ingram."

"He was what in the ALMS?" I asked.

"Something technical regulations. Not quite at the top, but close."

"Who made the decision to not hire him?"

Holly raised an eyebrow at me. "A committee headed by USCC's VP of Operations."

"Stuart. Keith Ingram could be mad at him."

"You'd think Keith would be over it by now." She shrugged. "One way to find out."

"You know him?"

"I must know someone at Benchmark. If not, I have two good friends at Carnegie, right next door."

"People talk to you more than they talk to me. How about you see what you can dig up on Arena, Monica, and anyone else on that team? Plus anyone who's got a problem with Stuart?"

"I'm on it. A gossip tour through the pits."

"Find out if there's anyone who's mad about the merger in general. And get anything you can about Tug and Elizabeth." I related what Elizabeth had said to me.

"There's some attitude under all that bland." She paused. "I'll try to figure out who the 'other guy' is, the one Tug said hadn't found a job yet. Plus see how mad Nik Reyes and any other drivers who lost out on rides might be." She frowned. "And I'll find out how Greg's doing."

I looked at my phone for the time: 11:30. This was turning into the longest day of my life, and I had hours—more than two of them behind the wheel—yet to go. "You going now?"

"Seems like a good time. You're not in for a while?"

I shook my head. "Colby for a triple, then me."

The phone buzzed in my hand, a text message from Zeke. I held it so Holly could see also.

"Shouldn't he be asleep?" She asked.

"You'd think."

We both read his words.

I remembered something I'd heard right after the Feds came calling for Arena early last year. It was questions about where the team's previous team computer/media guy had gone. Someone said the Feds wanted to talk to him and even asked people from other teams if they'd seen or heard from him, but no one in the paddock knew where he'd gone. Speculation ran wild Arena had gotten rid of a witness to stuff Arena wanted kept quiet. That's all rumor and my bad memory, but FYI.

Holly and I looked at each other, eyes wide.

I found my voice first. "Are you *kidding* me?"

Chapter Twenty-seven

The phone buzzed in my hand again, and another message appeared from Zeke:

Got a note from a media friend who said, Feds aside (Arena only questioned, remember), the closest Arena has ever been linked to illegal activity was his brother's doing. Brother (Julio) killed someone—details unknown—in retaliation. Arena not involved. Brother disappeared before he could be arrested, out of the country, never heard from again. Arena questioned, not charged. Otherwise, Arena's clean. Lots suspected, never any real evidence.

Another buzz. Same pal knows about Calhoun. Word is he's a cowboy. Totally unorthodox, hardly ever plays by the rules, but gets results. Also brilliant. Watch your back.

I looked at Holly. "Did I tell Calhoun he couldn't quote me in his article?"

She shook her head.

I typed a quick message to the reporter: I'm off the record. Don't quote me unless you ask first.

The phone vibrated in my hand five seconds later, Calhoun this time. Can I call you an "unnamed source in the paddock?"

I messaged back my agreement, then added, Explain again why Arena would hurt Stuart if YOU are writing an article?

The response: I'm not entirely sure. Best I can figure is Stuart might have given me information on the team—financials? Supplier companies? But I know there's something to find, given the reaction.

"Unethical behavior doesn't sound like Stuart," Holly noted.

"But it does sound like a cowboy who doesn't always play by the rules. I don't like how it takes someone being hurt to prove his point."

A new message: Thanks for the names you sent. Anything else for me?

My brain was full, and the image of Stuart getting hit started playing in my head. I offered the phone to Holly. "Can you update him? And maybe send Detective Latham screenshots of what Calhoun says?"

"Sure. You go chat with Jack. Drink more water."

I climbed up next to Jack on the command center, nodding a hello to Bruce on his other side. Jack filled me in on the car per Mike's reports—the important detail was no sustained damage from the two cut tires. Colby was about to get in for her three stints of approximately an hour each.

"We'll need to do the brake job in the next couple hours," Jack went on. "They're wearing like we thought they would—rears will go the distance, fronts will be good for fifteen or sixteen hours. Since we're in the zone now, we'll change the fronts when we get a good, long caution. Could be on your watch."

"No problem."

He studied me. "You look tired. Did you rest?"

"Too much going on. I'm not physically tired. It's the mental part—Stuart, Ian. When I get in and focus on the car, I'll be fine."

"Reilly, if you're not in shape to be in that car, say so."

I smiled. "No heroics. I'm good."

He grunted and settled the radio headset back on the ear nearest me. I took that as agreement and dismissal.

I parked myself in front of the monitors with a bottle of water as a Ferrari slipped past Mike on the back straight. A quick check of the timing and scoring chart told me the Ferrari was nine laps down, not fighting for position. Mike was holding onto seventh place, one lap down to the leaders. Still time to climb back up to the pointy end of the order.

Five minutes later, Holly joined me and returned my phone. "Read the messages when you want to refresh your memory." She lowered her voice. "Calhoun mentioned looking at who's next door—he asked for photos, if we can swing it—but also where that team is interacting with people. Other pits, the paddock, motorhome area, or wherever. I'll keep an eye out."

As a best friend, Holly was worth her weight in gold. "Thank you. Listen, go sleep if you need to. Just because I can't doesn't mean you have to stay awake."

"I've been storing up rest for the three months of off-season. I'm doing fine. Text if you need me."

She headed out in search of information, and I returned to the television screens with relief. I followed Mike from monitor to monitor for four or five laps, watching to see if he'd modified his line and searching for evidence of changes to the track itself. The dirt and debris in the Bus Stop was a given. New, but not unexpected, was the grass on the outside of Turn 3 being torn up, which also contributed to debris off-line.

After a while I scrolled through the messages Holly had sent to Calhoun, telling him who we'd seen where and who my father reported being with the team. She'd also forwarded Zeke's information about Arena's brother.

I thought for a minute about what I knew and didn't know, then typed a message to Calhoun myself. Tell me something about your article. So far you say he's bad and rumors here say he's pushy. Why should we believe you? Why should we do all this for you?

I was surprised by the quick response.

Fair enough, he wrote. Bottom line is Arena's laundering money, and I can almost prove it. I know for sure he's made a career and a fortune out of preying on the already downtrodden in our society. Deliberately targeting poor decision-makers and profiting from their actions. Not crimes, but not nice.

One arm of his business enterprise is Laundromats: some with machines known to break often, driving business to the associated dry cleaning or laundry service. Some with exorbitantly priced coffee shops or salons attached to sell services while you wait. Some with pawn shops attached.

Another arm is home security companies with a twist. His sales team tends to show up in neighborhoods where there's been a rash of burglaries a couple months prior. They make sales capitalizing on residents' fears. I don't have solid proof, but circumstantial evidence suggests he's behind the burglaries in the first place. And his security systems suck.

The idea of crossing Richard Arena was less appealing now. I texted back: Is he dangerous? I heard something about a missing witness.

He wrote: Funny thing, he isn't personally a violent guy. He's even mocked for being afraid to get dirty. Won't carry a gun. But he's got scary friends, and he condones violence on occasion.

I guess his brother got the violent gene? I returned.

Calhoun didn't reply for so long, I thought he'd shut down. Then a reply: I'm an idiot. It was Arena's brother who tried to run me off the road on the drive home last night. I saw him in Daytona Beach and didn't realize it—though he must have recognized me. But that won't be enough to stop me from exposing his brother as a vulture picking over the bones of human misfortune.

"A little overblown for your article," I muttered, typing a response: Focus, Calhoun. How would Julio recognize you? And why would he go after Stuart?

Reply: I interviewed him face-to-face before his trial, story went national. Stuart? Julio thinks Stuart knows who he is also or Julio wanted to stop Stuart giving me information on Richard. Or thought Stuart's accident would stop me. Pick one, they all work. A pause, then a follow-up: Do you trust me now, Kate?

I checked the monitors again. Mike was reeling off the last couple laps of his third stint, and the pit crew was ready next to the wall for an imminent stop. I went back to the messages, telling myself it was stupid to feel guilty about doubting this guy I didn't even know.

I typed back: I trust you more. But this is hard for me. Stuart's in surgery, and some guy I've never met shows up on his phone claiming all kinds of out-there stuff. It's a lot to take in.

Understood, he typed back. Sorry about your team driver also.

I didn't reply, but lifted my head to the monitors as I blinked back a sudden welling of tears for Ian.

The phone buzzed again.

I'm not trying to tell you who to trust—

"The hell you're not," I muttered, reading his words.

—but be careful with Stuart's subordinates, Tug and Elizabeth. No evidence, a gut feeling. Something odd there.

Agreed, I returned. Only Holly and the cops know about our conversation. Not exactly true, since Zeke, my father, and Gramps knew there was a conversation happening, but no one else knew the details. I didn't feel like thumb-typing the full explanation.

Another buzz, this time a message from Detective Latham asking if I had any new information via the reporter. I checked the time, grabbed a radio and headset, and told Latham to meet me in the Fan Zone near the stage in twenty minutes. I had a pilgrimage to make first.

Chapter Twenty-eight

It was no time for me to leave the pits, with Mike handing the car over to Colby and my shift on-deck starting. But I took off anyway, commandeering a golf cart and heading toward Vendor Village.

I ignored a traffic guard's shout of protest and zoomed out the top end of the Fan Zone, where open-sided trams loaded people for trips around the track's interior. Two minutes later, I made a purchase from a vendor then hopped back in the cart and backtracked. I managed to squeeze the cart between the row of port-a-potties and the parked trucks and SUVs pointing at the International Horseshoe, Turn 3. I nosed the cart up to the fence and turned off the headlights.

I sat there breathing, swallowing past the lump in my throat, and blinking away the tears. I watched drivers pilot a dozen different cars through the turn in front of me, and I cheered for Colby and Leon as they went by in Sandham Swift Corvettes.

I finally opened the package of kettle corn and ate some, thinking of Ian and our innocent bet from the start of the race. Wishing he was beside me. Celebrating him. Mourning him. *As Gramps would say, Godspeed, my friend. You are missed already.*

My phone buzzed with a message from Polly at the hospital. Surgeons were prepping Stuart for the next surgery. She'd tell me when it got underway.

I shed a few tears for Stuart as well as Ian, and I sent all the strength I could spare in the direction of the hospital. Then I pulled myself together and got back to my job.

I left the golf cart at the pits and found both officers at a picnic table in the Fan Zone. They looked tired, but they had notepads ready. Detective Latham scrolled through the texts on my phone. Both he and Webster-the-track-cop wrote everything down. I sat across from them and stared at the pits, wondering where Holly was and what kind of information she was digging up.

When they reached the point in the exchange where Calhoun asked us for photos, Latham spoke for the first time. "No photos. No spy games. Forget it."

As accompaniment, Webster made a slashing motion across his throat with the fingers of one hand.

"No spy games," I agreed. "Will you go look for Arena's brother now?"

Latham gave me that impassive look again, which I took to mean "Don't tell us how to do our jobs," "We're already doing that," or both. He looked down at the phone. "A new message arrived. He asks, 'Who is Ed Grant?'"

I made a "gimme" motion with my fingers. When he handed the phone back, I typed and spoke aloud for everyone else's benefit. Ed Grant is Edward Reilly-Stinson, associated with the official Series bank sponsor.

A return message. That's the kind of connection I'm looking for.

My spirits sank.

Another message. Uncle Eddie doesn't have much of a work ethic, and his son and pal Holden spend a lot of money on lost causes, don't they? Ever wonder where they get all that money?

I covered my eyes, not sure why I hated having the connection known. Because my relatives might be crooks, I supposed.

"What? What?" Latham inched forward to see the phone.

I held up a hand, as I typed a short response. How did you know?

Investigative reporter, he returned. Not relevant for my story. Probably.

Please keep that quiet, I typed.

Deal, unless relevant. I'll warn you if so, he said. What I'm interested in is how chummy Ed and Arena are. Can you find out?

I'll try, I told him. Why do you trust me, anyway?

Gotta trust someone. Checked you out. You're straight as an arrow. Going offline now, more later.

My assistant Holly will have my phone when I'm in the car. You can trust her too, I typed quickly, ignoring the cops' exasperated questions.

One last message: I do. Over and out.

I sighed. Latham looked ready to yank the phone from my hand.

"Don't keep this from us," he growled.

"Relax, detective," I snapped. "This is personal. Give me a second." I leaned forward, elbows on knees, and simply breathed.

A minute later, I sat up. "I know you don't blab, but I have to reiterate I don't want this spread around. I really, really don't want it running through the paddock."

Latham raised an eyebrow. Webster shook his head, his arms folded over his chest.

I read them the full exchange. "Satisfied?"

"Thank you." Latham held out his hand for the phone and they wrote down the rest of the messages.

I heard Jack talking to Colby on the team radio, checking on the car.

Then I saw Webster start to type something.

"Hey!" I jumped up and snatched the phone from him. "No way. You're not sending anything from my phone. You can tell me if you want me to ask him something. But no one sends messages from me but me." *Or Holly.*

Webster jingled change in his pocket. "Worth a try."

"Not if you want me to trust you." I scowled at him.

Latham gave his former partner a small shake of the head. He turned back to me. "Truce and apologies. We won't try to take the phone or type anything, all right? Keep working with us."

I thought I saw sincerity. I hoped I did, anyway. "Sure, fine."

"We need to agree on something." Latham looked stern. "You are not to take photos of or in any other way do surveillance on any team in the race. Is that clear?"

I frowned at him. "I won't do anything stupid."

"You're not going to do *anything*," he commanded. "I won't hesitate to post a guard to monitor your behavior if you don't assure me you won't attempt any surveillance. You leave that to us."

I stood, hands on my hips. "You aren't part of the race world—the racing family. You can't be inconspicuous in the pits like I can. Plus, you can't hold me here, and you won't stop me driving that car." Some of the fight went out of me. I spoke again, less vehemently. "I don't want to get hurt. We won't do anything dumb."

Latham stood. "I'll tell you one thing, all right? Whoever did this to your boyfriend, it wasn't Richard Arena or Monica Frank. They were surrounded by people all morning."

I absorbed that, feeling disappointed, yet unsurprised.

"We've had no luck trying to find Calhoun," Latham said. "How about you ask him to meet us here at the track in the morning? Would you do that?"

"I don't know why he'd change his mind, but I'll ask. Have you found the car that hit Stuart yet?"

Track-cop Webster looked at Latham, who shrugged. Webster shook his head. "We've got people searching every lot around the track. Nothing yet."

Latham pointed a finger at me. "Contact us the second you hear anything else." They walked off toward the garages.

I sent Calhoun the request to meet the cops at the track. Then I headed to the bathroom. When I emerged, Sam was waiting for me. I couldn't avoid him.

"Kate!" He hugged me before I could stop him.

I patted his back, trying to be polite and not shove him away. Trying also to ignore how good it felt to be held and comforted, even by him.

Sam pulled away and moved his hands to cup my face. "Kate."

Then he kissed me.

I stiffened, not responding. Resisting. And then I gave in. I kissed him back. Enthusiastically. Frantically, perhaps. So glad for a minute to simply feel wanted and desired. He whispered kisses over my face and neck, murmuring my name, telling me he'd missed me. I clutched at him as he kissed me like I was the most beautiful woman on the planet and he was the servant paid to keep her happy.

I felt great. My brain disengaged, and I simply felt—then reality set in. *What the hell am I doing?*

I broke away and pushed him back, both of us breathing heavily.

"Kate—"

I stopped him with a hand in the air. Physical attraction had never been a problem between us—clearly still wasn't. But it had always been like this: him as protector and worshiper, me as the idolized and protected. Never as a meeting of equals. Like it was with Stuart.

Oh my God, what about Stuart? What have I done while he's comatose in a hospital bed? Did I do this to get back at him for kissing Monica?

"I'm sorry, Kate, you're—I came over to talk to you for a minute. Please?"

I held up a hand again. "I've got to get back to the pits."

"Give me a minute."

I sighed. "Stay over there."

He squared his shoulders. "I want to apologize to you. For two years ago. I treated you terribly."

Figured it out, did you? "All right."

"I didn't have enough respect for your career. For you. All I could see was my opportunity and my wants, and I didn't take yours into account. I can't tell you how sorry I am." He stepped closer, took my hand, and looked me in the eye with that Sam Remington laser-like focus. "How much I miss you."

I felt my eyebrows go up.

"It's clear we're still good together. You enjoyed that kiss, too." He kept watching me. "Say something, Kate. Tell me I'm an idiot. Tell me you forgive me. Tell me you miss me also."

Am I stuck in a bad movie here?

He squeezed my hand. "Don't leave me hanging. Tell me I'm not too late."

I snatched my hand out of his grasp. "Too late for what, Sam? You're *engaged*, remember? Not to mention I've moved on. I'm happy with my life."

Sam shook his head. "Paula…that's not going so well. And seeing you—kissing you, having you come alive in my arms—makes me realize what I gave up. What I could have had, how much better my life would be with you back in it. You're amazing, and I'm such a fool." He hung his head.

My skin crawled at the thought I'd ever found his behavior appealing. I crossed my arms over my chest. "You're doing it again."

He looked hopeful. "Winning you back?"

I burst out laughing, suddenly free of the sexual haze I'd been in. "Not in a million years, champ. You're making it all about yourself again. Nearly every word out of your mouth has been about you and what you want. You haven't asked me what I want, how I am. What my dreams are."

At his stunned expression, I delivered the final blow. "No, Sam, you need someone who's as all about you as you are. Maybe Paula's that person—I hope so, for both of your sakes. But I'm not."

I studied the beautiful, talented, and self-absorbed man I'd loved for a time. "Have a happy life, Sam."

I walked away, rounding the corner into the Fan Zone and immediately running into Paula. That she'd heard our conversation was evident in the fury boiling off her. I swore I saw steam coming out of her ears.

I put my hands up in front of me. "He's all yours."

"Bitch!" she spat.

I didn't stick around.

Chapter Twenty-nine

I hightailed it back to pit lane and ran into Holly as she exited the CPG tent.

"Sugar, did something light your tail on fire?"

I grabbed her arm and marched her down the walkway—away from Sam's team—making her laugh as I described the scene with Sam and Paula. She sobered as I related my conversations with Calhoun and the cops. "I didn't promise *you* wouldn't take any photos," I noted.

"I'm sure the detective didn't miss that."

I felt my phone buzz again and saw a long email from Gramps.

"The way he types, it must have taken him an hour." I angled the phone so Holly could read the words with me.

Dear Katie, he wrote. I talked to two pals of mine from back in the day to see what they knew about Richard Arena. They've both met him—and don't worry, I've sworn them to secrecy and didn't say why I asked.

Holly paused in her reading. "It's not hard for his pals to figure out why he wants to know."

"Gramps might not have realized he was doing it—but too late now." I glanced at the pits—no sign of yellow flags—before continuing to read.

They've both worked with Arena a lot doing driving coaching work. Both have nothing but good to say about him.

Holly and I blinked at each other in surprise. I let out a shaky breath. With those few words, Gramps had turned everything I thought—and felt instinctively—inside out. And deprived me of my favorite suspect for attempted murder.

I shook my head and read the rest of Gramps' message.

Sure, he's got some aggressive assistants who're probably paid to keep his life interference-free. They swear he's a friendly guy, once you get past the protective walls around him. He can be direct and sometimes tough...but remember, that's going to be true of any CEO of a large corporation. They're paid too much to waste their time on the little stuff.

Anyway, Katie, the impression I get from my pals is Arena's basically a good man and certainly a good businessman. He apparently loves racing and wants to be accepted as a legitimate part of the racing world. This doesn't sound like what the reporter is telling you. I guess I'd say be careful to stay cordial with anyone who's got a lot of skin in the racing game. Drive well. Hi from Grandmother.

By "skin in the game," I knew Gramps meant "money in racing." He'd never wanted me to be a doormat, but he'd drilled into me during my early years at the track that supporters and sponsors could come from anywhere. I'd learned to be calm and considerate in victory or defeat, and more than once I'd driven for a team I'd battled fiercely with the year before. I wonder if he'd think I'd burned bridges with Monica? I didn't care.

Holly finished reading. "That was unexpected."

"No kidding."

We watched a crew hustle a prototype's replacement nose down pit lane.

I shook my head. "I can't believe how different Gramps' information is. That guy could be someone completely different than Zeke and Calhoun told us about."

"We only met Arena briefly. Mostly you've seen Monica and

your uncle. She could be one of those over-protective assistants. As for your uncle, you don't choose your customers."

"Arena's a great guy, but he's surrounded by people who do terrible things? And he's blind to it all? That's hard to believe."

Holly shrugged. "How do embezzlers succeed? They're trusted by higher-ups. Maybe Richard Arena trusts his minions too much."

"If that witch and other assistants are who he chooses to surround himself with, maybe it doesn't matter if he's really a nice guy. Charles Manson might have been really nice to someone."

Holly laughed. "You notice when you like someone, they're tough, and when you don't, they're aggressive?"

"Five people interpret the same event five different ways. People with a stake in Arena being successful in racing—Gramps' pals who want to get paid for consulting work, the Series who wants his money—will see what they want to see." I felt my face heat. "For that matter, I want to think he's a villain because there's a picture of his assistant kissing my boyfriend. We know someone hurt Stuart. I want a person to focus on, so I can be mad *at* someone, not just mad at the world."

"I guess we need to keep an open mind about him. Maybe not about her, but about him."

I took a deep breath. "I can believe I'm wrong about Arena, but I can't trust that Monica woman. Not gonna happen."

"I'd call you crazy if you could." Holly patted my shoulder. "Speaking of them, I'm only partway through my rounds, but I have one interesting tidbit."

She looked both directions before speaking again. "More than one source said they heard Stuart was behind the push for bigger, multi-car teams. That he didn't mind forcing out smaller operations like Western or WiseGuy."

My jaw dropped. "That's not true."

"You and I know it."

"If people really think that…"

"It's possible a lot of people are mad at him. Like Greg."

"Mad enough to try to kill him?" I almost choked on the words.

"It's the people who've already been squeezed out—who aren't at this race—who'd be the most angry." She patted my shoulder. "I'll ask about them, too."

"How do you keep all the details straight? I think you need a raise."

"Sugar, gossip to me is like breathing—takes no effort or concentration." She fluttered her fingers and headed back up pit lane.

I made it back to the Sandham Swift pits in time to catch Mike and ask him how the car and track were handling.

He shrugged. "Still nuts with traffic, cars everywhere. Lots of cautions. But it went well. Had some fun."

"How're track conditions?"

"Loads of dirt in the Bus Stop. People have been bombing over the curbs onto the grass so much there's no green left, only dirt. Plus the few offs there. Really have to watch your footing. The West Horseshoe's gotten a little slick too, though that might have been from someone laying down some fluid. Might be gone by the time you're out there."

I added his information to my mental image of the track.

"Also, watch for the front swaybar when you get back in," he added. "Colby likes the suspension softer than you or I do."

"Good to know."

"You hanging in there?" He lightly punched my shoulder. "We're all torn up about Ian, but you've got the double-whammy of Stuart also. He doing okay?"

"Holding his own in surgery, last I heard. I've talked to the cops some—they still don't know who did it. I'm glad to have the race to focus on." I paused, considering the new pangs of guilt layered on top of worry and grief. Anger made up an ever-larger proportion of my emotions.

I shook my head. "I'm getting through. Now go clean up and rest."

"Shower, meal, sleep. Catch you in the morning."

I followed him out to the walkway and looked around at the various activities taking place. Farther down pit lane, at the pit-out end of things, one team celebrated a birthday, singing, unboxing a cake, and taking photos with pocket cameras or phones—which gave me an idea.

I swiveled around, thinking about angles to get a view into the Arena tent. I came face-to-face with Monica, the woman who'd kissed my boyfriend last night.

Chapter Thirty

My heart leapt into my throat, and I froze.

"Kate! We meet you again!"

Vladimir, Pyotr, and Vinny accompanied Monica. Or she accompanied them, since the Russian brothers were the only ones with a goal.

"Please, to take more photos with us?" One of them asked.

I agreed, then winced as he smacked the other brother on the back of the head.

"Vladimir try to save earlier photos and instead delete." Pyotr shook his head and hit his brother again.

I smiled. "It's no problem, we'll take more."

I waved to Tom in our tent and made a photo-taking motion. He appeared a minute later to accept the camera from the brothers. I handed him my phone camera also and told him, in a low voice, to get as much of the pit lane in the background as possible. Vinny stood next to Tom, ready with two cameras of his own. Monica stood to the side, arms crossed over her chest, smirking.

I positioned myself between the brothers with our backs to the Arena pits. They each put an arm around my shoulders, and I rested an arm on each brother's waist—shifting position to avoid identical hard, bulky items at each waistline. One brother jerked away and shifted my arm to his shoulders. A couple photos in, I realized I'd felt guns.

They need guns at a racetrack?

I didn't tense or drop my smile—thanks to years of photos with every kind of fan and sponsor imaginable—but I wasn't comfortable with them anymore. I was relieved when they crossed to Vinny to review the photos.

I swallowed my nerves and pride, then offered my hand to Monica. "We haven't met. I'm Kate Reilly."

"Hard not to know who you are," she returned, in a tone I couldn't decipher. She shook my hand and smiled. "Monica Frank. I work for Richard Arena."

"It's an impressive setup you have. Do you help organize it?"

She chuckled and brushed some of her thick, wavy, perfect hair behind a shoulder. "I'm his chief financial officer and an advisor."

I was impressed, and I didn't want to be. I was also jealous because she was everything I wasn't and usually wanted to be. A couple inches taller, voluptuous, sultry.

She looks like Salma freaking Hayek, for pity's sake.

Not to mention she'd kissed my boyfriend—while I'd only argued with him.

"You work in an industry other than racing?" I asked.

She raised an eyebrow. "Across a variety of them, according to Richard's business interests."

"Sounds interesting."

She studied me for a moment. "Perhaps I should offer my condolences to you and best wishes to Stuart? We're all missing him today." Her tone held all the warmth of the polar ice cap.

I caught my breath. *It seems like a game. I'm here in this artificial world of the race, collecting photos and writing down names. Then I remember the reason: Stuart, so badly injured in the messy, sprawling, real world. Dammit, Kate, do not cry in front of this woman.* "We're waiting to see how he pulls through."

"You don't seem very concerned. I thought I'd heard you're his girlfriend?" Her lips curled with a touch of disdain on the last word.

I looked at Monica Frank as coolly as possible. "My relationship with Stuart Telarday isn't something I want to discuss."

She lifted a shoulder in a graceful shrug. "I was only surprised not to see you more distraught."

I was dumbfounded.

Smiling broadly, she crossed to Vinny, Tom, and the Russians. "Time to go boys, I'm sure this team needs to get back to more important tasks this evening. So nice to meet you, Kate," she called as she ushered them back down the lane.

Tom headed back into the Sandham Swift tent, while I remained frozen in the walkway. I didn't know what to do with the rage filling me. Hitting something—or someone—wouldn't be productive or good form. I wanted more space and more air. Different scenery. I spun around and jogged past the dozen pit spaces between Sandham Swift and the bottom of pit lane.

I stopped in the triangular space formed by the end of the pit stalls, the last section of grandstands above them, and the curving wall of the pit exit road. Two medical workers sitting in a motorized cart glanced my way. A crew member from another team banged out of a port-a-potty to run back up pit lane. I grabbed onto the fence that separated me from the track and leaned my forehead against cold chain-links.

The problem was, I finally admitted, I doubted I was reacting appropriately to Stuart's condition. I wasn't sure how I was supposed to feel—especially because I didn't know if he was going to live or die. My lower lip started to wobble. I reminded myself to breathe.

Did I assume Stuart would survive and get on with my life and job knowing I'd have time with him again? Or did I prepare for the worst, the idea I might never see him again, never be able to resolve the hard words and hurt feelings between us? Should I still have these bouts of tears that hit me without warning? I fumbled for a tissue in my pocket.

We'd been dating. We'd made love. We'd been on the way to falling in love—no, only I'd been in process. Stuart claimed he'd loved me for a year already. That was another brick on the Kate-guilt pile. Would I ever have a chance to catch up? Even if he lived, he'd have months of healing and rehabilitation ahead. Everything would change, no matter the outcome of his injuries.

I couldn't pretend everything between us had been perfect. We hadn't been on the way to the altar. I hadn't been ready for the kind of relationship he wanted. I wasn't ready to be settled. I loved him, but I didn't know if I was *in love* with him.

I felt a microscopic trickle of relief filter through my grief and guilt. Stuart's accident meant a reprieve from the pressure I felt to make a choice I didn't know how to make. A break from hurting him more. From disappointing him. My chest heaved. I blew my nose.

A Ferrari exited pit lane, and I got a whiff of rank port-a-potty smell as someone entered the plastic hut. I tensed when a man cleared his throat next to me.

Vinny from the Benchmark team apologized. "I wanted to make sure you were all right—I know you've got a lot going on, and I'm sorry for all of it. The whole team feels terrible."

I was torn between my need to blame someone for Ian's death—and who better than the team that ran him off the road?—and the knowledge that what happened was an accident. The look of concern and sorrow in his eyes sealed it. I let it go. "Thanks. I guess that's just racing."

He exhaled with what seemed like relief. "Plus if the Kuliks are bothering you, I can keep them away."

"They're fine. As you said, a lot going on." Everyone knew about Stuart and Ian, but there was also Sam to fend off. My relationship with my father—and now a half-sister—to negotiate. Cousins to avoid.

"You needed a break, I bet. Me, too." Vinny sighed.

We stood in silence for a minute, watching a Porsche exit pit lane and a couple dozen cars shoot toward the braking zone for Turn 1.

Vinny spoke again after a loud group of cars went past, entering the turn. "Sometimes I have to slip away in the middle of a race, for a break from the needs of everyone around me. The expectations."

I spun to him. "That's exactly it. Everyone expects something out of you. Me. I mean, my job, that's one thing. But family, friends, press, fans, strangers." I listened to myself. "Now I sound like a bratty child. Being responsible is simply being an adult."

"Sure, but sometimes being an adult sucks." Vinny grinned at me.

I laughed. "Agreed."

"This may fall under 'none of my business,' but Lara Reilly, who's working with my team this weekend, is she…?"

I closed my eyes, and he instantly backtracked. "Sorry, forget I asked."

"It's all right." I looked at him again. "Yes, related. Can I leave it at that? Will you keep it confidential?"

He raised an eyebrow, but nodded. He didn't ask why, but I could see the question in his eyes.

"I don't know how to deal with her yet," I admitted. "I can't manage to do what people want."

He turned to face the track again and spoke with great feeling. "Believe me, I understand."

"You, too?"

He blew out a breath, his expression going from open and friendly to cold and shuttered. "In my family, nothing I do is ever good enough."

"I can't believe that. You're running a team here, aren't you?"

"I never quite measure up." He shrugged.

"You seem successful. Maybe you should ignore your family. Follow your instincts."

He turned and smiled at me. "And maybe you should ignore what others think you should do about…your relation. Do what feels right."

I studied him a moment. He had the trim, muscular build of a racecar driver or a long-distance runner. Everything about him spoke of an easy, friendly guy on the surface, with a core of steel underneath. I might have been wary of him as a representative of the team that ran Ian off the road, but I felt comfortable with him. I liked him.

I held out a hand. "I will if you will—and if we keep it between us."

"The pit lane code of silence? And friends? Deal."

We shook on it. After a check of the time, Vinny set off back up pit lane. I followed a minute later, feeling more centered.

Holly was watching for me as I approached the Sandham Swift pits. "Where've you been, sugar?"

"Had to take a walk after I met Monica Frank."

"What did she say?"

"She accused me of not being sad enough about Stuart's accident. She thought I should be more torn up about it."

"That insufferable *bitch*!"

I smiled. "True."

Holly peered at my face. "It was more than that."

"It was everything. Mostly I had to admit some unpleasant truths." I might not be proud of how I felt or how I had handled Stuart. But I'd never lied to him or deceived him. I'd always been honest about how I felt. God willing, he'd understand and forgive me.

I focused on him for a moment—who he was and what he valued. I realized he probably would forgive me. Moreover, he'd tell me to get out there and do him proud in the job I loved. To make my mark in the world we're both passionate about.

I said it aloud. "Today, he'd want me to focus."

"Not only focus. He'd want you to give 'em hell."

"That's what I'm going to do. For me. For him. Focus on racing tonight and tomorrow. Deal with emotion when we know something. "

Holly pulled out her phone to show me photos and notes she'd taken up and down pit lane. "Maybe along the way," she began.

I finished her sentence. "We'll find the bastard who ran him down."

Chapter Thirty-one

As Colby came in for a green-flag pit stop—fuel only, double-stinting the tires—Holly and I again found seats at one end of the 30 car's abandoned pit cart. A representative from Sandham Swift's main sponsor, BW Goods, sat at the other end of the bench seat, wearing a team radio headset and watching the monitors mounted above the desk.

Holly and I studied the photos she'd taken, wrote down names and connections, and sent everything to Calhoun.

I shook my head. "By the end of the race we'll have sent information on every single person in the paddock to him. I don't see what good that'll do."

"One of them might connect with something he knows that we don't."

"We're still not getting the money shots inside the Arena tent. I don't know how to go about that."

Holly tapped a finger on her cheek. "Certainly neither of us can waltz in there and start snapping."

I started to laugh. "Wrong. Take your boyfriend to meet his fans."

"Miles has fans there?"

"Doesn't he have them everywhere?"

"Good point," she said. "Gotta love our all-access pass, Miles."

"I could also ask my father who he saw there. I wonder if he'd tell me what the group of them was discussing."

"You've already asked him for more than that. It shouldn't be a big deal."

"Did you uncover anything else?"

"Mass suspicion about Arena, but nothing concrete."

"Arena the guy or the team?" I asked.

"Both. About Monica, the men leered and the women rolled their eyes. She's not a female other women like—only cares about men."

"That's misogynistic of her."

"Everyone had heard the rumors of her affair with Willie the Michelin rep, but that was the unusual hookup. She's not sleeping with Arena, but no one's sure why. She's usually fawning over the biggest VIP of the race weekend. While I can't confirm that means sleeping with them, on at least two occasions it did."

I frowned. "Home-wrecking tramp."

Holly sighed. "Much as I hate to go against the feminine code of support for behaving how you want, not how society dictates, I have to agree with you."

I crossed my arms over my chest. "What else?"

"Other than general complaints about Ed Grant, nothing about that team. Except, my goodness, you wouldn't believe the team services. Apparently, what's available to the whole team, not only the drivers, is a masseuse, a chiropractor, a medical doctor, a dietician, and a gourmet chef." She nodded at my stunned expression. "What that chef is working with? Fresh fish for every meal. They're flying in fresh berries and whatever other delicacies they want."

"Maybe Arena doesn't know teams don't actually make money in racing?"

"Either that or spending it is the point?" She waggled her eyebrows at me.

"Money laundering?" I breathed it.

She shrugged. "All I know is he likes living in the lap of luxury. Otherwise, I got more confirmation Stuart was supposedly the one trying to run small teams out of the Series in favor of big teams." She put up a hand to stop my outrage. "I know he wouldn't do that—even the people repeating the rumor agreed when I challenged them. But it's what people are hearing."

I let out a frustrated breath. "I wonder where that's coming from."

"Two people pointed to other teams. One guy told me Tug implied it and swore him to secrecy. Another woman said Elizabeth mentioned something. Overall, the sentiment on pit lane about Stuart—accident aside—is more favorable from the big teams than the small." She grimaced. "I'll be honest. Greg is outright furious."

"At Stuart?"

"At everyone. It's ugly, Kate. I'm so sad it's come to that for Greg. I wish I knew how to help him." She bit her lip. "I didn't see him, but the team said he's been in and out of the pits. On top of his grief over Ian, he's angry at the Series for trying to push him out and welcoming people like that Ricky Amick from the 77 car instead."

A prototype whined its way down pit lane after making a stop. I kept quiet until it passed, glancing at the monitors to see Colby on the tail of a Porsche through the infield. A check of timing and scoring indicated she wasn't jockeying for position—as the Porsche was third in class, one lap ahead of us—but it was interesting to see how our cars compared on speed and handling.

I turned back to Holly. "Leaving aside that Greg and Stuart are people we know, I'd say Greg has a lot of motivation to be mad at Stuart and maybe even lash out. But Stuart's accident was before this race. Before the worst had happened to Greg."

"I don't think Greg tried to kill Stuart. But if *he's* that angry, who else is?"

"Did you get anything on disgruntled former ALMS employees—or participants?"

Holly held up fingers as she related names. "Jonathan Charles, of the right hook, was last seen in Seattle and isn't around this weekend. Nik Reyes is spitting mad about his driver ranking changing—thanks to Stuart and others—which kept him out of the race. As a side note, Cecilia at CPG is no longer involved with Tug—though 'involved' was an overstatement."

"A revenge hookup?"

"She loathes the Arena team with a passion, especially your favorite female. Any mention of them gets Cecilia riled up—I guess they closed ranks and denied any inappropriate relationship between Willie and Monica. Then went out of their way to belittle the Redemption team and Cecilia. She's convinced the Arena team was behind pranks like garbage dumped in front of their tent overnight and a bunch of stolen flats of soda and sports drinks."

Holly saw my look of disgust and went on. "No proof, just suspicion. Back to Keith Ingram, in the Benchmark tent next door to her. Cecilia hasn't interacted with him, but from what she's seen, he's an angry guy. On the other hand, Cecilia wouldn't mind being extra friendly with your friend Raul. She was sneaking peeks at him when he was over at Benchmark."

I ignored whatever it was inside that felt like jealousy, because being jealous would be absurd. "I thought he drove for Redemption Racing?"

"He does, but he was in Benchmark when I went past." She paused. "He was in the Arena tent before that."

We were both quiet a moment, watching the 28 car on the monitors.

Holly stood up. "I'll head back out there. Spend more time at CPG and Redemption, get closer to Benchmark, and maybe get some scoop on Joe Smith."

"Be careful of the Kulik brothers and their guns."

She raised an eyebrow at me.

"Small of the back. You know, arms around waists for photos? Creepy." I looked around the pit space. "Do lots of people here carry guns? I've never thought about it."

"I'm sure they're around, but I don't know anyone who actively carries—besides security guards or cops."

"I suppose I shouldn't be surprised—maybe that's another question I shouldn't ask." *All the same, I wonder about the brothers.*

I climbed down from the pit cart and headed for the port-a-potty again. Holly was waiting in the walkway for me when I got back.

"Give it a minute, then look casually," she whispered, pointedly looking away from the dark area of the former WiseGuy Racing pit space.

I glanced into it—then quickly away. The light shining out from the open side of the Arena tent illuminated the faces of my uncle, two cousins, and Monica standing closely together. Talking, maybe arguing. The men looming over the woman—not that she needed backup. Predators took care of themselves.

"I'd love to be a fly on the tent wall to hear what they're saying."

Holly froze. "Maybe you can be."

"How do you figure?"

She worried her bottom lip with an index finger. "Maybe there's a way to hear what they're saying."

"Tin cans on string don't work, Holly."

"Webcams do." She pointed to Tom, who sat on a plastic chair inside our pit space, directly behind the bank of monitors. He was busy typing on his laptop—a post to Twitter, Facebook, or the team blog, no doubt.

Then I remembered. Part of Tom's media efforts for this race included a live, streaming Webcam of the team in the pits. Right now the little ball-shaped camera was pointed at the team sitting around the screens.

I tamped down on my growing excitement. "But we can't use—"

"He's got a spare, and I know where there's an extra laptop we can connect it to."

We turned enormous smiles on each other.

"You're brilliant," I said.

"I've always told you, my mama didn't raise no fool. I'll check that out."

She looked both ways prior to crossing the walkway—we'd seen plenty of collisions between running crew or speeding carts and unwary pedestrians. She took one step, stopped, and turned back to me.

"Remember how you said sources might come to you?" She gestured down pit lane, to Scott Brooklyn, SGTV pit reporter, walking toward us. He was clearly off duty and in no hurry.

I grinned at Holly. "On it."

Chapter Thirty-two

Holly disappeared into our pits. I waited for Brooklyn's approach. When he was close enough, I waved him over.

"What can I do for you, Kate?" He leaned a shoulder against the chain-link fence next to me, an amused look on his face. "Ready to make a statement?"

The man behind Racing's Ringer, the current hot motorsports gossip blog, managed to stay anonymous to the racing world to everyone but me and Holly. Even after he tipped me off to his identity at the ALMS championship banquet last October, I'd never confronted him about it directly.

Now I looked him in the eye. "This isn't about SGTV, Scott."

"Even better. You have an eyewitness account for me?"

I pictured the cartoon of two eyeballs in a racecar that accompanied any news originating from him or his trusted lieutenants. "No. I hate that graphic."

He shrugged. "Part of the brand."

"I need information."

"What do I get in return?"

"You owe me." I crossed my arms over my chest, intending the combative gesture.

"If I don't help you? What then?"

"Ask someone else? I don't…" Then I understood.

He nodded. "Is this the first step of blackmail? Do I need to be in constant fear you'll tell the world?"

"Blackmail!" My voice was louder than I intended in a lull between nearby racecars.

"Hahahaha!" Scott looked around at the heads turned our way and pretended the word had been a big joke. "Laugh, you idiot," he hissed at me.

As I forced a few chuckles and a smile, I saw three of our crew members go back about their business.

I dropped the pretense. "I have ethics. Unless you slam me for no reason again, I'm not going to gossip about you. However, you owe me for being a jerk last year. If I need to know something, I'm going to ask. Like I'm *asking* now."

He looked me in the eye. "Sorry. You have information that could damage me. I don't know what you'd do or who you'd tell."

"You *gave* me the information that could damage you. I only told Holly, and she won't say a word."

"You told a girlfriend, not Stuart? Your own boyfriend?"

"You're questioning me keeping your secret?" I felt my face heat. I'd had more than one opportunity to tell Stuart about the Ringer's identity. I hadn't done so, for reasons I wasn't sure of.

Scott let loose with a genuine laugh this time, quietly. "No, sorry again. Thank you. Peace? Uneasy friends?"

I considered his outstretched hand for a moment, then shook. "Maybe not friends. Yet. Peace, sure. Some trust. I'll keep your secrets if you keep mine."

He tucked his hands in the pockets of his SGTV windbreaker. "What kind of secrets do you have, Kate?"

"You think I'll spill them that easily?"

Another smile. "Worth a try. What kind of information are you looking for?"

"What do you know about Keith Ingram, lately of the ALMS, now working for Benchmark Racing?"

"I know he felt underappreciated and angry he didn't get a job in the new administration. But he's not one to adopt the party line, so I'm not surprised he wasn't brought over."

"He doesn't like to play by the rules?"

Scott rubbed his chin. "He's not a rule-breaker, exactly, but he likes doing things his own way. He's maybe more of a renegade than the new Series would want, especially given the media scrutiny it'll have for the first couple years."

"Is Ingram still angry? At anyone in particular?"

He caught on quickly. "Is that what you're looking for? Who might have hurt Stuart? It wasn't an accident?"

"You can't use this—at least not yet." I waited for his nod in response. "I've talked to someone who saw a car with a track parking pass hit Stuart. I'm trying to understand who might have a grudge against him."

"Or who benefits from him out of the way, right?" I nodded and he went on. "Hard to tell with Keith. He seems to be settled at Benchmark, but I get a weird vibe from that team. I'm not sure if it's from him, their media guy, or what." He eyed me. "Want me to ask around?"

"Depends on what you want in return."

"This one's a freebie. The next one, I'll take out in anonymous tips."

I sighed. "Here's the next one. What do you know about Tug Brehan?"

"Good old Tug. Stepping into Stuart's shoes for this race—shoes he might have felt should have been his in the first place, which is undoubtedly why you're asking. Good at his job, if not quite as smooth, polished, or experienced as Stuart. Job history before Grand-Am unknown—I'll see what I can find out. Extremely popular with the ladies—the resident player in the Series."

"More than Marco?" I referenced an Italian Ferrari driver I knew from the ALMS who was notorious for having a new girlfriend on his arm at every race—despite a wife and children at home in Italy.

"Marco's got overt charm—you know you're being hit on. Tug has a more subtle approach, apparently—the kind of guy who can charm the pants off you without you noticing. What I've heard, anyway."

"That sounds like coercion."

"My impression is there's no need for coercion. Plenty of options out there for him—and no single one important enough to chase if they're not interested."

"That's sad."

He shrugged. "Sex without the heart being involved—isn't that what all men want?"

I heard bitterness in his voice and wondered if he was still smarting from the breakup of his last relationship. I didn't feel comfortable asking. "Maybe we all want that once in a while, but not as a permanent lifestyle."

"Doesn't seem to be hurting Tug—or the women he's involved with, who he tends to stay friendly with."

"Like Cecilia, down at CPG?"

"Exactly—though he's usually smart enough to stay out of messes like her divorce. I'm surprised he's still on good terms with Willie and the Arena folks—but charm is Tug's superpower."

"How ambitious is he?"

"I wouldn't say ambitious enough to run his boss down."

"What about Elizabeth Rogers?"

He raised his eyebrows. "Her either—though I agree. Something odd there."

"Any idea what?"

"Other than a blank slate, no. I'll ask around."

"That's two I'll owe you. Let's go for the trifecta: what do you know about why Joe Smith fought with Arena last year? For that matter, who is Joe Smith?"

"Joe Smith's real identity—second biggest mystery in the paddock. I have no idea who he really is, but I know he comes from a whole lot of money. Do you know anything?"

I told him no.

"No one's talking about last year's blowout between Arena and Smith," he continued. "But if I had to guess, I'd say it had to do with Smith wanting to bend the rules, and Arena not allowing it."

"Really?" I lowered my voice, leaning toward him. "Arena? Isn't he halfway to a crook already? Federal investigators and all?"

Scott started nodding halfway through my questions. "Except I hear he's squeaky clean with the racing team. Unnecessarily so."

I knew most people in racing followed the old saying, "If you ain't cheatin', you ain't tryin'." Personally, I abided by the rules I was given for driving and on-track behavior. And I believed my team owner that—like any team in the paddock or in racing—our team might push the rules, but didn't break them. I knew different teams interpreted the rules more strictly or more loosely than others.

But I wouldn't have pegged the resident bad guy as least likely to cheat.

"He's extremely vocal about it, too," Scott went on. "Or, I should say, his spokesperson is, as Arena himself doesn't talk to media. But Arena's hatchet man-slash-media guy Ryan—"

"'Hatchet man?'"

Scott shrugged. "It's what everyone says about him."

"Seems like everyone says the same thing—the same phrase."

"Maybe he puts it out there, so people don't mess with him or the team?"

I shrugged.

"Anyway," Scott said, "Ryan makes such a point of how the team adheres one hundred percent to the technical specifications, I figure they're either cheating like crazy or not cheating at all to compensate for cheating in the rest of his business enterprise."

"The latter's my guess."

His eyes sharpened. "What have you heard?"

"Anonymous source?"

He whipped out his phone to type notes.

I glanced around again and spoke even more quietly. "Lots of shady practices in his other businesses. Search online about his security system company and a fugitive brother."

"How do you know this?"

"The guy who saw Stuart get hit told me. He's on the case."

"What case?"

I didn't respond.

"I can work with that." He slipped the phone back in his pocket. "I'll let you know what I find out. Keep me posted on any other details I can use."

"Deal. You didn't hear this from me."

"That'd be impossible, since everyone knows you hate the Ringer."

"True. By the way, what's the first biggest mystery in the paddock?"

Scott grinned. "The Ringer's identity, of course. Catch you later."

Chapter Thirty-three

I texted Holly the broad strokes of Scott's information and suggested she nose around more about Arena's insistence on aboveboard race tactics. Then I collected another bottle of water and climbed up to the second level of seats in the main pit cart where I had a good view of the monitors and our pit spaces, as well as access to talk to Jack if necessary.

I settled in to study the rhythm of the car, track, and race as much as possible by watching the camera feeds. My attempt was short-lived. Only five minutes later, someone did something stupid again—and Colby had nowhere to go.

As it so often had, the trouble involved the Arena Motorsports number 54 car—Uncle Eddie's car, though he wasn't behind the wheel.

The amateur driver, Brody van Huff, was clearly headed for disaster in the infield. Perhaps he was pushing hard to make up the handful of laps he was down. Or he overestimated his own driving ability. But he was driving over the edge, which no one did for long.

Colby was in exactly the right place to be a target for van Huff. First she was a goal car to reach and attempt to over-take—not that doing so was likely for an amateur driving in a lower-level class. Second, she served as a catcher's mitt for van

Huff's out-of-control car. In later hours and days, many would ask Colby if her actions and the outcome of the clash between cars was accidental or deliberate. She'd merely smile.

I knew better. I knew no one was quite that good—and we'd been lucky.

Van Huff blew his line and speed for the Kink, and got sucked offline, driver's right. His Porsche skated over the wet grass, careening out of control toward Turn 5, aiming straight for the 28 Corvette. Colby was a sitting duck. All she could do was brake as hard as possible. And maybe pray. All of us in the Sandham Swift pits held our breaths, pressed our right feet to imaginary brake pedals, and prayed with her.

It worked, barely. Van Huff's Porsche skittered across the front of the 28, ripping up the bumper but avoiding serious damage. Then something strange happened. As van Huff's car cleared the Corvette, the Porsche jolted and its back end spun away from our car, almost as if Colby nudged the throttle mid-slide and flicked van Huff's car off of hers. Except that would have required near-impossible reaction times.

Whatever the reason, van Huff continued his slide-and-spin into the tire wall outside Turn 5, impacting heavily. Double-yellow flags. Full-course caution.

Our crew's cries of dismay over the damage to our car turned into self-righteous mutterings of "Bastard had that coming" and "Now will they park that car?"

I thought van Huff might have saved the Series the trouble.

Even as our crew members made those comments, they readied tools and car parts and scrambled to don their protective gear. They brought forward the spare nose—bumper, lights, front undertray, and more—along with racks of tools and supplies for fixing or changing suspension parts, taping together or cutting off body panels, and making any other repair that might be required. The crew that would remain behind the wall also prepared foot-wide strips of extra-thick, super-sticky crash tape.

When Colby pitted with the GT classes, we were relieved to see only superficial bodywork damage and a slow leak in the right-front tire. The crew used five sheets of crash tape to hold the bumper together and keep the right-front headlight in place. Four new tires and fuel, and Colby was back out. Lucky.

Duncan Forsythe, driver of one of the other GTLM Corvettes, walked up clapping his hands. He half-climbed the stairs at the back of our cart to pull himself up next to my ear. "You tell Colby 'well done' from all of us. Van Huff needed to be put in his place—which turns out to be the tire wall."

But she couldn't have...smile and thank him, Kate. Once Duncan left, I leaned forward to check on the car.

Jack pulled the earmuff away from his ear and spoke. "Flat tire, body damage. That's it."

"Duncan said to pass on his kudos for teaching them a lesson. He seems to think she helped him along." We both paused to watch the sixth replay on the live SGTV feed.

"Sure looked like it, didn't it?"

"She couldn't have, Jack."

He frowned. "Dammit, I know that. I'm pissed off though, because I'll have to go make nice."

"You never apologize to another team."

"Not true. Depends on who the other team is. How much I like them." He paused, his frown lines digging deeper into his face. "How connected they are." He mumbled a curse and put the headset back on both ears, turning again to the monitors.

I climbed down from the cart, needing to be on my feet, and watched the live feed with the rest of the team as the field collected behind the safety car after pit stops.

A buzz in my pocket. I retrieved my phone to find a text from Polly, the Series office manager at the hospital. Stuart's still holding his own, starting the second surgery. His family just arrived. I'll keep you posted.

My throat constricted. I hadn't yet met his parents or his sister, and I wondered if their arrival meant I'd get more information or less. I wondered what they knew and thought about me. *It's not about you, Kate. It's about Stuart in surgery.*

I texted a thank you back to Polly, then hesitated, considering my words. Before I could second-guess myself, I texted her again, asking her to tell Stuart's parents my thoughts were with them and him. By then, Tug's message with the same update had come in, and I thanked him also. Then I resolutely turned my attention to the monitors, which showed the accident replay one last time before the field took the green flag.

It still looks like Colby did it on purpose. Community response could go two ways: Colby and Sandham Swift could be vilified for retaliation or we could be seen as heroes standing for everyone wrecked by overanxious, green drivers with more money than skill.

The live feed switched to a camera trained on the Arena pits, where the 54 car was being worked on. *I know how that team will react, for sure.*

Sure enough, the next shot was of an SGTV reporter standing at Arena's pit wall, interviewing someone associated with the car.

Uncle Eddie.

Chapter Thirty-four

I couldn't hear what Ed Grant was saying—I didn't think we even had audio in our pit feeds—but he was fuming. Red-faced and sweating, he held up a clenched fist in a menacing way, then turned to speak to the camera, jabbing a finger to emphasize his words. I presumed he was speaking directly to Colby.

A tire changer stood next to me, shaking his head. "Madder 'n heck, but not frightening."

I chuckled. Uncle Eddie was tall but soft. In contrast, the tire-changer hauled seventy-five pound tires around one-handed and had bench-pressed *me* once as a joke. I'd stay near our crew until the 54 car got back up and running.

At 1:30, the race went back to green. The undeniably skilled Arena team had fixed the 54 car, but they were eight laps down. I worried they'd be out to get us. Jack obviously shared my concern, because after the race went green again, he descended from the command center, sighed heavily, and set off to make peace.

I couldn't help myself. I followed, though I stayed at the entrance to the Arena tent, watching as Jack approached the big boss on his own command center pit cart—a larger, more opulent one than ours.

Jack wasn't one for warm fuzzies, and he didn't appear to offer them to Richard Arena. But his attempt to shake hands over a racing incident—one we hadn't caused—counted for something. Or would have, with any other team.

Richard Arena was stone-faced on his lofty perch as he looked down on Jack. He ignored Jack's proffered hand and spoke only a couple words. Jack said something else, was met with silence, and then left, shaking his head. Unfortunately, Jack walked past Ed Grant, who shoved in front of him and shouted. Uncle Eddie was turned away from me, and cars were passing on the front straight, so I couldn't hear his words.

I heard Jack's response clearly. "Grow up."

Which made me laugh. The problem was, Uncle Eddie turned to watch Jack exit the tent and saw me laughing. His face went beet red. The look in his eyes turned vicious.

I didn't consider running, because I wouldn't cower in front of him—big money, "family," and connected to Series brass? I didn't care. He was a bully.

He took four quick steps in my direction. Stopped, too close to me. Trying to intimidate. I could almost see the fury boiling out of him.

His face twisted with hate. "You little piece of shit."

"You don't impress me." I turned to walk away.

Uncle Eddie grabbed my arm and spun me around to face him again, snarling, "You're a conniving, interfering whore— same as your mother. Stay away—"

I didn't hear anything else, because my ears were full of a roaring sound. I pried his thumb off my bicep and yanked it back—and back and back. Not caring how much I hurt him. Wanting to hurt him. He grunted with pain and buckled into a kneeling position as I bore down on his thumb.

I looked him in the eye. "Leave. Me. Alone." I let go and turned away.

He bellowed with rage. I spun quickly, ready for an attack. Instead, I saw Ryan Johnston restraining him and talking to him quietly. I tensed, ready for a fight. Ryan caught my eye and calmly shooed me away with one hand.

Surprised, I did as he indicated and got the hell out of enemy territory. But one last obstacle lurked outside the tent. Monica Frank glared at me, none of her earlier fake-pleasantness in evidence.

"What the hell is your co-driver thinking? Can she think? Because clearly she can't drive," she spat.

"Did I hear correctly? Colby should have been *another* punching-bag for your car of inept drivers? Fix your own problems before you tell me I have any." I shook my head. "I'm not going to listen to this."

"You're only standing up for her because she's female. Same way you both get special dispensation around here. Everyone's afraid to say anything bad about you because you'll claim they hate women."

I stared at her in disbelief. *It's exactly how Holly described her behavior to Greg—harassing me while claiming I'm bullying her.*

"Don't bother denying it," she went on. "It's plain as day."

I found my voice. "I'm standing up for her because *she's right*, not because she's female. And I've never once claimed anyone hates women." *Not officially, anyway.* I shook my head. "I'm not discussing this with you. Colby was right. You and your driver are wrong. Have a nice day."

Without further confrontations, I made it back to my own team's pit space. I sat down in a chair and finally got the shakes. When Holly returned from her latest rounds, I described the scene for her.

She opened and closed her mouth three times before speaking. "I have no words vile enough to describe Ed Grant or that witch. You need to stay far away from both of them, sugar. She'll stab you in the back any chance she gets. He sounds unbalanced. Dangerous."

"On-track and off."

"Will you tell your father what Grant said?"

I was shaking my head before she finished the question.

"Why not?"

"My father and I haven't talked about my mother yet. I haven't been ready."

"Seems like the kind of thing he'd want to know." She saw my reaction and added, "Think about it. Meantime, let their psychosis and paranoia roll off your back. Focus on the car."

I stood. "One interesting note. That Ryan guy seems all right. For a minute, I expected him to help the jerk come after me, but Ryan didn't even look angry."

"Not everyone in that organization is a crook or crazy?"

I laughed and moved to stand in the entryway of our tent, where I could see both monitors and pit lane. "Maybe only some of them."

"And then there are those two." Holly gestured at Tug and Elizabeth, who were entering the Arena tent.

"It's hard to figure out exactly what game everyone's playing."

Holly wandered into our tent, and I remained at my post watching the track monitors and occasionally glancing up pit lane to observe the comings and goings. A couple minutes later, I noticed Tug and Elizabeth standing in the entryway to the Arena tent, talking with someone I couldn't see. I focused on the monitors showing track feeds, willing myself not to stare at them.

Then Elizabeth was at my elbow. "Kate, I wanted to touch base and be sure there wasn't any lasting issue between your team and Arena Motorsports. I understand you and Jack both made the gracious gesture of going over there to apologize."

"Jack did. I observed. I wouldn't have spoken to anyone if Ed Grant and Monica Frank hadn't both yelled at me."

She made a face, something between a grimace and a pout. "We hope you won't take that seriously. I'm sure you know how high passions can get. The team has assured us they don't bear you any ill will."

I raised an eyebrow. *How magnanimous—and what an about-face from a few minutes ago.* "May I ask who that message came from?"

"Richard Arena himself."

I looked past her and saw Tug and Ryan Johnston speaking outside the Arena tent, Tug darting a furtive look behind him. Ryan reached out to shake Tug's hand, but it was Tug who bobbled the pass of a small piece of paper. Green paper. Money. He pulled his hand away, cupping it awkwardly, the bill visible perhaps only to me.

I snapped my eyes back to Elizabeth. "Interesting."

Chapter Thirty-five

"You'll let bygones be bygones? Agree it's just good, hard racing?" Elizabeth sounded eager.

If she finds a personality, she could go far in this business. She's already got the platitudes at her fingertips. But Stuart would have handled this better. I ignored the ache in my chest. "I have no desire to get into anything with that team. I've got no grudge." I took a deep breath and offered her a half-smile. "No vendettas on top of everything else."

She shook her head. "I'm sorry this adds to such a terrible day for you. Grief is hard enough without trying to be polite to other people as well." She touched my arm before she left, adding, "Thanks for not escalating things between teams. I'll check in later."

I still wasn't sure I could trust her, but I felt comforted.

My phone buzzed in my pocket. An email from Zeke. I waved Holly over and started reading, unsure how to react. Zeke's information contradicted every word from Gramps, which made me sad if Gramps had been misled. On the other hand, my spirits lifted, because Zeke's source had come through with deeper background info on Arena that validated everything I felt in my gut.

Zeke's bottom line: Richard Arena was crooked up to his eyeballs.

The collective attitude in the media center toward Arena is mild suspicion, Zeke wrote. Like many other men with money, he's come racing. He's used to wielding influence and knows how to charm people who are important. But the list of "important people" doesn't include the media. As I mentioned before, Katie-Q, no one's gotten an interview with him. Ever.

Which isn't to say he's not polite, Zeke went on. He's polite to anyone he sees—from flunky to CEO. Except no one ever sees him—at least no one in the media. He hides away in his paddock complex until the Series comes calling. Because of all that, everyone here wonders what he's got to hide. The topic was never confirmed to be Arena when federal agencies talked to the Series. We all know better.

A check of the monitors told me I had seven minutes until I needed to be ready. I went back to Zeke's email.

The case against Arena is mostly hearsay—like those articles you said Calhoun talked about, which I found and read. But hearsay or not, how many voices do you have to have asking the same question before you believe it? I smiled. Off-camera, Zeke had a tendency to get side-tracked into philosophical questions.

He stayed focused this time. There's nothing to pin on Arena legally about those stories or companies. But there's enough to make you question his ethics. Which probably explains why he doesn't want random reporters asking him questions. No idea if the Feds came calling because of these issues—if there are serious complaints in multiple states, they might have. One guy up here seems to know more than the others, but he's not talking to me. Yet. Links to articles below. More later.

I looked at Holly. "Back to where we started."

"Depending on who you decide to believe."

"Gramps is the lone voice of praise in all of this, which isn't much compared to the rest."

"I agree." She studied me. "But I know how much you trust Gramps."

I shrugged. "His is still second-hand information." I dumped the phone plus my helmet and gloves in her hands. "Enough."

My preparation for my stint started with drinking a last bottle of water and making a quick run to the port-a-potty. Exiting the plastic stall, I came face-to-face with my half-sister, Lara. She was bundled up against the night air, her long, blond hair tied back in a ponytail. I was disconcerted to see my own eyes—our father's eyes—in her face.

"Kate!" Her face was flushed. "I had a break—I came down here to say hello."

I had no idea how to respond. *Is she going to hug me? Don't shake hands, you just left the outhouse. You've got no time for this now—it's time to focus on the car!*

"Hi." I held up my hands and flipped them front to back. "I need sanitizer." I went past her to the Sandham Swift pits and one of the many pump containers of antibacterial gel. *Talk to her, Kate! Dammit, I would if I knew what to say.*

She'd followed me and stood nearby as I slathered more gel on my hands than necessary. "You're about to get in the car again?" she asked. "How long this time?"

I glanced at the monitors. Thirty-five minutes left in the fuel window. I should be suited up by now, not dealing with awkward family issues. "About to get in for a double or triple stint—and I've got to be getting my gear on in about a minute." *Give her something, Kate.* "You pulling the all-nighter with the team?"

"I'm going to try, anyway." Her giggle reminded me she was a nineteen-year-old college sophomore. I felt a lot more than six years older.

I checked the monitors again. "I'm sorry. I have to get ready."

"Sure. Sorry I'm bothering you. Could I—I mean, maybe we…" She bit her lip. "I wanted to talk with you a little, that's all."

Jack waved at me from the pit box and crew members jumped up to prepare for a stop—my heart rate jolted into high gear. *Must be a problem with the car.*

I reached past Lara and scooped up my gear. "Maybe tomorrow morning. Car's coming in now." I dashed over to Jack, not looking back to see her leave.

Jack leaned down to me. "Colby's having an issue with her seat insert—one of her legs is going numb. Bringing her in to hand over to you."

I pulled on my balaclava. "I'm ready. Anything else?"

"Status quo. Three laps down because of the issues earlier, P10. But the car's running fine. Push but don't be stupid. Plenty of time to make it up. We'll give you fresh rubber and fuel, then probably double- or triple-stint the tires. Let us know how it feels."

Jack straightened up, refocusing on the monitors. Holly helped me sling the HANS over my shoulders and pull on my helmet. "Was that your half-sister, by the way?"

I held up a finger in front of my helmet to quiet her.

"No one heard. Poor kid looked disappointed." Some of the frustration and guilt I felt must have shown in my eyes, because Holly held up a hand and spoke again. "I know you had to get ready."

My voice was muffled under my helmet. "Too many people want too much from me this weekend. I can't take it." *Focus on the car now.*

The crew stepped up onto the wall, which meant three laps to go. I pulled on my gloves and looked at Holly again, feeling a thin current of shame wash through me. "I acted like a bitch."

Holly raised a single eyebrow.

"Tell her I'm sorry, and I'll see her tomorrow. I'll make it up to her." *Even if I don't really want to.*

"I'll get her the message." She tilted her head to the side. "I know it's a crappy day all around, and I know your family is a difficult topic. But she seems like one of the good guys, not a villain."

I rolled my shoulders to slough off thoughts of family. *Focus on the car.*

A moment later, the track went full-course caution because of a Ferrari stalled in the inner loop—driver's right before the Kink. The tension dropped as we waited now for a yellow-flag stop, instead of a full driver change and service under green.

I saw Holly tapping into a phone and sneaking glances at me, and I waved her over. I wanted to know if the reporter had any more information.

She forestalled my question. "It's Zeke again."

I took the phone and held it up so I could see it through the opening in my helmet.

More about the missing witness. Not sure if testimony would have been about illegal businesses, fraud, money laundering, association with the Mob, or all of the above. Word is the kid was gotten rid of because he'd have talked about stuff Arena wants kept quiet.

I put my helmeted head close to hers. "The Mob?"

She took the phone back and shrugged. "I'll pass everything to the reporter. And if the reporter writes back, I'll let the cops know. You go out there and take a break from this."

She pointed to the pit wall where the crew was gathered. The tire changers started to step up onto the wall, to be ready to leap into the hot side of pit lane when the car appeared. I had a couple laps to be ready.

I closed my eyes. Breathed deeply three times, concentrating on the car, imagining every shift and turn, every braking point and apex around the track. Thought through the driver change procedure. Refused to entertain a single thought about comatose boyfriends, crooked teams, pushy reporters, or terrible family members. None of them. Putting away all of that emotion, confusion, and…yes, I admitted it, fear.

The freaking Mob?

I pounded my fists on the sides of my helmet. None of those thoughts.

*Up on the wall, waiting. Car stops, jump down, wait by the back. When Colby's out, settle my seat insert, climb in after it…*I got up on the wall next to Bubs and repeated the process silently over and over until Colby pulled up with a whoosh of carbon fiber brake dust.

Then I followed my own instructions. Bubs holding the door open. Right leg over the side frame, left leg follows. Grab the frame rail over the door and lower myself into the seat, twist to face front. Find right shoulder and lap belts, fasten them into center mechanism. Bubs fastens the other belts, then plugs in my radio cable and air conditioning helmet hose and fastens the window net. Meanwhile, I tilt the steering column down into place.

Bubs shuts the door with a thump. The tire changers move to their second tire—only seconds left. Watching the air-hose guy in the mirror. Reach up to make sure my shoulder belts rest on top of the shoulder pieces of my HANS. Tighten the belts. Air hose guy in motion. My hand moving to the ignition button.

Car bouncing down onto its tires. Fuel hose disengaged. Push the button. Car firing as I hear "Go, go, go!"

Wheel right, engaging clutch, throttle on. Tires chirping as I clear the pit box. Slot in behind a Porsche and in front of a BMW. Check the pit lane speed limiter is engaged. Fumbling for the drink tube as I head down the pits.

"Radio check," says Bruce in my ear.

Push the radio button. "Copy."

Breathing. Tightening belts as I navigate the twisty pit lane exit. Tightening wrist straps on my gloves. Testing the drink button gets me water. Breathing still. Onto the track. I get quickly through the inner loop and catch up with the field in a ragged, single-file line on the back straight.

I approached the Bus Stop on the caution lap and felt a wave of unease and grief for Ian.

How could that happen? Why did it happen? What if it happened to me?

My thoughts terrified me more than seeing Ian killed in front of me. Doubt couldn't be in the car with me—wouldn't be. Wasn't.

I talked myself through the laps as we circulated. I listened to the music and rhythm of the car. I centered myself with smooth, even breathing.

By the time the green flag flew five laps later, I was settled, focused, and happy. I felt at home.

Chapter Thirty-six

I took the green flag in the middle of the GT pack, which trailed the prototypes. I was hyper-focused on everyone around me. Looking well ahead on the track and trying to divine trouble before it happened. By this point, almost halfway through the race, no one was flush with the adrenaline we'd felt at the race start, nor anxious or panicked about pulling off a miracle by race end. We all behaved and got through Turn 1 cleanly.

In years past, cars and teams would race the first twenty-one or so hours at something less than ten-tenths, only going all out for the last hours on Sunday. Mostly that was to preserve the cars. Modern technological improvements, however, meant our equipment could withstand the full twenty-four hours of pounding. We now raced all twenty-four hours as they used to race the last three—at full tilt. Ten-tenths. Qualifying speeds.

Each team still followed their own strategy, pit stop sequence, and driver rotation, rather than responding to what other teams were doing. The outright heroics we saved for late Sunday. But we all pushed as hard as possible every minute of the race.

None of us on track—at least during that restart—felt the need to play the hero at two in the morning. We all simply wanted to put in time and solid laps. To not do anything stupid or damage our cars irreparably. My job was to get the Corvette

through the wee hours of the morning and hand it over to Miles
to drive through the dawn. No heroics, no emotion. Quick,
precise laps.

I settled into a rhythm quickly, finding my groove on the
artificially brightened track and negotiating the constant stream
of faster and slower cars around me. I couldn't claim the track
was as bright as day, but every nook and cranny of pavement
was floodlit. Driving in the nighttime here at Daytona meant
adjusting to the different depth perception and flatter shadows
cast by the banks of lights, but at least I could see who and what
I was dealing with around me. Old-timers—I included Zeke in
that number, to his annoyance—liked to reminisce about the
days when the lights didn't illuminate the infield. When drivers
had to move from the lighted banking to the darkness of the
infield road course and back again, every lap. Plus deal with the
flare of headlights from overtaking cars in your mirrors. That
sounded tough on the eyes.

Even with the track lighting, we all ran with headlights: yellow
for the GT classes of sportscars and white for the prototype
classes. The headlights helped with the forward illumination,
but we also relied on them to show us the edges of the track. By
splaying the lights at a forty-five degree angle, we lit up braking
markers, turn in points, and anything else we might miss off to
the sides of our field of view. Like the marbles from deteriorated
tires offline driver's right in Turn 1. Like the long path of dirt
offline driver's left throughout the Bus Stop. There were plenty
of hazards for me to avoid.

After three laps at speed, Bruce radioed. "How's the car feeling, Kate?"

I pushed the transmit button. "Good and fast."

"I'll check in with fifteen to go before the end of the fuel
stint. Otherwise, let me know when you want information."

"Sounds good."

I got comfortable between a Porsche in front of me and a
BMW behind, about four car lengths' gap in both directions.
We were well-matched on pace, though we were all on different

laps and not competing for position. We remained in formation, bobbing and weaving through traffic, one after another. After a while, I verified the other drivers with Bruce and asked him or my spotter—Millie was on the radio—to pass the word I was happy to stay tucked between them for a while.

We three were all pros, and we knew each other well. Heinrich Engel, a German driver who used to drive prototypes in the American Le Mans Series, was in the BMW behind me, having been picked up by the manufacturer's factory team in the off-season. He was a precise, clean racer who I'd never gone head-to-head with—we'd driven in different classes in the ALMS—but who I respected. He wouldn't pull anything dumb.

In front of me was Dave Hacker, a small, tow-headed guy from Indiana who used to race a Panoz in the same class as my Corvette. I'd been wheel-to-wheel with him plenty in the last two years. I trusted him completely.

I followed the same line as Dave through the tri-oval and under the start/finish stand, staying low as we approached Turn 1. Braking from max speed of 175 miles per hour, downshifting from sixth gear to second. A big, lighted signboard was parked in the middle of the unused portion of banked track with a giant arrow rolling from right to left—our reminder to turn into the infield, not continue straight on the oval track. Road racers like myself didn't need the reminder, but maybe the visiting NASCAR and IndyCar drivers did. Whatever the reason, the flashing lights attracted attention at night, and I obediently turned left to Turn 1. The weight of the car shifted through the transition from banking to flat track, loading each of the four tires in turn, and I was careful not to lock up any of the wheels under braking. A flat spot could be disastrous.

Second gear. Moving to the left side of the track at the point where the track passed alongside pit lane. Braking more, holding the wheel straight for a moment, then turning in, touching the apex at the tire wall. Feeding the power back on. Upshift to third. Throttle flat on the floor through the narrow Turn 2, staying as close to the pit exit wall as possible, but trying not to get into the dirt collecting there. Fourth gear.

Looking at Turn 3, braking early. It was more important to be quick out of Turn 3 than in, and especially with its low-grip entry, the horseshoe-shaped Turn 3 wasn't a corner to overshoot the braking on. Down to first gear, late apex. Unroll the wheel all the way to the left side of the track on exit, throttle on, upshift to second. I followed Dave back to the right side of the track, seeing Heinrich do the same behind me. Full throttle. Fourth. Turning left through the Kink, brush the second half of the left curbing. Fifth gear.

I felt the compression as I went over the dip in the middle of the turn, and the front end of the car got light—like it would understeer and send me off track to the right. That dip caught out plenty of rookie drivers who tried to avoid the unsettling compression, but were thrown off the track to driver's right because of the way the track tilted. I was reassured, not worried. Sure enough, a moment later, the Corvette settled, and I powered forward to Turn 5.

Hard on the brakes, staying right on the approach. Downshifting. Long right-hander, stay tight in the turn, late apex. Another turn to be slow in and quick out of, wanting to get the tires planted and the power down as soon as possible on exit. I followed Dave's lead and touched the left-side curbs on exit, riding the bumps, then nailing the throttle for the short chute down to Turn 6.

More hard braking into 6, the goal to get turned and back to the throttle as fast as possible. I eased the throttle back on as I unwound the wheel, staying low on the banking—and almost immediately, the faster prototype I'd noticed looming up behind our trio zoomed past us on the high line. Upshift twice, building speed to 175 mph. Holding the steering wheel almost straight, letting the banking turn the car. Watching for the braking markers for the Bus Stop. Watching. Pouncing on the brakes.

Downshift three times under braking. Left, right turns, then ease into the throttle in the middle of the Bus Stop. Hope the car sticks on exit. Right, left, back onto the banking. Nail the throttle to the floor. Flying through NASCAR 3 and absorbing the dip through NASCAR 4. Through the tri-oval and back down into Turn 1.

Thirty-five minutes into the stint, I lost my leader, but that was the only event of note, other than dealing with nonstop prototypes passing me or slower GT cars to go around. It wasn't long before Bruce started counting down the laps until I'd make a green-flag pit stop.

"Five laps," he warned me.

Then "Three laps."

"Pit next time by."

Finally, "Pit now, Kate. Pit now."

I'd stayed low on the banking coming out of the Bus Stop, still hard on the throttle in top gear, but diving onto the apron out of NASCAR 4 and braking hard for the pit lane commit line. Downshifting quickly to first gear, pushing the pit lane speed limiter.

Bruce guided me into our pit space, reiterating instructions for me and the team. "Full fuel, clean the windscreen. Replace Kate's water bottle. No tires. Repeat, no tire change. Three, two, one, box now, Kate. Box now."

My heart rate spiked as I pulled to a stop, the cars on-track speeding away from us. My crew scurried into action.

Chapter Thirty-seven

Our pit stop went smoothly. I merged back onto the track with improved visibility, a full load of fuel, and no more BMW behind me, since Heinrich had pitted three laps before I did. I roared out of pit lane and dove into the middle of a flock of Porsches. I was careful, but took the opening I saw—though I suspected the less-experienced driver behind me didn't realize he'd left an opening, from the way he acted aggressive and angry after I moved in front of him.

"You hesitate, I move in. Your tough luck," I muttered under my helmet.

The other car wasn't impeded. We didn't bump. His options were push the issue and go two-wide with me through Turn 2—a losing proposition for both of us—or check up a fraction of a second on the throttle when I slid into line. He'd chosen the latter course, but the way he snugged up on the Corvette's bumper told me he had issues with me.

Deal with it, that's racing.

Bruce radioed me. "That's an Arena Motorsports car. FYI."

My heart sank. "Tell me it's not the 54."

"Negative. It's the 47, the cupcake car." We'd chuckled over the car all week, logoed as it was with giant images of the dessert.

"Guess we won't get any freebies." I steered onto the banking after Turn 6 and breathed. *There's our excuse.* "Maybe Holly can take Miles down there. Make nice." *Take some photos.* "Bring back some treats."

Bruce was laughing as he keyed the radio. "Copy, I'll suggest it."

The Porsche behind me settled down and backed off. I dismissed it and everything but racing from my mind. I focused on the road ahead. And the car ahead, another Porsche—one I'd need to pass soon before it held me up too much.

But a lap of pulling close and considering a run on him in Turn 1 or Turn 5, it was clear he was deliberately making his car as wide as possible. Deliberately trying to keep me behind him. A ridiculous effort for this hour of the race.

I called Bruce. "Who is this guy blocking me? He's not even in the same class. This is BS."

"Copy. Arena Motorsports, 50 car. Arena himself behind the wheel. Jack's talking to Race Control about it. Keep your cool."

"I won't hit him."

What I did was keep the heat on him. I stuck to his bumper, dogging him in and out of every turn. He paid so much attention to staying in front of me he slowed us both down. The three Porsches I'd thought firmly in my rearview mirror got closer. But unlike Arena, I could ignore the cars behind me and focus on the one ahead. I was betting I could rattle him into making a mistake that would allow me by.

And I did. On the next lap, he wavered through the Kink, carrying too much speed for how late he turned. He drifted to the right side of the track in the turn and his momentum kept him going in a straight line, off track into the grass. I sailed through the left-hander, free of him at last. I smiled under my helmet and focused on regaining the ground I'd lost.

"Nice work," Bruce told me. "Race Control was going to talk to them. This was better."

"I'd like to know if I have a target on this car because Colby got into it with the 54."

"Copy," he responded. After a couple minutes, Bruce spoke again. "Series assures us the Arena team holds no grudge. Holly says Colby's been elected prom queen."

I focused on navigating the Bus Stop before working out what Bruce and Holly meant. Team radio was monitored by the Series, other teams, the media, and even fans, so we had to be careful what we said.

Colby's popular in the paddock. Everyone's glad she taught the guy a lesson.

"Copy." I still believed Uncle Eddie and his co-drivers—maybe other Arena drivers as well—might be out to get me or anyone else in the 28 Corvette, regardless of the official Series message. But at least I didn't fear retribution from other cars on-track.

I settled into a good run over the next ten laps, overtaking a dozen slower GT cars and letting faster prototypes fly by on the banking. I was hard on the throttle going down the back straight when the speedway lit up like a Christmas tree. Pairs of yellow lights flashed under the start/finish stand. Every safety vehicle in the facility had its light bars in motion.

"Full-course caution, Kate. Big, big wreck in Turn 1."

I didn't respond, focusing on downshifting and slowing down through the Bus Stop.

Bruce gave me more information. "Pace car's going to pick up the leader behind you, so you'll pass the wreck on your own. Race Control is directing everyone to be extra careful and stay well left through Turn 1. Safety crews are off-track driver's right at the wall, but they want all cars to stay in line and stay left going through Turn 1."

"Copy, Bruce. Thanks."

As I followed orders, tucking up next to the inner wall, I was alarmed at the array of safety vehicles in Turn 1 completely obscuring the involved racecars. The track could mobilize four types of vehicles for every accident: safety trucks, ambulances, tow trucks, and giant tractor/forklift combinations. At least two of each vehicle were off to the right. Their continuously flashing lights seemed especially garish against the black night outside.

"What happened?" I asked Bruce.

"Two Porsches in Turn 1. One is Arena in the 50 car—his fault. He overcooked it, went in too hard, ran right over one of the CPG prototypes, who never saw it coming. The 50 car has massive front end damage, going to need a flatbed tow. The other car though…"

It was never good when someone describing an accident paused.

"Which CPG car, Bruce?" *Don't let it be Sam.* I surprised myself with the intensity of my fear about him.

"The 17 car—not the one with the NASCAR guys. It's stuffed under the tires, probably impacted the wall. They're trying to get to the driver still."

Not the NASCAR guys means not Sam. But the driver can't be seriously hurt. He can't be. Ian was enough for this race.

"Gonna be a long caution," I finally replied.

"Agreed. Once they get him out and take care of the car, they'll have to fix the tires, maybe even repair the wall behind them. Again." He paused. "We'll do the front brake swap when you pit."

"Copy the brake swap."

I tooled around with the field for a bunch of laps before the Series deemed us collected and orderly enough to open the pits for stopping—if we weren't all together when the pits opened, some cars could be considered to have an advantage. First the prototypes pitted, and next time around, the GTs.

I pulled into my pit space, steering carefully around the 29 car, which parked behind me but had been ahead of me on track. I stopped the car and turned off the engine. The mechanics went to work.

The fueler plugged in as the tire-changers pulled off the old rubber. Bubs also hopped over the wall to open the driver-side door. He leaned in front of me to clean the inside of the windscreen, then shut the door and walked around to the passenger side to clean that half of the thick plastic.

Thirty or forty seconds after he'd started, the fueler disengaged. Two pairs of mechanics were already halfway finished changing the full brake assemblies on each front wheel. Brake pads, calipers, and even the brake discs were pre-assembled into a single unit with quick-release connectors that could be changed in three or four minutes. Up and down pit lane, teams performed similar, if not the same, maintenance, all of us taking advantage of the long caution.

I pushed the radio button. "What's going on with the accident?"

This time Jack responded. "Maybe a minute left on the brakes. Arena got himself out of the 50 car and seems to be fine. Not sure if that car's done for the day or not. They're still working on the other car."

"I can't believe it's the Arena team again."

Chapter Thirty-eight

"Brakes done, tires going on." Bruce warned.

I tightened my belts again and breathed deeply. Focused on the Corvette.

Three seconds later, I pushed the ignition button as the released air jacks bounced the car back onto its new tires. The crew member at the front left corner of the car checked for oncoming traffic and waved me out.

"Take it easy this first lap," Bruce instructed. "You're still under yellow."

"Copy, where's the field?"

"Coming out of NASCAR 2 onto the back straight. You'll have most of a lap to catch up and feel out the new brakes. Should be no one around you."

I focused on hitting my marks as I exited pit lane—careful on my cold tires and brakes not to make the rookie mistake of running into the pit wall. I gave the throttle a quick burst when I joined the track in Turn 2, then pounced on the brakes harder than I needed to for Turn 3. Did the same into Turn 5. Reported to Bruce that all was well.

"Great," he returned. "Stay careful while you get everything up to temperature and catch up to the field."

"Copy."

Coming out of the infield onto the banking again, I saw more vehicles headed to Turn 1, one more safety truck and a tractor loaded with tires, obvious replacements for those damaged in the accident.

I caught up to the pack and cruised around at 60 mph behind a silver prototype with white and red stripes. That speed was a walk in the park compared to race-pace, which gave me time to notice the eerie flickering of active fire pits in infield campsites. I also had time to try to make sense of what I'd learned.

A variety of things didn't sit right with me—Ian's accident and Monica Frank's existence, for example. Foster Calhoun's narrow focus on Richard Arena was another. Not that I believed Arena was a good guy. I thought he ran his businesses in nefarious and underhanded ways, right up to possible dealings with the Mob and investigation by the Feds. Plus the brother on the run for killing someone. Gramps aside, all evidence pointed to him being crooked, to a higher level than the mild wickedness sometimes exhibited in the other paddock inhabitants.

On the other hand, Arena supposedly eschewed violence himself and insisted on his racecars operating strictly within the rules. The irony was rich: a crook goes straight in an environment where pushing limits is the job—where trying to break the rules is expected and best practice. I couldn't decide if I thought he was a fool or I admired him. But I didn't think he was impulsive or stupid. Trying to kill Stuart—in broad daylight while wearing a race team shirt—seemed like both. Plus, he had an alibi for the time of Stuart's attack.

It could have been Arena's order and an underling's doing. It wasn't a stretch to think ill of anyone involved with that team—even the likeable "hatchet man"—and I knew first-hand how some people in that tent ran high on emotion and violence and low on thought.

Could my cousins or uncle have tried to kill Stuart?

I shook my head as I played follow-the-leader through Turn 3. I expected Holden, Billy, and Ed to be up to no good, though

I didn't really believe they'd run Stuart down. But other people in that tent?

I clenched my fists on the wheel, wondering why Monica had cozied up to Stuart. And why he'd let her. I felt twin stabs of guilt and grief over missing dinner with him—and for the first time I wondered what would have been different if I'd been there. Would Monica have been around? Would Stuart have met with Calhoun? I wondered if Monica had been the one to see Stuart with Calhoun and pass the message to Arena. If she'd been the reason Stuart was injured. If I'd been there, would the timing have been different?

I swallowed hard. *If I'd been at dinner, would Stuart still be fighting for his life?*

This wasn't helping. I flipped up the visor on my helmet and rubbed my eyes. The rough feel of my gloves reminded me to focus on facts, logic, and driving the car.

Fine, Kate, you don't like Monica. Maybe you should swallow your pride and ask about her conversation with Stuart. I blew out a breath and flipped my visor closed again. Doing so sounded like hell, but might be worth a try.

Bruce's voice cut through my thoughts. "Driver of the CPG car is out and walking around. Going to the medical center, but seems to be okay."

"Great to hear, thanks." I felt a weight drop off my shoulders at the news. That's what I expected from even a dramatic-looking accident—that the safety systems in place would minimize impact and injury to the driver. Ian's accident had been a tragic fluke.

Bruce spoke again. "The Series still anticipates a long caution. They need to fix tires and the wall, now they've cleared the car."

"Thanks." I took a deep breath, then took another.

Long caution means plenty of time to think. Back to Stuart. Look at it another way. Why would someone try to kill him? I could only think of three motives.

The first was to stop him. Calhoun thought this was Arena's motive, to stop Stuart giving Calhoun damaging information about Arena. But I couldn't imagine Stuart having access to information so damaging to Arena he'd be killed for it. Plus, I knew Stuart's ethics and integrity. Team information would be confidential or proprietary to the team and Series. He'd never share that with an outsider. Not even me. He wouldn't have told Calhoun anything. *If* any damaging information existed. If it was in Series files. If Stuart knew it.

That seemed like too many ifs to me, but I didn't have a secret I'd hurt someone to keep. An individual who didn't know the extent of Stuart's moral code *might* think information existed and *might* think Stuart would hand it over. *And might send his hatchet man after Stuart.*

I frowned. It seemed farfetched.

The second motive was revenge. I didn't think this applied to Arena and friends, otherwise the hypothetical damaging information would already be out—and Calhoun wouldn't be asking for my help. But revenge suited others in the paddock like Greg Davenport or another small-team owner who thought Stuart favored the big teams at their expense.

Then there were people who didn't get hired by the new Series, such as Keith Ingram, Jonathan Charles, and Perry Jameson. I wondered how many other disgruntled former ALMS or Grand-Am employees were out there and how many blamed Stuart for their lack of employment. Not to mention drivers who were out of a ride, due to fewer teams in total or revisions to driver rankings. Like Nik Reyes.

The third motive I could imagine was someone who'd benefit with Stuart gone. Tug Brehan leapt to mind. Between his near giddiness at assuming Stuart's role and his secretive conversation with Ryan at the Arena team, Tug might deserve a little investigating.

As did Elizabeth Rogers, especially given her current taste in men. Which brought me back around to wondering what my cousins were up to. Were they here simply as spectators and moral support? I snorted under my helmet. Doubtful.

Who else was acting weird?

My uncle wasn't the only driver from the Arena mega-team who was unstable and potentially dangerous on track—though

Uncle Eddie was the same off-track as well. *Could he have tried to run Stuart down?* I was positive he was capable, but would he have a reason? How could I find out? I heard his voice in my head, bitter and hateful, and I stiffened. That really couldn't be in the car with me.

Sam Remington was also acting weird, but that was personal—and a couple years too late. My father being helpful, no questions asked? My half-sister wanting to get to know me? Unusual occurrences. Weird for me, maybe, but nothing a normal person would classify as suspicious.

I steered through the Bus Stop. Then I remembered Joe Smith, and I wondered if he'd have information I could use— which brought me back to Richard Arena. Maybe Arena was the focus of everything, after all.

Who had the opportunity to hurt Stuart? Who wasn't around yesterday morning?

I knew Arena and Monica were in the clear, thanks to the detective. But I considered Tug and Elizabeth, Uncle Eddie and the cousins, and even Greg. Maybe the Kulik brothers? Then I wondered who else I should consider.

"Hi, Kate."

I blinked. Holly wasn't who I expected to hear on the radio.

Chapter Thirty-nine

"What's up?" My heart was in my throat, even though I knew she wouldn't give me bad news about Stuart like this.

"Everyone's fine. More on the same topic," she replied.

My pulse rate slowed. *Stuart's still okay, and there's more dirt on Arena.* "Copy."

"Confirmation on all but the pals stuff. Plus some background."

All the bad stuff we'd heard was true, but not the good stuff from Gramps' friends. Background might be Arena's own history.

Holly spoke again. "Found out more about the missing item."

I was silent, steering my way through Turn 3, the Kink, and Turn 5. Wondering what she meant. *Missing? His brother.* I pushed the radio button. "Found hi—found it?"

"No, though it might be home at your favorite beach. Apparently it went missing after a car accident." She paused. "Lot of that today. Also, Stuart's still holding his own."

I felt the rush of relief at the news about Stuart first. Then I frowned, surprised she'd delivered that tidbit over the radio. I thought back through her statement. *The reason Arena's brother is on the run is because of a car accident? But I thought he'd killed someone…other car accidents today and Stuart.* She meant Julio Arena killed someone in a hit-and-run accident. Like someone tried to do to Stuart.

I gripped the steering wheel tightly as I followed the field through the Bus Stop. *Was Calhoun right? Was Julio Arena in Daytona? Did he run Stuart down?*

I took a deep breath. Holly said Julio Arena might be home at my favorite beach. I didn't think I had a favorite, only a beach I'd hated and would never go back to—that's what she meant. Holly and I had taken the road trip from hell one spring to Rosarito in Baja California, where everything that could go wrong had. We'd hightailed it out of Mexico, and I'd sworn never to drive across the border again. Translation: Julio Arena was supposedly living in Rosarito. Another good reason never to go back.

My brain was scrambled. The car in front of me swerved hard sideways. I braked quickly. *Get the emotion out of your head, Kate. Take in the information, but focus on the car.*

"Any other messages?"

"Nope," Holly replied. "I'll tell our friends. Have a good stint."

She'd share the reporter's information with the cops. I let the details she'd given me roll around in my subconscious as I circled under caution. I thought about anyone I'd seen in the Arena tent who could be Arena's thuggish younger brother. Hiding in plain sight as a crew member, maybe? Could he really be here? Why would he risk it? Better to stay safely in Rosarito, God help him.

I yawned. Two more laps down. The caution was doing nothing to keep me awake.

I called to the pits. "Anyone got any jokes?"

"Nothing clean enough for the radio," Jack responded.

"I've got a story that'll entertain you all." This time it was Cooper, my spotter.

"Keep it appropriate." That was from Jack.

"It's a *story*," Cooper returned. "Hypothetical. Because if it had *really happened*, it would be seriously messed up."

Cooper's voice made it clear it wasn't hypothetical. "Entertain me," I radioed.

"Once upon a time," he began, making me chuckle. "There were two heroic guards at the top of a great castle—the world's greatest castle—doing their jobs to watch out for the great fighters inside the castle walls. Even in the middle of the night, regardless of wind, rain, fog, or any other discomfort."

He paused, then went on in a more serious tone, "Track update. Only a couple trucks remaining at the wall they've been fixing. Shouldn't be long now." He paused again. "Anyway, the story. These heroic spotters—I mean, guards. They knew their place and never asked for glory. They knew their job was to watch and call down messages, but never to fight, for though they had the hearts of warriors, they hadn't the skills."

Jack snorted. "Does this have a point?"

I keyed the mic. "It's keeping me awake. Keep telling me the fairy tale, Coop."

"Thank you, fair maiden. These brave guards were minding their own business one night when two crafty, malicious, and wealthy men scaled the heights of the guard tower and tried to bribe the guards to betray their, er, king. And princess?"

"What the hell?" All traces of amusement were gone from Jack's voice. I echoed his sentiment under my helmet.

"But those loyal guards wouldn't be swayed. They drove off the dastardly villains, with the help of their colleagues, and returned to their posts to spin tales like the bards of old for the royal court."

I was torn between shock and amusement. He'd been entertaining. But if what he said was true, someone tried to bribe them to not do their jobs. Who did that kind of thing?

I pressed the transmit button. "Coop, what's your day job?"

"English professor, city college."

That figured.

"You tell anyone else that story?" Jack asked.

"Not yet. Waiting for the main guard to come back on duty in the tower here," Cooper told him.

"I'll get that expedited." Jack paused. "Thanks for the… entertainment."

I considered. Two men, crafty, dastardly villains. Rich. Trying to subvert my spotter. I might be paranoid, but I thought I knew who fit that bill. "Coop, you know who the villains were?"

"We're getting that offline, Kate," Jack broke in. "Holly says to tell you your guess is correct."

I didn't respond. *My cousins are up to no good and are actively trying to damage my race. Fantastic.*

The radio went silent after that. I kept circulating with the rest of the field.

All the coded messages made my head hurt, though some of that was the coffee I'd had wearing off. Plus a long, fatiguing day of suppressing emotion. I was fine when I was focused and racing. But the downtime under caution like this was tough. Boring.

Fortunately, there were fewer track vehicles in Turn 1 this time by, and I began to hope we'd get back to racing soon.

Bruce confirmed it a lap later. "Series is telling us five more laps of caution. We're going to bring you in to top up with fuel. You good to stay in another stint?"

"Thank goodness. Yes, I'll stay in." It would be my fourth actual stint, but one had been half normal length and one had been thirty minutes of caution. Regulations barred a driver from staying in the car more than four consecutive hours, so I was safe. I was awake. I wanted more time behind the wheel.

Chapter Forty

At least two-thirds of the cars in the race rolled down pit lane with me three laps later. I paused for a few seconds of fuel and pulled away again, eager to get back up to speed.

Two laps later, we finally saw the green, for the first time in three-quarters of an hour. I quickly found my groove again.

The laps I put down during my last stint that night were even better than the ones before. All of us on track found our rhythm, and we had an uninterrupted hour of racing with no calamities, no pushing each other off track, and no blown engines. Good, hard driving in the deepest hours of the night.

The prototypes that restarted behind me went past and, in turn, I passed two slower cars ahead of me. The new brakes and tires were responsive and balanced. I got into a zone, trying to put in the perfect lap. Hitting that apex just right. Getting on the throttle a fraction of a second sooner there. Setting my hands once for the sweeping, banked turns and not moving them again until the road flattened out. Getting through each turn better than I had the lap before.

When Bruce radioed me for his fifteen-minutes-to-pit warning, he also told me I'd lowered our team's fastest lap mark four times, one lap after the other. Two laps later, I set fastest lap of the race for the GTLM class. I was lucky with traffic on those laps. I was having a ball. These stints were why I raced, for the feeling of being one with the car and the track. Nothing beyond my view out of my windscreen registered or mattered. I was plugged into that Corvette.

It seemed like only moments before Bruce was prepping me for the hand-over. "Pit in five laps," he informed me.

I focused on keeping the car smooth and clean. On the last half-lap before pitting, I removed my drink tube and the air hose feeding cool air into my helmet. At the pit line I downshifted to first and engaged the pit speed limiter, then disconnected my radio cable, loosened my belts, and unfastened the window net while I steered down the lane to our box. I concentrated on being precise, not pulling too close to the wall.

Focus was important, because I could feel exhaustion seeping in. I'd been in the car for three and a half hours—more than we'd intended because of the long caution. It had now been a very long time since I'd slept. Only a few tasks remained before I could allow fatigue to make me clumsy.

I stopped the car smoothly on my mark and shut down the engine. Removed the steering wheel and hung it on the ceiling hook. Twisted the dial to release my belts. Aimed my head at the opening Bubs had cleared, and heaved myself out. Reached back in for my seat insert and scrambled out of Miles' way, over the wall into the pit box.

Full service: fuel, tires, windscreen and headlights cleaned, and driver change.

I tugged my helmet off, seeing my warm, wet firesuit steaming in the cold night air. I watched the crew finish their jobs, sending Miles roaring away.

I traded Holly my helmet for a cold, wet towel and wiped down my sweaty face and neck. "How's Stuart? Did I miss much?"

"Sugar, you wouldn't believe. Stuart's the same. Let's get you debriefed and cleaned up, and we'll talk about the rest."

I stared at her dumbly for a moment, in disbelief that she looked as fresh as she had twelve hours earlier. *How did she do that?*

She took my other gear from me, and I snapped out of it. Time to chat with Jack and Bruce. I grabbed my jacket and slung it around my shoulders to ward off the chill, then climbed up the side of the pit cart.

Five minutes later I was back on the ground, as another full-course caution was called, for a car off in the grass in the inner loop. I watched on the monitors with the rest of the crew as a bunch of the GT field pitted, not including Miles, which meant we got another of our laps back. We gave each other thumbs-up and smiles. Only two laps down on the leaders now.

Holly and I headed out of the pits. I needed a shower, food, and some sleep, but I also needed to unwind. I was still keyed up from the focus and adrenaline of my hours in the car.

We passed the Arena tent, and I looked at Holly. "Miles?" "Yep."

A motorized cart roared past us, towing a rack of tires faster than the rack should go, judging by the skipping and chittering of its wheels. We kept walking without discussion, exiting the pits and heading through the Fan Zone. Two unwelcome faces appeared out of the shadows ahead, walking our direction.

I gritted my teeth and kept going. I watched as Billy Reilly-Stinson and Holden Sherain recognized us, shared a look, and came to a decision. They stopped in front of us, forming a wall of tall, self-important, over-indulged twenty-something male. Holly and I tried once to step around them, but when they moved sideways to block us, we gave up. We crossed our arms over our chests and glared up at them. They had us on size, but we made up for it in attitude.

For the first time in my experience, Holden spoke first. "Stay away from our family." Talking was unusual for him, the perpetual glower he wore wasn't.

I gestured around us. "You're the one who stopped me. I didn't want to talk to you. Come to think of it, I've never wanted to talk to you."

Billy smiled. "We want you to understand how the rest of the family feels—besides James, of course. No one's interested in the prodigal daughter's return—no one's interested in you at all."

"That's plain unfriendly." Holly's eyes were fierce.

"Why should I care what they think?" I asked her. I turned to them. "Listen up. My relationship with *my father* is none of your damn business. Since I have less than zero desire to be part of any family that includes you, there's no problem. Besides, you've got your parables wrong. For me to be a prodigal daughter, I'd have had some inheritance for me to squander in the first place. I've gotten nothing from your family. Ever. And that's the way it'll stay."

Holden smiled, which was even more disconcerting than when he scowled. "Apparently the golden child doesn't know everything? Ask your precious grandparents what they did with the money they took from my family."

He saw some reaction on my face, and his smile got broader. "That's right. My family wanted so little to do with you they paid your grandparents to take you away. Your grandparents took the cash and ran. I guess your hands aren't quite so clean of Reilly money after all."

"Don't think you'll ever worm another cent out of us," Billy warned. "Don't think a sponsorship is yours for the taking. We'll make sure that never happens."

I knew, logically, there was no reason to feel rattled by the news of Reilly family money in my past. But I'd always been proud of receiving nothing from my father's family, so I was shaken. Frustrated and annoyed. Because *of course* Billy and Holden had to throw the information in my face.

Except they'd given me a clue why they lashed out at every opportunity. They were afraid of me.

Chapter Forty-one

I tapped a finger on my cheek. "Is that what you're worried about? That I'll try to get sponsorship money from the bank? Play on the old family connection? Scoop up the available funds that might otherwise support your dad's racing? Or…yours?" I looked questioningly between the two men and saw Billy dart a look at Holden.

"Holden, sugar," Holly drawled, "are you racing, too? All in the family?"

Holden bared his teeth. "You stay out of this, you ignorant hillbilly."

I stepped in front of Holly. "Don't ever be rude to her again, or I will go directly to my father and tell him every disrespectful word you've ever said to me. Or said to my spotters. Then we'll see who has access to the purse strings."

The threat was a stab in the dark. But I suspected my father was both the spiritual and financial patriarch of the family—plus I thought the cousins wouldn't want every detail of our interactions made public. I looked from one to the other and decided my message had gotten through.

I turned to Holly. "Let's go." I pushed forward roughly between Billy and Holden. They parted, though I knew better than to assume they were permanently cowed.

I waited five paces before asking Holly what the hell she thought she was doing.

"Being part of the discussion."

"Don't get them mad at you, too. Stay out of it."

She stopped, her hands on her hips. "You think they'll be nice to me if I'm nice to them? No chance. No good friend would stand by and let them try to tear you to bits."

I gave in. "Thank you."

We stopped at the team lounge to check in with Aunt Tee. I told her I'd be awake by nine in the morning and in the pits by about nine-thirty. My goal was three hours sleep. With that much, I knew I could function, even if I'd be exhausted after the race.

"You both go rest," Aunt Tee urged. "Though I have to admit, Holly looks like she's had a full night's sleep already."

I looked at my friend. "Seriously, what's that about?"

"Deal with the devil, sugar. Plus clean living, under-eye concealer, and a couple catnaps."

"Do the devil and clean living go together?" I asked her.

Aunt Tee laughed and shooed us out of the garages back to the motorhome. I was starting to feel the chill of the cold night air through my soaking-wet firesuit.

Holly and I hurried out the paddock gate, across the speedway road, and into the gated community of team motorhomes, waving our credentials at a lone guard as we passed.

Colby had assured us that at a race like this, she slept with earplugs in, so Holly and I didn't worry about the noise we made. I went straight to the shower, and a few minutes later, Holly and I were seated in Linda's food tent, digging into a breakfast casserole with croissants and fruit salad on the side. Plus a sports drink for me, to replace lost electrolytes.

"Catch me up?" I asked Holly, as I waved to a driver down the table.

"The simplest item first. I took Miles down to Benchmark, CPG, and Arena not long after you got in the car. Those Kulik brothers were so happy to see him, you'd have thought Miles was the second coming. Everyone was happy to have us there except for your snotty cousins, Uncle Eddie, and that witch, Monica."

"Even Richard Arena?"

She waggled her fork at me. "Never underestimate the power of a celebrity. Arena himself descended from his perch to speak with Miles."

"Never underestimate the power of NASCAR's Most Popular Driver four years running, is more like it. Did he mind going over there with you?"

"Shoot," she smiled. "Not at all."

I'd seen Holly mildly infatuated before, but this was more serious—and with NASCAR's four-time Most Popular Driver. He'd better play fair with her, or he'd answer to me.

"Anything good in the photos? Did you spot the 'missing item' there?"

"Not that I'm aware of." She took out her phone and scrolled through the images.

I rolled my eyes when we came to the one of Miles with Sam and his fiancée Paula. "I guess she's forgiven him?"

"I didn't ask, but she's still there." Holly shrugged. "In other news, I got Tom's spare Webcam set up in the empty pit space between our teams."

I got up and took another helping of the egg casserole, yawning as I sat back down. "Did you hear anything?"

"We're not recording constantly, but we can record clips by hand. When I saw people of interest talking in that pit space, I'd record and save the video. It's not perfect audio, with car noise and all, but you can hear a bit of what they're saying."

"Video?" I asked.

"Comes with the audio. The way I was able to hide the camera though, all we can see is shoes to torsos, depending on where they stand, so video isn't useful. There was only one conversation I caught while you were in the car: Tug and two other men talking about strategies for the end of the race."

"What kind of strategies?"

She shook her head. "Wasn't clear. We saved it for you."

"We?"

"I had to have Tom's help, but swore him to secrecy. I told him we were worried the other team was out to get you. That a couple guys had tried to bully you already—I didn't mention they were related to you."

I waved a hand, swallowing a bite of food. "Whatever you think. Did I understand you? Julio Arena killed a guy in a hit-and-run and ran off to Rosarito?"

"That's what Calhoun dug up. Quite a coincidence, isn't it?"

"But how could he be here?"

She shrugged. "Maybe he isn't."

"I've got to sleep." I yawned. I couldn't cope any more. Didn't care what information or secret Calhoun had sent while I'd been in the car. "Let me catch up on the other stuff later. It was more background, you said?" I yawned again.

"It's nothing we didn't suspect. More about Arena's history. You can read it in your message queue when you get up." She took the dirty dishes I fumbled with. "I've got these, go on out to the golf cart."

I nodded at her, smothering another yawn, and walked to the exit at the end of the long tent. I turned the corner, tripped over the ropes strung to hold the tent up, and would have fallen on my face if Raul Salas hadn't caught me.

"Are you steady, Kate?" he asked.

"And embarrassed. Thanks."

He put both hands in his pockets, but continued to stand close in the darkness, smiling at me. Studying me.

"What is it?" I felt flustered, and my stomach jumped around. *Holly, get out here.*

He narrowed his eyes. "I'm trying to understand what it is that draws me to you."

I tried to form a response, but he kept talking.

"You are beautiful, of course. But it's not your beauty that makes you extraordinary. No, that is because of your talent, your strength. Your spirit that sticks out its chin and dares the rest of the world to keep up."

I was frozen in place. Poleaxed, Gramps would say.

Raul stepped closer—close, but not touching. "Men will want to harness or own you for that. And you may be tempted, but that's not what you need." He shook his head. "The truly intelligent and worthy man will want to be your partner, to encourage you to greater heights."

He paused, lifting a hand to frame my face, but stopping a fraction of an inch away. Still not quite touching.

He leaned close. "Perhaps someday that lucky man can be me."

Raul walked away, but not before whispering, "Rest well, Kate." Not before reducing me to a puddle of mindless lust in front of Linda's Catering Services.

Holly didn't notice my daze as she ferried us back to the motorhome.

Where did that come from? And why did I let that happen? I can't believe what a hypocrite I am after being mad at Stuart for kissing—wait. Raul didn't touch me. He'd nearly seduced me without ever touching me—except to keep me from falling. *Wow, he's good.*

I shook my head as I followed Holly into the rig. *Deal with it later, sleep now.* "Twenty-two hours is too long to be awake. Good night."

"I'll set your alarm."

With a wave, I made my way into the bedroom at the back of the motorhome and curled up on top of the twin bed next to the one Colby occupied. I pulled a blanket up to my chin and went out like a light.

Chapter Forty-two

Three hours later I woke with a start, a question for Calhoun clear in my mind. Outside, the buzz of racecars circling the track was well into its eighteenth hour.

I found my phone plugged into its charger on the bedside table, where Holly must have put it after setting the alarm, and I typed the question to the reporter. **What did you think Stuart would tell you about Arena?**

I knew Stuart wouldn't have told Calhoun anything. But I wondered what Calhoun thought he'd learn about Arena's racing endeavors that were relevant to his article—especially given the reports that Arena kept his racing team clean.

The motorhome was completely empty. Colby should be a few minutes away from getting into the Corvette for a double-stint. The only evidence of Holly was a note to text her when I woke up and to meet her in the pits.

I took a lightning-fast shower, more to feel awake and refreshed than because I needed to be clean. I knew I'd gotten enough sleep to perform well in the car today, but I wasn't exactly rested. I suited up in a clean set of Nomex undergarments and a fresh firesuit, added my sunglasses against the glare of daylight, and headed to Linda's for breakfast.

En route, I received twin text messages from Tug and Polly, both telling me Stuart was out of surgery and listed in critical condition. Polly added, He's stable so far, Kate, but he's in a coma. They fixed everything they could. Now it's up to him when he wakes up. I'll keep you posted.

I heard the words she hadn't said: "If he wakes up." I closed my eyes and prayed hard for Stuart to come out of the coma. He'd made it this far. I chose to keep believing he'd survive. I took a few deep breaths and kept walking.

Once inside the food tent, I drank my first cup of coffee while standing at the pot, then filled my cup again and scooped up more egg casserole.

While I ate, I scrolled back through the message stream from Calhoun. He'd started by sending highlights of Richard Arena's life history. Arena grew up poor in one of the bad parts of Long Beach, California, the oldest of five. Father killed in a drive-by shooting when he was nine, then his mother remarried. His step-father was sent to jail when he was eighteen, and Arena himself followed a couple years later, but only for nine months on an embezzlement charge.

That seemed to have turned Arena around, wrote Calhoun. He's never been seriously in trouble with the law again. And one thing he's a stickler for: he never carries a gun. No one can even say if he knows how to shoot one, though all suspect he doesn't need to, with hired muscle around.

Calhoun outlined a progression of Arena's growing business empire that tallied with what Zeke had told us, starting out with local Laundromats, then buying more individual sites, tying them together into a chain, opening associated services with them—everything from nail salons to car washes to electronics stores. He then added security patrol service to the businesses and expanded to other cities across the Southwest and then the South. Split out the security services into its own patrol and residential systems company. Much later, he added the company that imported olive oil and the racing team.

Calhoun's last words about Arena's background information weren't reassuring. There's no single, definite connection to the Mob, but there are at least seven tenuous, possible connections.

One source wouldn't name names but mentioned a money-maker and money launderer who the Mob bosses called "the Midas of home security." I've got no doubt he has friends in the family.

As I scooped up a pile of fruit salad and a blueberry muffin, I considered the idea of Arena—a poor boy from Southern California—becoming a money man for the mafia. I expected it could only be done by the kind of ruthless businessman Arena was reputed to be. *Does the Mob only stick to Italians, or is that only in the movies? For that matter, could the Mob be the Russians, not the Italians?* Maybe the Kuliks were involved with Arena. I'd seen them with Arena and Monica enough.

I sighed and broke open the muffin. I could speculate in circles for hours.

"May I?" I looked up to see the hatchet man himself, Ryan Johnston, pointing to the seat across the table from me.

"Be my guest." I tried to hide my surprise. Linda's provided long rows of open-seating tables, and there were plenty of unoccupied open seats. I wondered what Ryan wanted.

He cleared his throat. "You're heading back to the pits now, correct?"

"That's right. How's everything for your cars?"

"Mixed." He sipped his coffee. "As could be expected."

Alibis, Kate. "You have so many sponsors your team must have to do a ton of hospitality work."

He nodded, chewing, so I went on. "Did you have pre-race stuff planned for your guests or only activities once the race started?"

"All morning also. Of course, some of our sponsors are also drivers, so they had obligations, but their guests would participate. For instance your—" he caught my involuntary tensing and changed course. "For instance, our main Frame Savings representative is also driving, but his son and nephew participated in the full slate of morning activities."

"You get them all doing everything together? That's impressive."

"All of them were with our hospitality leader from nine in the morning to the green flag." He looked me steadily in the eye, as if he knew the information I was trying to get out of him. "The drivers, on the other hand, were on their own until the mandatory driver's meeting at eleven-thirty."

That meant Billy and Holden couldn't have run Stuart down—but Uncle Eddie might have had time. If he had a reason.

Who else had alibis? The cops told me Richard Arena and Monica did.

Ryan stood up and retrieved a blueberry muffin. He gestured to the half-muffin remaining on my plate as he sat down. "That looked good."

I broke off another piece. "Someone told me you were the media guy for your team, is that right?"

"Whatever Richard needs, really. Some media work." He nibbled on his muffin. "Yesterday it was negotiations with the Series—Tug and I were hashing details out right up until the autograph session." He stopped picking at his food and looked at me. "In fact, Stuart Telarday left us together for the offsite meeting where he was hurt. Such a shame."

I caught my breath. *That meant Tug couldn't have done it. Nor could Ryan. Elizabeth could have, since she was called to the track after the accident.*

Ryan looked at his watch, jolting me out of my thoughts. It was time for me to be on my way also. We both stood up.

To my surprise, he held out a hand. "It was nice to chat. I hope the rest of your race is smooth."

I shook, but warily. I knew what I'd gotten out of the conversation, but I didn't know what he'd found interesting or useful. I'd given away my connection to Ed Grant and the cousins, but I didn't think that was news to him.

Unless he could tell I was after alibies for the time of Stuart's attack?

I didn't have time to figure it out. I needed to find how the 28 Corvette was doing—and how soon I could get in it again.

Chapter Forty-three

9:30 A.M. | 4:40 HOURS REMAINING

Five minutes later I was in the transport trailer, talking to Aunt Tee, catching up on what had happened in the race while I'd slept through the dawn.

Miles had a brush with a curb that started to make the right front tire go down, but he'd gotten to the pits before it did any damage to the car or before losing more laps. The 28 car was one lap down to the four cars remaining on the lead lap and one lap up on the two cars behind us, with Mike currently behind the wheel. We were all encouraged by how well the car continued to run—also that we'd stayed out of trouble so far. But no one was counting any chickens.

Colby was due to get in the car in fifteen minutes, so I picked up a radio and headed that direction, with a short detour on the way through the Fan Zone. I climbed the stairs to the Fan Deck on top of the garage building and joined scores of race fans peering down on the activity below, looking out over the infield, and catching sight of the racecars zooming around the banked curves at both ends of the track.

The Daytona Speedway was a city unto itself. It had a carnival, a family fun zone, a food area, a lake with boats on it, and multiple camping areas, including a quiet zone, a rowdy area, and a gated community for the teams. As Holly had put it, the only thing missing from Speedway-world was a bowling alley. Campers lined the track in the infield, most of them sporting rooftop observation decks from which fans watched the action. I knew most fans would have been awake many hours already—if they'd ever slept—and would be huddled for warmth around their fires or stationed atop their rigs, clutching coffee or beer, and following the action.

In the silence between cars on the front stretch, I heard shouts and the revving of an engine below me. I looked down to the paddock lane to see crew and fans scatter—the latter doing so less adeptly than team members—as a prototype rolled toward the garage. I recognized the silver machine with white and red stripes I'd followed during the long caution the night before, one of the three cars battling for the overall race lead at the time. Team members in silver and red firesuits arrived on a run from the pits, followed shortly thereafter by media representatives. Within seconds, a crowd five deep had formed around the opening to the car's garage space.

I turned my back to the railing and looked across the infield, across the lake, to the back straight. Took deep breaths of crisp air scented delicately with fuel, rubber, and hot oil. I was sorry I'd missed the sunrise over the track, a magical time for drivers and teams after the long, cold night before. But even three hours after sunrise, I felt a sense of rebirth. A sense of a fresh start. Sure, cars and teams looked worn and bedraggled, but in the way of warriors who'd fought long and hard and knew their work wasn't yet done. I wished Stuart were here to experience the moment with me.

Time to get back to work.

My phone buzzed with a message as I went down the stairs nearest the pit lane. I deleted the new piece of spam email, but in doing so, I discovered an email that had arrived overnight from Calhoun. A long one, with a draft of his article attached. He'd sent the article to his editor, but he also wanted me and Holly to see what we'd been helping him with. He'd somehow anticipated my question about Stuart, writing, I hoped Stuart could tell me something about the company or team backing Arena's race entry. Looking for a money chain from one corporation to another. Maybe also who the sponsor companies are. Backing corporations, not only what's on the car. I didn't get anything from him.

"No surprise there," I muttered.

What Calhoun did have was a list of what looked like nine company names, starting with Arena Motorsports and including three others I recognized as sponsors of various Arena cars. The three sponsor companies belonged to two different parent companies I'd never heard of. Both of those belonged to a single corporation: Belmont Enterprises. Another one I'd never heard of.

Calhoun's brief explanation at the end was clear. This is what I hoped Stuart could verify or confirm. Info and connections I've constructed from various sources. Proves money laundering.

Then a final surprise: I've finished my article, so I'll come to the track to talk to the cops. Looking forward to meeting you, Kate. Thanks for the help.

I stopped at the bottom of the stairs. "Looking forward to meeting you, too, Calhoun," I muttered, typing that reply. I wanted to meet this guy face-to-face.

A text message came in, the notification appearing on my screen over the email. It was Latham, asking if I had anything new and where I'd be for the next hour.

Holly should have passed on the stuff from last night, background on you-know-who, I typed back. Also got an email from him with his article and a list of companies possibly involved in money laundering.

Latham responded with his email address and a warning: Easily a motive for murder. We'll come find you soon.

I told him I'd for sure be in my own pits in twenty minutes, then asked if they'd figured out yet who attacked Stuart.

Not yet. Getting closer, was his reply.

I had to be content with that. I started toward Sandham Swift, but a text message from Holly diverted me to the Redemption Racing pits instead. I poked my head in the double-wide setup a few spaces above the Arena tent. Holly stood with two men and waved me over.

"Kate, meet Joe Smith." She gestured to a short, dark guy who didn't look the late-twenties Holly estimated. Nor did he look rich and famous enough to need anonymity. He did look smart and confident. We shook hands.

Holly went on. "And Jason Carnegie, who runs Redemption." I shifted and extended my hand to a man only a few years older than me. In contrast to Joe Smith—or whatever his real name was—Jason had the open face and easy grin of a businessman. Or a salesman.

Jason shook my hand. "Kate, a pleasure to meet you."

"Carnegie? Related to the Carnegie of CPG?" I asked.

"CPG is Daniel, my older brother," he said easily. "Welcome to Redemption. Our *casa es su casa*. Make yourself at home."

I thanked him and looked at Holly. I wasn't sure what her plan was.

"I was talking with Joe and Jason about some of the difficult interactions we've had with the Arena team at this race. I knew they've had their issues in the past. The big question is," Holly said, looking from one man to the other. "If there's anything in particular we should know in dealing with them. Frankly, any leverage we can use if they try to pull rank or size or intimidate us?"

Jason looked at Joe Smith and spoke carefully. "I would recommend being careful trusting them."

When neither one said anything more, I offered, "We're having problems with some of the people on that team. Specifically, Ed Grant, who started to get violent. Only one person under that tent seemed to care. The rest acted like I deserved it. We didn't know if that was a pattern of behavior. If there's anything to be done about it."

Give to get, Gramps always said, and it worked this time.

Joe Smith shook his head. "In my experience, there's nothing to be done. On that team, more than anywhere, only money talks. They think money solves everything—lack of experience, lack of respect, you name it. Pay for what you need."

"That contradicts something else we'd heard," Holly put in. "That Arena keeps his race team operating on the up-and-up. Won't allow any bending of the rules or cheating."

Jason agreed. "Everything that team does is well within the rules—for all the good it does him. Most people understand there's money and there are the intangibles. Some groups of people won't ever work together well, no matter how much you pay for salaries, training, or equipment. Other groups of people can come together with sub-par tools and little practice, yet create magic."

"Believe me," Joe said. "That team doesn't understand the magic. They try to bulldoze their way forward with money." He shrugged. "In the end, I couldn't operate that way. I could play that game, but that's not how I want to go about racing. Plus, I don't want to be around the kind of people he's bringing into the team. Like Grant."

"I get that," I muttered.

"I'll tell you a secret of theirs," Joe offered. "They're connected to Benchmark Racing—partners or something."

Holly echoed my thoughts. "So?"

Joe grinned. "I know, right? They treat every useless bit of information like a trade secret." He gave a sharp laugh. "Like who some of their less-than-savory guests are for a race weekend. Some of them look like stereotypical mobsters—no idea if that's what they are. But between the drivers and the guests, I wanted no part of the team."

I could see why he'd gotten out fast.

Jason returned a wave from one of his crew on the pit box, then turned back to us. "Thing is, Arena's 'don't cheat' reputation took a beating overnight. You hear about the spotter scandal?"

Chapter Forty-four

"I'd forgotten about the spotter thing," I said. "I was in the car at the time. Two guys? Around three in the morning?"

"Idiots," Jason said. "Got up there and started throwing around hints about favors and payoffs for telling drivers the wrong thing. Who thinks that will work?"

Holly smiled. "People who think money talks louder than anything else. Is it for sure they were from Arena's team?"

"Our guys saw an Arena badge when it slipped out of one of the idiots' pockets. Not sure exactly who they are, but one of them called the other 'cousin.'"

I'm sure of their identities. I kept my disgust off my face and the information to myself. "Anything going to happen to them?"

Jason shook his head. "No real harm done, because no one took them seriously. I'm not even sure how the Series would handle something like this." He glanced at the monitors above his pit box again. "Anyway, you guys be careful with that team. Let us know if you need anything—like backup." He smiled and left us.

"I've got to go prep, myself," Joe said, offering a hand to both me and Holly.

"Have fun out there," I said. "And thanks for the info."

"It goes no further than us," Holly promised.

I waited until we were out of the Redemption Racing pits before exploding. "I can't believe my loser cousins will get away with their behavior. There's got to be some way—" I turned to Holly. "Our favorite racing blogger should hear about it."

Her cheek-splitting grin matched mine. "Genius, sugar. I'm on it."

"I owe him. I'd better tell him." I spent ten seconds congratulating myself and starting to compose the text message I'd write, when I saw who was traveling up pit lane in our direction. First was Lara Reilly, looking anxious. But I was more concerned about the two men behind her, also headed toward me. Detective Latham from the Daytona PD and Officer Webster from the Speedway looked even more gloomy than when they'd told me about Stuart the day before.

Is Stuart—no, he's all right. Polly or Tug would tell me if he wasn't, not the detectives. What else is wrong?

"Kate, do you have a minute?"

Lara stopped in front of me, a little breathless.

I jerked my eyes from the still-advancing detectives to Lara. "I don't think so." Her face fell, and I remembered how I'd treated her the last time. "I'm sorry. I'm not trying to avoid you. I swear." *Of course, that's what I'd tell her, even if I were.* "I've got to talk to these guys, and then get to my pits. Can I find you after my stint?"

She turned and saw the cops standing three paces away, waiting for me. She got more nervous. "That's fine. I hope you're not in trouble or anything. I don't even know if what I wanted to tell you is important—maybe it's not, so listen, don't worry about it. It's just—talking to the guy from the car, and something should be wrong but nothing really was, you know? No brakes, no nothing." She stopped abruptly. "I'm sorry. It's probably nothing. I'll find you later." She took off up pit lane.

I looked a question at Holly.

"No idea either," she responded.

I shook my head, squared my shoulders, and approached the officers.

"Are you going back to your pits?" Latham asked.

At my nod, he stood to the side and gestured. "Let's get you both down there." He and Webster fell in behind us as we made our way past three prototype pit spaces and then the Arena Motorsports team. It felt like we were being trailed by bodyguards.

We arrived at Sandham Swift, where the crew was cleaning up after the stop to change Mike to Colby. I gestured the officers to seats or coffee. "Give me a second to check in, then we can talk." I let Jack and Bruce know I was there and patted a sweaty Mike on the back. Then I returned to the cops, ready for whatever questions they had about interactions with the reporter.

I dug my phone out of my pocket as I approached them. "I haven't gotten anything else from Calhoun since that email. He hasn't responded to our last texts."

Webster nudged us to the side of the tent, farther away from the rest of the team.

Latham frowned. "You're not going to hear anything else."

I didn't understand. "Since he's done with the article, you mean? Did you guys get to him and arrest him? Confiscate Stuart's phone?"

Latham shook his head. Beside me, Holly sucked in a gasp of air.

I started to feel a heaviness in my chest and shoulders.

Latham spoke. "Calhoun's dead."

I heard Holly muttering, "Shit, shit, shit."

I agreed with her and wiped my eyes. I wasn't sure why I was crying, since I didn't actually know the man. "What happened?"

"Bludgeoned with a regular ol' tire iron," Webster told us. "Over in the infield parking by NASCAR 3, other side of one of the bathroom buildings. 'Round dawn."

"You're sure it's—" Latham's nod cut off Holly's question.

I shuddered. *While I was sleeping a few hundred yards away, Calhoun was killed.* "No wonder we had no more messages from him."

"About that," Latham began. "What's the last thing you got from him? Can we see?"

I handed over my phone and tried to process Calhoun's death—his murder—while they copied the information down in a notebook and took screenshots. I felt disconnected, unnerved by the news. Calhoun was a cipher. He'd only existed for me via text message—yet he'd been a real person, killed deliberately.

I didn't know how to mourn him. If I should. *Too much injury, death, and grief this weekend. It's all too much.* I wanted the race over. I wanted to get the hell out of Daytona Beach.

Holly broke the silence. "What was he doing at the track? He was the one wanting to stay away."

"He turned in his article overnight and sent it to me, also. Said he was coming to the track to see the cops and meet me," I told her. I looked to the cops. "Shouldn't you have Stuart's phone? I'm sure Calhoun would have kept it with him."

They exchanged a glance, and Latham answered. "We're trying to determine why he was here and why he was in that parking area, but we don't know. I was hoping we might find a clue in your interactions with him." He sighed. "We didn't find Mr. Telarday's phone with Calhoun. Nor was it in the car we've identified as his. We've got to assume his killer has that phone and a record of your conversations with him."

I gasped for breath. Some faceless, heartless creep had run down my boyfriend, killed Calhoun, and now knew I'd been trying to identify him. I shivered. I didn't know who to guard against.

"You need to be very careful now, Ms. Reilly," Webster said. "Don't go anywhere alone." He looked at Holly. "You either. Get someone else to go with you if it's only the two of you."

"What if someone tries to get to Stuart?" I asked.

"We've got an officer at the hospital," Latham assured me. "And before you ask, we're looking into the team Calhoun was focused on. Tell us if you have any information we can use. And be careful." With a final nod, he and Webster left the pits. Holly and I sat down in the nearest chairs.

"Wow," she finally said.

"No kidding." My thoughts were an incoherent jumble of everything I'd learned in the last thirty minutes. *When in doubt, focus on the car.* I stood to watch Colby on the monitors, and I asked Tom how the 29 car was doing.

"They had a close encounter with an over-excited prototype driver. It had to be towed back to the garage—heavy rear end damage. But both crews pitched in, changed out the left-rear suspension, and got bodywork replaced or taped down. Took about twenty minutes off-track, so we're down something like a dozen laps."

"At least they're still running."

"Right, not like the thirteen cars that have parked and closed up shop so far."

With just over four hours to go until we saw the checkers, the rising tension was palpable up and down pit lane. The nerves I felt about a murderer on the loose were a bonus.

Chapter Forty-five

Holly nudged my side. "Videos," she mouthed, and waved to me to follow her to the unused pit box.

She handed me a pair of earbuds as she opened a folder on the laptop and double-clicked one of two video files. I plugged the earbuds in and tried to understand what I heard and saw. The video was only the vague outline of three pairs of shoes next to the metal structure of a tire rack. The audio was more interesting—Tug and two other male voices, one of which was completely unintelligible. But the third was familiar. On the second time through the recording, I identified my cousin Billy. That made the third one likely to be Holden.

Unfortunately, I couldn't make out much of what they said. Tug asked what he could do to help them, Holden said something short, and Billy possibly elaborated with, "We want to be sure there are no…make sure we have strategies in place to prevent that."

Tug: "I've already gone way beyond—I'm not sure what more I can do. But you know I'm happy to help you."

Billy: "So you understand the situation and are ready to step in, should it be necessary.…disastrous for all of us…word might get out you weren't where you were supposed to be."

A car went down pit lane on the tape, drowning out everything but one last statement from Billy: "We'll check in with you later and let you know what we need."

Where was Tug supposed to be? And when? Was he outside the track running Stuart down? Not according to Ryan, unless he'd lied to me. I shook myself. *Billy's statement could mean anything. It could be completely innocuous—though with Billy and Holden involved, "innocuous" was unlikely.* Either way, I needed to keep an eye on Tug's interactions with them and anyone next door.

I pulled an earbud out of one ear. "I'm not sure what that told me."

"Seems like how to make sure Grant gets money to keep racing."

"Does that mean Tug's crooked? If he was offering to help them?"

She shrugged. "Or he could be listening and not planning to help."

"I'm not sure about that guy. Is he what he pretends to be?"

"He's a tough one to read."

I shook my head and put the earbud back in, then clicked on the next file. It was a shorter clip, but I could tell immediately who was speaking: Richard Arena and Monica Frank. They'd whispered, but they must have been closer to the microphone, because every word was clear.

Arena: "What are you doing about the situation?"

Monica: "Making sure we're covered for the appropriate time. Making sure no one has any reason to connect us to him."

Arena, forceful: "That might be hard to do. You're not keeping a low profile with those photos online."

Monica, unconcerned: "That's nothing. Two consenting adults, who cares? No one knows about *my cousin.* Everything's under control."

I unclenched my fingers from the headphone cables and forced myself to stay calm. *Was she ensuring they had alibis for the time of Stuart's death? For the time of Calhoun's death? And who's her cousin?*

"Two consenting adults," my eye! I handed the earphones back to Holly and went out to the pit walkway. I leaned my forehead against the metal of the fence and breathed. Reminded myself Stuart was honorable and logical. Even if he was mad or disappointed in me, he wouldn't have initiated a kiss without severing ties with me first.

I wondered if Monica had an ulterior motive for ending up in those photos with him or if she couldn't resist trying to corrupt the incorruptible.

"The day can't be that bad already." I turned to see Miles grinning at me. "The car's still doing well."

I stood up straight and held out a hand to shake. "Nice drive, partner."

He ignored my hand and hugged me. "Great drive to you, partner. What a fantastic race to be part of."

I patted his back and stepped away. "You starting to like these endurance races?"

"Yeah, I'm getting the hang of this car and this kind of thing—with all the classes, especially. It's really different than Cup racing."

"Car's pretty different, anyway. And we're on the twisty stuff, not only lefts." I elbowed him in the side to let him know I was teasing him about the lack of road courses in NASCAR's season.

"I wish we did more road courses, silly as those Cup cars are on them. I'm sure enjoying this car."

"It's feeling better?"

"Sure is. When I got in the car for my second stint, right after you this morning, I finally felt like everything had slowed down. Felt like I could really contribute to the team, now that I'm better at driving the car."

"Shoot, Miles, you were good at driving the car from the beginning. I'm not sure I can stand you getting much better—you'll take my job."

"Look who's talking, Ms. Fast-Lap of the Race." He grinned. "Last I heard that was still holding." He headed into the pit tent with a wave.

I felt pure pleasure for the first time in the whole race. *All the crap going on in the outside world can't stop me from doing what I do best: kicking butt on the racetrack.*

Flush with that boost of confidence, when I felt my phone wiggle in my pocket and pulled it out to see a long email from my father, I took a leap. I sent a text message asking if we could talk briefly, because I had something to tell him. I was tired of tiptoeing around him and, by extension, covering up for his family members. He deserved to know what his nephews were up to and what they and his brother had to say to me. I needed to know if he endorsed their attitudes.

The thought of my cousins reminded me to contact SGTV reporter Scott Brooklyn, aka Racing's Ringer. Since I didn't have his cell number, I typed a quick message via the Ringer's site to find me.

Only then did I skim the information my father sent. He'd given me some of the same facts about Arena's background I'd heard from other sources, but from the business world's perspective. The only new tidbit was details about Arena founding a non-profit organization aimed at stopping juvenile recidivism.

It was the first mention of any charitable offering from Arena or his organizations. I wondered if he was trying to help his brother—or his younger self. Richard Arena had been a young parolee and had managed to become a success in the white-collar world. Perhaps he was trying to turn other lives around. I felt grudging respect for him, if that were the case. I had my doubts he was still law-abiding, but he couldn't be all villain if he was trying to keep young people from committing more crimes.

Helping his brother…could he have helped his brother to a new career? Nik Reyes walked past me, headed for the bottom end of pit lane. My heart skipped a beat. *Could Nik Reyes be Julio Arena? Or was I starting to suspect everyone?*

A bigger and more frightening question occurred to me. *Could Raul be Julio Arena? Could I be attracted to a murderer?*

Holly must have seen the stricken expression on my face. She scrambled down from the pit cart and crossed to me. I explained my thought process.

"Don't freak out about it, sugar. Let me do a little digging." She pulled out her phone and started tapping away. "Besides, wouldn't it make more sense to use a non-Latino name? Something no one would think twice about?"

I considered her point, and we turned to each other with the same thought. I said the words aloud. "Something like Joe Smith?"

"You know who else fits age and general appearance?" She looked amused. "Tug Brehan."

"Talk about hiding in plain sight. I wonder…"

She went back to working her phone while I turned over different possibilities. Then she stopped and held up her phone.

Under the photo of Raul Salas were lines of biographical data. He was two years older than me, and he'd been born in July. In Rosarito, Mexico.

Chapter Forty-six

After I fought down my alarm, I sent a message to Detective Latham asking if he'd looked into Raul Salas at all. If Raul could be Julio Arena.

I crossed back into our pits to pour myself some coffee and watch the action on the monitor. Cup in hand, I watched Colby take the car around the track. I also let my mind drift over the new information.

I wasn't going to touch Calhoun's evidence of Richard Arena's involvement in money laundering. Maybe it was wrapped up in a motive for hurting Stuart and killing Calhoun—but I'd leave that one to the cops. Or maybe the Feds. At least to Calhoun's editor to run the story.

I couldn't say I was surprised by the information from Joe Smith and Jason Carnegie, that money ruled the world in the Arena tent—witness my grasping, greedy cousins' attempts to throw it around to bribe spotters. *The Arena team and that part of my father's family are a match made in heaven.* I *was* surprised Arena didn't have the imagination to understand money alone couldn't solve racing problems. That would ultimately limit his team's success.

But none of that knowledge brought me closer to figuring out who'd run Stuart down. Or who killed Calhoun—because I assumed the two were connected. I pulled out my phone and sent that question to Latham.

Our conversation at Redemption Racing confirmed Arena was everything I didn't like about the racing world: money-grubbing, arrogant, and focused on winning. We all wanted to win, but for most of us, the fun was in *racing*, not only winning. If it was only about the dollars and the trophies, you missed something. Joe Smith got that, too, which impressed me.

I wonder if we'll ever know who he really is. It seems like he comes from some serious money, but doesn't want to use much of it. Wants to earn his way, instead. I could respect that.

"Kate?"

I looked up at my father. My heart leapt into my throat, and I led him over to the pair of plastic chairs at the quiet side of the tent.

He spoke before I could gather my thoughts. "What's wrong? How can I help?"

"I'm not sure there's anything you can do. But I felt like you should know…." I sighed. "I'm no good at this."

"At what?"

I waved my hand around. "This family stuff. Do you keep quiet when people are being assholes? Do you tell someone about it? Whose feelings am I trying to save? I guess it's yours, not theirs—"

"Kate, tell me whatever it is."

"Billy and Holden. And your brother."

He sat back, either relaxed or resigned. "Now what?"

"The boys were apparently up on the spotter's stand in the early hours of the morning, trying to bribe spotters from other teams to sabotage their cars."

He didn't speak, only rubbed a hand over his eyes. I went on. "No one knows their names, but someone up there saw the Arena team name on a badge. And there can't be too many pairs of young, wealthy, arrogant cousins associated with that team."

"Likely not. Thank you, I—"

"There's more. They're trying to scare me away from you and your family. Holden's made comments about always watching me. Most recently, they made threats about staying away and not trying for any Reilly money."

In spite of my father's aghast expression, I added, "Then again, I didn't know there ever *was* Reilly money, which is a conversation I'll have with my grandparents sometime soon."

"I'm finding this hard to believe." He waved a hand as I bristled. "Bad choice of words. I believe you. I'm simply astonished by them." He cleared his throat. "When did this begin?"

"It's how they've always been, since I met them. Back at Petit."

He sat forward. "They made threats then?"

"Then, now." I shrugged. "It's how they are. I couldn't figure out why, until they said something last night. They seem to think I'd take sponsorship money they or your brother would otherwise get."

He blew out a breath and sat up straight. "Let's get this straight. They've been acting aggressively and threatening you for three months, and you haven't said anything to me?"

"I haven't seen them between Petit Le Mans and now. At first it was silly squabbling, schoolyard kid stuff. I could handle it."

"It has changed?"

"The stuff with the spotters and the intentional physical intimidation—" I saw anger flash over his face. "Blocking the walkway, so we had to talk to them, that's all." I paused. *He really wouldn't like the story about his brother.* "They didn't touch us or threaten to. But it got to be too much. I felt like I was covering up for them, which I have no interest in doing."

"Good. They're also trying to bribe other teams' crew to sabotage cars?"

"That's what I heard, from my spotter and from another team whose spotter was also involved. It was around three in the morning. I've also seen them in close conversation with Tug Brehan and Monica Frank—the kind of discussions that look like plotting or scheming."

He shook his head. "You asked why they might be doing this. I know of a possible explanation, but frankly, theirs is not a reasonable response to the situation."

I'd never thought Billy and Holden to be much troubled by reason, but I kept my mouth shut.

He went on. "I need to request you keep this information to yourself—it's probably confidential board information I shouldn't be sharing, but it's clearly impacting you."

"Of course."

"It's true Edward's racing is sponsored by the bank— 'sponsored' is the polite word," my father explained. "'Primarily funded' is more accurate. Has been for almost two decades now. It was his interest in racing that led to the bank sponsoring the American Le Mans Series in the past and now the United SportsCar Championship. And the bank feels it has benefited from its participation in racing. That's not the issue."

"There's an issue?"

"For some years now, the bank hasn't seen any benefits to its funding of Edward. No return on its investment—due in equal parts to lack of finishes, exorbitant costs for equipment, and unfavorable mentions on-air or in print. Edward was given funds for this race with the option for more if he finished fifth or better and generated good publicity or mentions. I expect that's what's behind his…determination, as well as Billy and Holden's efforts."

"Does Holden race also?"

"He and Billy both, in lower ranks so far. They also receive bank sponsorship, but not as much as Edward."

"Maybe they think if your brother loses sponsorship, they'll have less chance of getting more in the future?"

"That's probably an accurate deduction." His smile was bleak. "Neither Billy nor Holden has proven to be a wise investment so far, which, while not involving the bank's money, is common knowledge."

"Maybe Billy and Holden feel challenged or intimidated by me, because I'm a better driver, with other, bigger sponsorships. Not because I'm going to take away the bank's money."

My father shifted in his chair and glanced away.

"James." I made him look at me. "I'm not looking for more sponsorship."

"I realize. But it hasn't escaped the board's notice there is a Reilly in racing who's quite good. Who has considerably more charisma than the other family representatives involved in the sport." He frowned. "It was mentioned to Edward."

My jaw dropped. "Why the hell would you do that?"

"You misunderstand." He shook his head. "It wasn't me, but another board member who came out with it during one contentious meeting. I couldn't stop it."

"No wonder they all act like they hate me. They think I'm going to take away their meal ticket." I thought for a moment. "Now the spotter thing makes sense."

"How so?"

"The other spotters they tried to bribe were cars in GT Daytona, the class your brother competes in. I assume the point was hindering other cars so your brother might advance to fifth place. But I drive in GT Le Mans, so trying to bribe my spotter wouldn't help."

"Except by making you look bad to the bank's board," James concluded. "It seems I will be having a few words with my nephews. And my brother."

"There's one more thing." I took a deep breath. "About your brother."

"What did Edward do?" His knuckles were white where they gripped the arms of the chair.

I started with the easy stuff. "Jack went over to the Arena tent to make nice, after the incident with Colby. I followed him. Your brother got in Jack's face, and Jack told him to grow up, which made me laugh. Your brother saw me laughing and charged over to get in my face. I walked away."

My stomach jumped around, and I drew another deep breath. "That's when he grabbed my arm and called me a 'conniving, interfering whore.'"

I finished the rest in a whisper. "Like my mother."

Chapter Forty-seven

My father froze. Didn't blink, didn't seem to breathe. Nothing moved except the blood that drained from his face. He looked older and madder at the end of thirty seconds than I'd ever seen him.

"Edward said that?" I could barely hear his words through his clenched jaw.

I nodded.

"He touched you in anger? Did he hurt you?"

I shrugged. "I hurt him more. I bent his thumb back to make him let go. The guy over there, Ryan, got hold of your brother so he didn't come after me."

My father stood, his movements small and controlled. I had the sense of him drawing everything in, harnessing rage. I didn't much care what he did to his brother, but I hadn't meant to hurt my father.

"Are you all right?" I asked.

He gave a single nod. "I'm sorry you had to hear that, Kate. It's untrue, and he had no right to spill his bile in your ears. We…I'd like to talk with you about your mother someday soon. But this is the wrong time."

I agreed with him. This conversation had been enough for the moment.

"Is there anything else I need to be made aware of, Kate?"

"Not unless you know anything about Stuart favoring bigger, richer teams over small ones."

He'd been eyeing the exit, clearly distracted by thoughts of his brother, but he turned to me sharply. "But he doesn't. He's very supportive of the smaller, privateer, single-car teams. Feels they're the heart of the Series and sportscar racing."

"The rumor going around says otherwise."

"I'm astonished and dismayed, once again." He came up with a wry smile. "This conversation hasn't been very uplifting, has it?"

I laughed. "Not so much."

"Regardless, thank you for informing me about all of this. I plan to…address some of the issues."

I didn't know whether to apologize or thank him.

Before he turned away, he waved a finger in the air. "Now I remember Stuart mentioning a concern about someone in his office taking that exact approach. He spoke of needing to educate an associate on that point. But I don't know who it was."

"I think it's Tug, but I haven't traced the rumor back to prove it."

"I'll see if I can do so. Be careful. And thank you. I'll be in touch."

I looked after him and wondered what he was going to do. I didn't envy him the complication of those particular family members.

Speaking of family members, I remembered Lara wanting to talk to me and her garbled message. *What had she said?* Something about the guy from the car, something wrong, nothing wrong, no brakes, no nothing. *What the hell did that mean?*

Holly tapped me on the shoulder as she dashed past and hopped up onto the pit cart. I followed her and took the proffered single earbud, as she clicked the record button. I had to lean close to the display to block out the glare and see the video feed of two men, from shoulder to knees. Holly breathed into my ear: "Arena and Grant."

I looked at her briefly, my eyebrows raised. We were lucky there weren't any cars on the front straight, so we could hear them clearly.

I heard Arena's voice in my ear: "That's not how this team does things. We race fair."

"Fair isn't getting me what I need, Arena," blustered Ed Grant. I could hear his voice through the recording and also faintly through the canvas wall to my right.

"Not my problem," Arena returned. His voice was icy and calm.

Grant again: "Your other team doesn't have a problem with pushing things, making things happen."

"There is no other team. If you want to work with a different team, I suggest you make those arrangements after this race."

"Right." Grant drawled the word, sounding more arrogant than usual. A car went down pit lane, and we missed whatever he said next.

"Pardon me." I froze at the sound of a new voice I recognized.

"James, what can I do for you?" Arena asked.

"I need a moment with my brother, if you don't mind," my father responded.

"Certainly." We saw Arena's firesuit exit through the opening into the Arena tent.

My heart pounded. *Would Grant know I'd said something? Would he be more angry and come after me?*

My speculations were cut off by the sound of flesh meeting flesh and a body falling to the ground.

My father stood over his brother and spat, "Don't you ever speak to her again or bring up her mother to anyone. You have no idea what I can do to you, so leave my daughter alone. And call off your son and his cousin, before they get arrested or thrown out of the Series." He stalked away, shaking his hand.

Holly clicked the button to stop recording. She turned to me, her mouth a perfect "O."

"I decided to stop keeping things from him."

"I figured that much."

"It's not how I expected him to react. I probably shouldn't feel good about it."

"But you do."

I chuckled, then got serious. "As long as Ed doesn't come after me."

"Let's hope he's not that crazy."

We stopped talking as the Sandham Swift crew stood, stretched, and began to prepare for the next pit stop. One more stint for Colby, then my turn.

Someone tapped me on the back, and I turned to see Scott Brooklyn.

"Got a minute?" he asked.

I climbed over Holly and led Scott out to the walkway. "You got my message."

"You really have a tip for me?" He grinned.

"It's people who really, really deserve to be outed. Maybe you've heard about it already? The stuff up on the spotter's stand overnight?"

He shook his head, and I smiled. "This is one I owe you." I told him every detail I'd heard about my cousins' failed attempts at bribery. Scott went from interested to surprised to downright gleeful. He thumb-typed notes into his phone as fast as possible.

He caught the oddity right away. "Why go after cars in different classes?"

"No idea. Maybe my spotter wasn't telling a first-hand story after all. I mean, you won't use my team name anyway, right? You'd better not." *No way am I letting Racing's Ringer in on my sordid family drama.*

"Nothing will connect to you as the source, Scout's honor."

I eyed him. "Were you actually a Boy Scout?"

He nodded, still typing. "This is great. It'll even get the eyewitness icon."

My favorite, eyeballs-in-a-racecar. "Glad I could give you something good."

He stopped typing. "One good turn deserves another. I followed up on some of your earlier questions." He held up his index finger. "Keith Ingram. Chatted with him before an on-camera. Asked how he was doing, if he still was mad at the Series or any Series representatives, and he said no."

"Isn't that an about-face?"

"I thought so, too, but his body language was relaxed and happy. He said he'd finally realized this morning, talking the drivers through the dawn and pushing the team to execute on their pit stops, how much more fun it was to compete with a team than being on the outside observing. He also said he's making more money." Scott shrugged. "Seems like he means it."

"Interesting."

He held up a second finger to go with the first. "Tug Brehan. Seems to be focusing his energies on two locations this race weekend: the Arena tent and the Benchmark tent—but the reason for the latter is trying to chase that cute little intern they've got down there this weekend. Lara, I think her name is?"

I stopped breathing.

Chapter Forty-eight

I coughed. "She's a little young for him, don't you think? She's, what? Nineteen or twenty?"

Scott shrugged. "Legal."

Great. My—it was hard to say it even in my mind—*half-sister being hunted down by the biggest player in the Series.* "That's disgusting, Scott."

He held up his hands. "*I'm* not trying to pick her up. Warn her about him if you want. That wasn't the information I had for you. I wouldn't repeat this publicly—so don't you either—but I talked to someone who knows him well. Apparently Tug was pretty angry he had to settle for second-fiddle to Stuart. Spitting nails, angry. But he decided to suck it up, play the game, and be ready to step up when the opportunity arose."

Scott shook his head to stop my exclamation. "But Tug was also visible in the paddock yesterday—from seven in the morning to race start. He didn't do the deed."

I sighed. "I really want to know who did this."

He held up a third finger. "Elizabeth Rogers." He paused. "Oddest one of the bunch. Such a non-entity, I had to do some Googling."

"And?"

"Couldn't find a thing."

"It's a pretty common name, right?"

"Sure, but no trails that looked like her. So I asked a contact." He winked at me, which I took to mean he'd asked a Racing's Ringer source. "He couldn't find anything either before she worked for Grand-Am. Neither of us wanted to dig too deep."

I shook my head. "I wonder if she's trying to hide something."

Our 28 car's crew stirred, hefted equipment, and leapt off the wall to service the car as Colby pulled in. Tire change—back to single-stinting them in the heat of the day—full fuel, and a clean windscreen. Colby pulled back out for her last stint.

I turned back to Scott. "You don't know if the Kulik brothers have an alibi for ten-thirty to eleven-thirty yesterday morning, do you?"

"Sure I do." He laughed at my surprise. "Social media is your friend, Kate. They were at yesterday's tweetup at ten—you were there, weren't you? Then they hauled everyone over to the Kulik vodka tent for free shots until the autograph session started."

"I didn't see everyone who attended the tweetup." I thought through the timing. "That was an hour and a half of vodka shots?"

"Closer to two hours, really." He smiled. "Sadly, I was on the job and didn't participate. But I was there documenting it all for SGTV."

Another suspect bites the dust. Not that I thought the Kulkis had motive, only guns. I glanced at Scott. "These questions are off the record, remember."

"No problem, I've got plenty. Thanks for the tip, catch you later, Kate." He waved at me and headed up pit lane.

I picked up a radio, told Holly I'd be right back, and took off at a jog for the main bathroom building. I exited the building two minutes later and jogged back into the walkway, only to bump into Sam Remington as I sidestepped a golf cart.

Sam grabbed my upper arms to steady me, stop me, or both. "I hoped I'd run into you, Kate, but didn't mean it literally." He was laughing.

I forced a smile. "You never know, do you? Sorry, I've got to get back and get ready."

"I'll walk you there. Wanted a minute."

I gave up the idea of avoiding him as he fell into step next to me. "What can I do for you?"

"Mostly I wanted to apologize."

Again? I looked at him, but didn't respond.

"For…bothering you last night." He grimaced. "I get it. I miss you, and you've moved on. My bad luck. I accept it."

I sighed. "Sometimes I miss you, too, Sam, but that's the past. And maybe it's your good luck—you know, Paula and all?"

"Maybe. Probably. I don't know." He shook his head. "I heard you've been dating Stuart Telarday recently. But then he was photographed kissing that Monica woman. Um, that sucks?"

I burst out laughing, because the Sam I remembered couldn't retain paddock gossip for more than ten seconds. "I'm not going to comment, because after you, I'd had enough of my relationship being publicly dissected." I eyed him. "But I will ask how you know."

He looked embarrassed. "Paula."

"I see." I took a deep breath. *If there's ever someone who should know you're off the market….* "It's not for public consumption, but yes, I've been dating Stuart. And yes, there were those photos, but they weren't anything serious. One of those things that looked like something it wasn't." I surprised myself by meaning the words. After all of the drama and doubt and emotion of the last day, I wasn't angry anymore about the photos—at least not angry at Stuart. I'd still like to drop-kick Monica.

At that moment, we reached the start of the Arena Motorsport tent. I averted my gaze, focusing entirely on Sam.

He was nodding. "That's good. Good. Stuart's a good guy."

So glad you approve. I kept my eye-rolling internal.

"I think you're right about that Monica woman," he went on. "I mean, I saw them interact yesterday morning, and there was nothing to it. No extra vibe or anything."

"What did you see?"

He glanced behind me, into the Arena tent, I presumed, and lowered his voice. "I was chatting to Stuart, and she walked by with the guy from the team next to ours? That Vinny guy?"

"Vinny Cruise at Benchmark."

"Right, him. Stuart greeted them, and they shook hands all around—you know, like they'd all met before. But there wasn't anything romantic or even awkward between Monica and Stuart." He paused and frowned. "No vibe directed at him at all, only at me."

We'd cleared the Arena tents and slowed to stop outside Sandham Swift. "She made a play for you instead of Stuart?"

He shrugged. "Some, but Vinny didn't seem to like it. I'd said something about how Vinny and Monica looked like they could be related. Vinny looked annoyed, got all stiff. Monica laughed it off and moved close. Put her hand on my arm, leaned into me, brushed up against—you know."

I did know, having watched it often enough from women on the prowl in pit lane. I heard my name called and saw Jack wave at me, without urgency, from the top of the pit box. I held up a finger to indicate one minute.

Turning back to Sam, I stuck my hand out. "Friends? Only?"

He looked like he wanted to hug me again, but he restrained himself. He shook. "I'd like that. Not sure about Paula, but I'd like it."

"Up to you, Sam. I'll see you around." I crossed the walkway and entered the pit space, then stopped and looked back to find him watching me. He had a strange expression on his face, a combination of pride, regret, and wistfulness. I raised my hand and turned back to talk to Jack. Miles had been watching the monitors, and he trailed me over to the command center.

I climbed up a step. Jack leaned over, pulled the radio headset off his ears.

"When Colby comes in, we're going to take a few extra seconds to check suspension linkages and clean out the grills. It's running a little warmer than usual, and Colby says there's some vibration in the left turns, which could be some pickup or marbles. We'll check everything out, maybe find some junk blocking a vent. Kate, it shouldn't mean more than five extra seconds after you get strapped in, but wanted you to know."

I gave Jack a thumbs-up, then I joined Holly at the monitors. I updated her on Scott Brooklyn's information. "Everyone suspicious is turning out to have an alibi and couldn't have hurt Stuart."

"Except Elizabeth."

"Or one of the guys who could be Julio Arena. Nik Reyes, Joe Smith, or Raul—we don't know where they were. But that's all wild speculation and possibly racial profiling, I don't know."

"I'll see if I can find out where they were."

I hesitated. "Did you ever find out if Greg was accounted for?"

"Don't get timid now, Kate. No, I didn't. But…" She cocked her head to the side and stared at the ceiling of the tent. "Ian's sister Jennifer stuck her head into our team lounge yesterday, hoping Greg was there with Ian. That was before the drivers' meeting, right?"

"Was that what she wanted? I couldn't hear. It had to be before, because we went straight from the drivers' meeting to the autograph session to the grid."

"Was it before the quick team meeting Jack held?"

It was painful thinking back to those pre-race hours, when we were all fresh, energetic, and hopeful. When Ian was still alive. Before Stuart was hurt. I thought back to Aunt Tee gathering us, Jack striding into the room, me looking for a seat. "It was right before. Jack had just come in the room, and Jennifer caught the door before it closed."

Holly frowned. "That was around eleven-fifteen, and Jennifer said she hadn't seen Greg for at least half an hour, if not longer."

"I don't want to even say it."

"I know." She sighed. "But that means Greg was missing at the right time. And he was mad at Stuart."

"Maybe you can verify he was gone?"

"I'll check up on it." She sounded as weighed down as I felt. Greg had been through so much, I felt terrible considering him as a suspect. He'd lost his wife, was being pushed out of his career, and then lost his son…how could I pile more on him?

Stuart didn't deserve to be hurt, no matter the reason. The voice in my head was quiet, but devastating. I reconsidered, refocused.

If Greg hurt Stuart, he needs to pay. I lived with that thought a moment, then nodded, satisfied my head was on straight again. I crossed to my shelf of gear and started suiting up.

I was ready with my helmet and gloves in hand, standing at the monitors with twenty minutes to go in the stint, when a prototype's suspension broke and the car skidded into the outer track wall. I pulled my helmet on as they threw the double-yellow to retrieve the broken car.

I gave Bruce a thumbs-up and pulled my gloves on as I walked forward to the pit wall, where the crew scrambled to their places. I stood to the side and closed my eyes, focusing on the sound of the cars circulating on the track and the feel of my own breathing. I emptied my mind of everything but the car.

This double-stint would be my last time behind the wheel in the race. I was going to make it a good one.

Chapter Forty-nine

The team's twenty-fifth pit stop of the race nearly proved our undoing. The crew had been more or less awake for twenty-nine hours by the time I got in the car that morning, and they'd stayed alert and on point the whole time. Until the fumbles hit us all at once.

First I sat down on the right-side lap belt getting in and had to fish it out from under my behind once I was in place. Then I jammed my right shoulder belt in the central buckle wrong, requiring Bubs to release all the belts and re-buckle everything. Finally, it took Bubs three tries to plug in my helmet air hose. That was only what happened inside the car.

Outside, everything went smoothly until the guy wielding the air gun on the right-rear tire—Eric, the North Carolinian—cross-threaded the single, giant wheel nut. Everyone moves so fast during a pit stop that by the time Eric could tell the others what happened, tell them to stop so he could fix the nut, the car had been dropped off its jacks and I was pulling away.

I'd like to claim I felt something wrong with the car at the first revolution of the wheels. But I didn't. The reality was Bruce shouting "Stop!" in my ear, which sent both of my feet to the floor on clutch and brake. I was two pit stalls away, in the central no-man's lane between the full-pit-speed, passing-through lane on the right and the pit spaces on the left.

"Stay in neutral," Bruce instructed. "Pulling you back. Wheel nut."

I took my foot off the brake and clicked the paddle behind the steering wheel to put the car into neutral. Four crew members were already pushing the car back into our pit space, because cars couldn't reverse in pit lane, but they could be pushed or pulled by hand.

In position. Air jacks pop the car six inches into the air. *Brrrrrrrrrt*, went the air gun. Silence. Tugging on the car. *Brrrrrrrrrt* again. Something metallic clanked on the wheel. *Brrrrrrrrrt.* Then the normal sound and sensation of a tire coming off, a tire going on, and a wheel nut being secured. *Brrrrrrrrrrt.* A hand in the air from Eric. Car bouncing down off the air jacks.

"Go, go, go, Kate." Bruce's voice.

I shifted into gear and roared out again, unchallenged this time. I checked to be sure the speed limiter was on, because the last thing we needed was a pit lane speeding violation and penalty to go with the rest of it.

Every nerve screamed at me to get out there fast, make up the time we'd lost. But I chanted, "Stay calm, stay calm," as I exited the tricky, curvy pit lane. Checked for traffic as I merged onto the track. Focused on the next turn in front of me, then the next one, thinking ahead to the one after that. Getting the new tires up to speed, feeling out the track again. Noting the changes since I'd been in the car and on the track six hours prior. I'd made it around the back straight and through the Bus Stop before Bruce checked in.

"Feel all right, Kate?"

"Fine. No wheel damage, right?"

"Good news is the wheel should be fine. Bad news is the leader in class is two cars behind you. If you can stay ahead of him, we won't go another lap down."

I glanced in the mirror. A BMW ten car lengths behind me. Five car lengths behind him was a Porsche, the GT class leader.

Bruce radioed again. "The crew's really sorry. Do whatever you can out there."

I thought about the crew who'd been up all night. Who'd fixed damaged cars with good humor and only mild complaint. I'd never worked with a more dedicated, talented group of people.

I pushed the radio button. "I'm on it, Bruce. Tell the crew not to worry."

Then I drove my heart out.

My last stint in the race. My last chance to make my mark on the GT field. My final opportunity in this race to prove a point to the racing world. And to myself. To celebrate racing and feel the joy I knew was there, as a counterpoint to the sorrow we'd been feeling.

Suddenly this drive represented my career. My essence. Performing well in this moment would validate everything I'd worked for—sacrificed for—throughout my life. Everything Ian had represented, everything Stuart worked to deliver.

I drove as if in a trance, with no radio traffic back to the pits and no stray thoughts creeping in. Only regular spotter bulletins delivered by Millie in a steady monotone. I poured every last scrap of my energy and emotion into focus on the corner ahead, the car ahead, and the car after that. One by one I worked my way up to and past the GT runners in front of me, until—with the help of a lot of traffic—I'd put half a lap between myself and the GT leader.

Then I got lucky with a yellow flag—which flew with the overall race leader behind me, seconds away from passing me. He dropped back at the flashing yellow lights, and when the safety car picked him up, I continued around to join the back of the pack. I was still one lap down to the top four cars in class, but the GT class leader was three cars ahead of me.

I pitted with the GT field, praying the crew were back to their typical sharp standards. I stopped the car on my marks. Fuel going in. Tires being changed. Bubs on my side and Eric on the passenger side scrubbing at the windscreen. They jerked away. Bruce in my ear, "Go, go, go!" The guy in front waving me out into pit lane.

That felt quick. That felt quick!

Bruce confirmed it, sharing even better news. "We leap-frogged the GT leader. We are now back on the lead lap."

He didn't have to add, "If Kate can stay there," because come hell or high water, as Gramps would say, I would.

I dropped quickly back into the zone and picked off cars ahead of me. I used all the power and performance that Corvette had to offer during the next forty minutes. I was determined and inspired. I made sure the racing world—especially our competitors in this new United SportsCar Championship—knew Sandham Swift Racing was a contender. As was Kate Reilly.

Deep down, I knew my determination to prove myself was directly related to the size of the stage I was performing on. The 24 Hours of Daytona tempted teams and drivers from all over the world and across every form of racing to compete. We had four IndyCar champions in the field, seven Le Mans champions, and three NASCAR champions—including Miles on my own team. If little Kate Reilly—short, slim, twenty-five year old *female*—could match the performance of those thirty- and forty-something champion men?

My lips curved into a smile under my helmet. *They wouldn't forget me.*

Those thoughts flashed through my head as I took a breath down the back straight. Then I wiped my mind clear of everything except the Bus Stop turn and the Ferrari ahead of me.

Six laps later, I snuck past the Ferrari into Turn 1.

Three turns later, Bruce radioed to tell me I was P4 in class and ten laps away from pitting to change to Miles. Two laps later, we got another full-course caution.

I savored the last laps at safety-car speed, enjoying the view of the track. Reveling in the music of the racecar.

Then I followed the GT leaders out of NASCAR 4 into pit lane, unplugging cables and tubes. Loosening belts. I stopped, got out of the car, out of Miles' way, over the wall. Pulled off my gloves, watching anxiously as the crew performed a perfect, smooth service. I pulled my helmet and balaclava off and watched as the crew sent the car away.

For a moment, as the car—the excitement—moved on without me, as the crew swarmed around the car and Miles, I felt bereft.

My sense of aloneness lasted only a nanosecond, because no sooner had the car disappeared down pit lane than the crew surrounded me, whooping, pounding me on the back, and picking me up in giant bear hugs of thanks. This time my eyes watered with tears of joy and relief.

Some minutes later, the crew dispersed to put away their gear. I collected a cold towel and bottle of water before climbing onto the pit cart to review my stints in the car. A quick chat with Jack and Bruce—who confirmed they didn't need me on-deck for the last stint of the race—and I sat back to drink a bottle of water and wipe my face down with the wet towel Aunt Tee had handed me.

That's when, out of the blue, I finally processed what Lara had been trying to tell me. What my gut had been trying to tell me since I saw Ian's accident.

She'd talked to "the guy from the car," who discovered nothing wrong, "no brakes, no nothing." I saw the accident in my mind's eye again and understood. The report was the throttle had stuck wide open, and the driver's attempt to step on the brakes hadn't stopped the car. But I'd seen no brake lights—that's what had gnawed at my insides since the wreck. I hurried down the steps of the pit box and found Alex Hanley, our brake expert, in the back of the tent.

"Alex, say my throttle stuck. If I stepped on the brakes, would they do anything to slow the car? Would the brake lights still go on?"

He put his hands to his hips, his splayed-out elbows mirroring his bowed legs. "You're not worried 'boutcher own throttle or brakes, are you?" The frown on his face didn't match the lines in his tanned face. Alex more typically beamed ear-to-ear at all times.

I shook my head. "A question, in general."

"I'd say yes, then. If yer throttle was wide open, but you pushed the pedal, the brakes'd still do something. Unless the brakes failed at the same time as the throttle stuck—but that'd be nigh on impossible." He scratched his head. "Maybe not impossible they'd both go, but mighty unusual." He considered further. "But if you stepped on the brakes, ye'd still getcher brake lights."

I thanked him, and he got back to work with a jaunty wave.

No brake lights meant the driver hadn't tried to stop. And given Lara's message of "nothing wrong," I wondered if the throttle had malfunctioned after all. The only conclusion I could draw was the driver had deliberately tried to take our car out. It was pure bad luck that he'd killed Ian in the process.

But why?

The 30 car had competed in the GT Daytona class. I knew some people who weren't above bribery and really needed a good finish in that class.

Were my cousins responsible for Ian's death?

Chapter Fifty

My next thought was to wonder if Lara could be in trouble. I also realized I'd forgotten to warn her about Tug. I pulled out my phone and sent a message to my father asking for her cell number.

He responded almost immediately, and I typed a message to her: Lara, it's Kate. What you said earlier, was that about the 77 car? Did you mean there really was no throttle problem? I sent that and agonized over the five other questions I had. That was enough to start with.

I sent a second message: Also, watch out for Tug. Big flirt, big player. Don't let him talk you into anything.

Holly breezed in, full of congratulations, but bit them off as soon as she saw my face. "Now what, sugar?"

I explained to her what I'd figured out. Her face fell also.

She stood up from the cooler she was on, reached inside, and brought out a water bottle. She exchanged it for the empty one I held in my hand. "You need to get cleaned up."

"I need to hear back from Lara. I may be spinning something simple into a big conspiracy theory. I'm not sure I understood her correctly."

"Then let's take a golf cart for the run back to the motorhome. We could stop by Lara's team after that. I was just next door in CPG."

Fifteen minutes later, I was showered and dressed in jeans, a team polo shirt, and a light jacket. Aunt Tee played chauffeur and dropped us off at the top end of pit lane. I waved the radio at her. "Tell Jack I'm listening if he needs me. I'll be back for the end, for sure."

She waved and glided off.

My cell phone finally buzzed with a return message from Lara.

Don't worry, I don't trust anything Tug says. Yes, 77 car. Overheard mechanic saying all systems were fine.

I tugged Holly out of the way of foot traffic and showed her the message.

You overheard? Does the whole team know? I typed back.

Secret. Couple people talking. I think the mechanic likes me, so I might ask him about it, came her return.

Holly read over my shoulder. "She's certainly your sister." I glared at her, and she added, "Sorry, half-sister."

I didn't mind the association as much as I had before. I typed back: **Don't investigate, don't get in trouble. Leave it alone.**

Lara's response: **Why not? You do. Besides, I'll be careful.**

I groaned.

Holly laughed. "Related to you. Maybe it's not a problem. Maybe it's all the driver's doing and the mechanic is covering his own ass."

"That might be easier to believe than a giant conspiracy."

"On the other hand, that team might not be a good place for her to be."

I typed back. **Can you get out of there? Meet me?**

She replied: **Not now. Need to run some numbers. Maybe in a bit?**

"I'm not sure what to do, Holly." I slipped the phone in my pocket and looked around us. "That's got nothing to do with Stuart or Calhoun, right? She found out someone lied about the accident. Like you said, the team could feel badly about it and be fibbing to make their mistakes seem less awful."

"My Spidey-sense tells me it's not as simple as all that. At least you should tell the cops and your father, don't you think?"

"Good idea."

I sent quick texts to Latham and my father. Holly and I headed down the walkway. Two teams later, we ran into my grandfather's industry friend, Jimmy Baker.

I introduced him to Holly, and he joined us to walk down the lane, chatting to Holly about teams they'd both worked with. Holly ducked into the Western Racing tent. Jimmy and I stood to the side to wait for her.

Jimmy looked at me with concern. He lowered his voice to speak. "Kate, I hope you'll forgive my presumption. You look a touch frazzled."

I touched a hand to my hair, then rubbed my forehead, imagining what he saw: three hours' sleep, no makeup or hair styling, radio headset slung around my neck. Jimmy, in contrast, looked like he'd gotten a good night's sleep. Today's bow tie was forest green with white polka dots.

He waved a hand. "It's not that you look unattractive, my dear. You look concerned. Upset. I merely wondered if there's anything I could help you with—in place of your grandfather. I'm sure he'd want me to offer. I'm at your disposal if there's anything at all."

Can he help? Is it even wise to tell him anything? "It's been a tough race," I started, cautiously.

"Indeed." He paused. "Perhaps it would help to let you know that over the years, your grandfather confided in me about your father's family. I'm aware some of them are here and that your grandparents would prefer you not interact with them. However, I know how to be discreet."

I was rattled to hear this near-stranger knew all about me. But he reminded me of Gramps. And I could easily imagine Gramps asking one of his pals to help me out on the sly. "Thank you. I'm not sure if I'll need anything, but I'll keep it in mind." I took a deep breath. "I think my father is working on keeping the idiots in his family in line. Though perhaps you could keep an eye out for my—" I faltered. I'd always drawn the line at saying the term aloud. I sighed, wondering why it mattered anymore. Wondering what good the privacy and independence I'd hugged to myself so fiercely had done for me.

I cleared my throat. "Keep an eye out for my half-sister in the tent next to yours. The little blonde. Lara."

"It would be my pleasure. It must be difficult to compete and do your job while dealing with family interactions, drama, concerns."

A short laugh popped out of me. "You're not kidding."

"Even though you see it so often in the racing world."

"It's really a family sport."

"I've always thought it's harder to treat racing like a business if your son—or daughter—is driving for you. If your brother is a car chief or marketing executive. If your cousin is your accountant. Or worse yet—if your close relation is giving you the money to race."

Yes, like my father and his brother or nephews. And wait, didn't Holly also say... "Jimmy, whose cousin is an accountant?"

He smiled at Holly, who emerged from the Western tent and crossed the lane to join us. "I believe Richard Arena and Monica Frank are cousins. Holly, how're they doing in there?"

She held her hand flat and wiggled it back and forth. "Coping, but strange. There's something going on, and they won't tell me what it is. Greg isn't blaming everyone as much as before, though he's still plenty angry at the Series." She chewed on her lower lip. "I'm worried he's going to go out in some big blaze of glory."

I glanced back at the tent. "Did you get confirmation?"

She nodded, a sad look in her eyes, as Jimmy gestured us on down the lane. My heart sank. *Greg was missing during the time of Stuart's attack. Could he really be capable of it?*

I wanted to ask Holly if she'd sent word of our suspicions to the police, but I didn't want to do it while Jimmy was with us. Instead, I listened with only half my attention as Holly and Jimmy talked about the race. I chewed on the idea of Greg as a killer.

It all comes back to family. Greg's family, whether it's the racing world or Ian. My family, causing problems. Other family...

Something nagged at me about family connections. I was worried about Lara, and my cousins could be in big trouble, but those issues weren't what my subconscious was stuck on.

We were steps away from Jimmy's destination, the CPG tent, when a stirring around us indicated something happening on track. We hurried into CPG and found the monitors in time to see the double-yellow thrown for a battered BMW that had given up the ghost and was stopped in the runoff area at the exit of Turn 3.

Something about cousins? Was that it? What cousins? I knew of my own. Arena and Monica. Thomas Kendall, aka Tommy Fantastic, and Chris Syfert, drivers in the Sandham Swift 30 car. Whoever Monica had referenced as her cousin in the video recording.

Holly nudged me, and we said goodbye to Jimmy. As we turned to leave, Jason Carnegie caught my eye. I returned his wave.

Was the issue other relations? Like Jason, younger brother of Daniel Carnegie? Certainly there was a younger brother out there, the missing Julio Arena.

We walked past the opening of Benchmark Racing's tent, and I spied Lara twisted around in her seat on the pit cart, smiling down at a crew member. She saw me and raised her hand in a subtle wave. Vinny, three seats down from her on the same bench, glanced over at Lara and scowled at her and the crew member.

A dozen details rearranged themselves into a new pattern in my mind. I gasped. Fortunately, only Holly heard me over the noise from the track.

"What?" She grabbed my arm.

I darted a glance into the tent again. Vinny still watched Lara and the crew member, who I suspected was the mechanic from the 77 car. Then Vinny turned and saw us.

I pasted on my brightest smile and waved at a man I thought was a killer.

Chapter Fifty-one

I shoved Holly farther down the pit lane.

"What's going on, Kate?"

I tugged her into the back of the next team tent, the factory Corvette group, wanting to be out of sight of Benchmark Racing, but desperate to tell Holly what I'd put together. If it made sense to her, maybe it was true.

Duncan Forsyth, one of the Corvette drivers, turned from his position in front of their monitors and walked over. "Ladies. Anything we can help you with?"

"Space for a quick conversation," I told him.

He raised his eyebrows. "Help yourself." He returned to the elaborate bank of screens mounted on the back of a pit cart even larger than ours.

Holly looked worried. "What on—"

"Everything we keep hearing is about family, right?" I spoke close to her ear, in a low tone I knew couldn't be overheard.

She nodded, and I went on. "Cousins and brothers. Half-sisters. All over the place. Mine, other people's. Plus people who aren't who they say they are."

"Joe Smith?" She whispered back.

"And maybe others. The point is, that was rattling around in my head. Arena and Monica are cousins. Monica talked about 'her cousin' to him, in a way that didn't seem like she was referring to him. Monica walking with Vinny. Someone saying they look related. People aren't who they say they are. The Arena and Benchmark teams connected, but it's supposed to be a secret. A missing brother known to have killed someone via a hit-and-run."

I could see the moment she added everything up and got the same number I had. "You think Vinny Cruise is Julio Arena?" She barely breathed it.

My knees shook as I added another piece of the puzzle. "Calhoun saw Julio Friday night—had to be at the restaurant with Stuart. Stuart saw Vinny and Arena together there—he said so to Vinny."

"Vinny thought he was going to be exposed as Julio," Holly added.

"Right. Vinny thought Stuart knew who he was, like Calhoun did." I considered. "Does it make sense? Too out there?"

She was silent a full minute. "I think you're right. I'm not sure we can prove it, but it makes sense. Tell the cops."

I yanked my cell phone out of my pocket and took twice as long as usual to type a message to Detective Latham, because my fingers trembled. *We think Vinny Cruise of Benchmark Racing is really Julio Arena, RA's brother. That he hurt Stuart and killed Calhoun to keep it secret.*

I also sent a frantic text message to my father warning him that Vinny might be dangerous and to get Lara out of there immediately.

Latham responded: We're on top of it. Stay with your team and keep quiet. Don't get in our way. We'll take care of it.

My sister's in that tent! I returned.

Latham's reply: We'll take care of it and her.

I realized my heart was pounding. I tried to calm down by taking deep breaths—which didn't help the way it usually did. With no better idea of what to do, we set off back down the pit lane.

A minute later, we ducked into the empty tent on the other side of the Redemption team—abandoned by another team whose race ended early—so I could read a fresh text message from Lara. Tino, the mechanic, was paid to lie about the throttle. He heard someone paid team owner to reduce car count in the class. Tino's having a hard time keeping quiet given what happened.

I covered my mouth with my hand, horrified someone would do such a thing. Tino was covering up after the fact. But the team owner, driver, and sources of the bribe…I couldn't believe they'd willfully damage a competitor. *What are you thinking? Of course you can believe that of Vinny Cruise. You think worse.*

I responded to Lara. Can you get out of there? Come see me? Let me meet you? Worried about you knowing that information. Worried about you in that team tent. Please, meet me?

It took a long time, but I finally got a return, a strange one.

Holly looked up from the screen. "'Not now sister'? That doesn't seem like Lara."

"It doesn't. It sounds like someone telling her what to say or responding for her. What if Vinny figured out she knows something?"

"Have you heard more from the cops? Your father?"

I shook my head. I paced back to the entryway of the tent and out into the walkway. Then I walked to the entryway of the Redemption tent where I could see their bank of monitors. I felt restless, unsettled. Helpless and irritated. I couldn't rush into the Benchmark tent on a rescue mission. I couldn't go meekly back to my own team pits.

Holly joined me. "You're not planning anything, are you, sugar?"

I kept looking around, searching for any sign of Lara, my father, or the cops. "Why am I worried about her, Holly? Why do I care?" I paused. "When did I start thinking of her as my sister?"

"For one thing, you'd care about anyone in the same situation. For another, she *is* your half-sister, and she seems nice. Nothing wrong with being interested in a family connection." She turned to glance toward the Arena tent. "Unless it's *that* family connection. But your father seems like a decent guy. Your half-sister's probably the same."

"When did I start caring about family?"

Holly sighed. "You've always cared about family. You simply didn't have much of it. You want what family's supposed to give you. Unquestioning acceptance and support." She held up a hand to stop my response. "I know you get that from your grandparents, but who doesn't want more? Also you want a sense of where you come from. Heritage. History. We all do. You've only had half the story so far."

I felt the familiar tightness in my chest at the idea of being sucked into my father's family. *I never wanted the burden—so many people, so many emotions and needs. Isn't it simpler and easier with only my grandparents?*

I followed the 28 Corvette through a full loop of the track on the monitors as I considered different scenarios. One, ignore my father and his family and have only my grandparents in my life. That gave me an itch between my shoulder blades. *Because what happens when your grandparents are gone?* I frowned. Fear of being alone was a stupid reason to open myself up to anyone. But the thought of never knowing where I came from made me feel…adrift.

Scenario two, I let my father's family in. At best, I might really like my father and his wife and kids. *Grandmother might never forgive me.* I shook my head. I couldn't let her feelings dictate my actions. If she had good reasons, she needed to share them with me, not darkly hint at evil.

At worst, I might be exposing myself to a hateful group of people—like Ed Grant, his son Billy, and Holden Sherain. I didn't know what emotional currents ran through that family. I didn't want to know. But I already had a champion and a defender in my father.

I closed my eyes and took a deep breath. *What do I want?* I exhaled and shook my head. I'd run from the decision long enough. My life with my grandparents might be simpler, but it was also incomplete. I wanted to know my father and his wife and children. I wanted to believe I could be part of his family.

I looked around, thinking it a strange time and place for such a momentous decision. The final hour of a grueling endurance race. The final push for weary, grieving teams. Culprits still uncaught. Stuart's condition still unresolved. And I was making life-changing decisions.

I still wasn't sure it would work. That any part of the Reilly family wanted me, that we'd find a connection. That I'd trust them completely—since I knew I didn't trust Ed, Billy, or Holden. But my half-sister? I instinctively trusted her, even if I didn't fully trust our father.

You can't trust him until you know what happened when you were born. I closed my eyes. I might never feel ready for it, but it was time for that information.

I looked at Holly, who'd turned her attention to the monitors while I wrestled with my thoughts. "All right, I'm interested in some of the family. The bigger issue is Lara could be sitting next to a killer."

"The cops told you they'd handle it."

"I hate feeling helpless. I'm not going to go barging in there, but maybe there's something we can do. I'd feel better at least if I heard from my father." I pulled my cell phone out of my pocket. No messages. "I can't believe he's not responding—now, when it's *his daughter* in trouble."

I stopped finally, because Holly wasn't listening. Something big was happening, that was clear from the shocked postures of the team in front of us and the stunned silence up and down pit lane. I followed Holly's shaking finger as she pointed to the monitors. It took me a few seconds to understand what I was seeing.

Greg Davenport was behind the wheel of his Western Racing Porsche wearing neither firesuit nor helmet. He drove down pit lane, waving out the window to the people he passed. Hand-painted signs festooned both sides of the car, the roof, and the hood, with messages proclaiming "Greed KILLS Teams and People," "Shame on USCC," and a much smaller "RIP Ian."

Greg ignored the madly waving red flag at the end of pit lane, warning him to stop. Instead, he exited, headed for the racetrack.

Chapter Fifty-two

Pit lane erupted into sound as teams watched in disbelief and crew chiefs scrambled to warn their drivers. Race Control overrode all radio communications, issuing terse instructions for yellow flags to put the race under full-course caution and for the safety car to deploy quickly to control the field. Then Race Control called for black flags—racing's equivalent of a penalty card—to be waved by all corner workers at Greg.

Holly stood wide-eyed. "What *in hell* is he thinking? He could get himself killed—not to mention be kicked out of the Series."

"He did say if they pushed him too far, he'd show them."

"But this is crazy."

I shrugged, thinking Greg had plenty of reason to be a little crazy. I was actually relieved this was how he chose to vent his outrage—rather than more lethal options.

His actions were still shocking. It was unthinkable anyone would be out on an active racetrack without proper safety gear— firesuit, helmet, HANS, gloves, and the window net fastened, to name only the ignored items I could see—let alone to have gone out there with a race in full song. In addition, Greg wasn't a registered driver for the car, so by going out there, he'd disqualified his car from contention. That didn't address the anti-Series messages he displayed for millions of television viewers, which were likely to get him tossed out of the entire championship. But with his son dead and the despair he'd felt even before that about his future in racing, I supposed he didn't care.

A strange thing happened on track, however. None of the drivers wanted to pass Greg, so he ended up leading the field around for a full lap, making it appear the other drivers wanted to honor his statements. Like Greg was the main attraction in the show, with the other fifty-five cars the supporting cast. I wondered if that was circumstantial or deliberate.

The strange parade lasted only until Race Control realized Greg wouldn't stop for the black flag and ended the spectacle by tossing the red flag and stopping everyone else on the back straight. Greg continued to drive at low speed, still waving to his rapt audience. The SGTV cameras and live broadcast continued to capture every moment of the drama. I didn't know what to think. I understood Greg's pain and frustration, but his actions were reckless and public. Permanent.

"He must really not care about ever racing again," I murmured to Holly.

She continued shaking her head, as she'd done since he first appeared on pit lane, her eyes glued to the monitors.

The spectacle didn't reduce my anxiety or restlessness. I watched as the Series sent out two big safety trucks—each loaded with four safety workers—to herd Greg into pit lane. Then they blocked pit lane with a variety of vehicles, from tractors to golf carts and an ambulance, to make turning into the garage area his only option. Greg almost got around the line of cars by steering onto the big stretch of grass separating pit lane from the front straight, but a quick-thinking driver in one of the safety trucks accelerated alongside him and cut off that option.

After that final spark of rebellion, Greg sedately steered his car through pit lane, through the garages, and into his garage space. It was clear from the TV broadcast the Series had mobilized all possible staff to keep the garage area clear for Greg's passage. They also had security staff waiting for him at his garage. I recognized

Officer Webster of the Speedway police and other uniformed officers who looked like the real cops.

The churning in my gut reached its zenith. I grabbed Holly's arm. "If Webster's there with Daytona police, who's up at Benchmark watching out for Lara?"

"Everyone seems preoccupied with Greg right now."

"I'm going down there."

"Don't burst in, Kate." Holly's words stopped me. "Let's go past Benchmark into the CPG tent. I know you don't want to deal with Sam—"

"Doesn't matter, plus Jimmy Baker is there."

"And Cecilia, who'll make sure the team helps us, no questions asked."

I put a hand on her arm. "Holly, find Scott Brooklyn."

"And his camera. Genius. On it."

I headed up the pits at a run. Right before the opening to the Benchmark tent, I slowed to a leisurely walk, trying to look casual and breathe normally. I took the radio headset from around my neck and put it over my ears, pretending to concentrate on what I was hearing.

I passed Benchmark slowly, stopping as I had a view into the tent and cocking my head at the imaginary voice in my ears while I searched for Lara. She wasn't on the pit box. I fought for breath. *There!* I caught sight of her standing at the far side of the tent, near the wall Benchmark shared with CPG, talking with four people. Big people who blocked my view of her. A crew member exited the tent and walked past me. I glanced around the tent to find a couple crew members watching me, including a big guy on the pit box next to Vinny.

I gave a faint smile and looked to the team's bank of monitors, putting my hand on my right earpiece, pretending to press the radio button, and mouthing some words. Then, careful not to let my eyes do more than scan past Lara again, I started walking. I ducked into CPG's tent, yanked my headset off, and zeroed in on Cecilia, a tiny, thirty-something blonde with a pixie cut.

"Holly said you could help us," I said into her ear. "Next door—someone may be in trouble."

"Whatever you need."

"Would you watch the walkway and make sure a woman with long, blonde hair doesn't leave?"

"Lara?"

"You know her?"

"She's been over here a few times. Sweet kid. She's in trouble?"

"I think so." I bit my lip. "Could you get her out of there?"

"Shouldn't be a problem." She darted out of the pit space.

I loitered by the doorway of the tent, one eye on the monitors, the other watching for Holly. I peeked around the tent opening into the walkway once, but didn't see anyone I was looking for. I checked my phone. Still nothing from Lara, the cops, the hospital, or my father. Nothing to calm my nerves.

I glanced around the tent, nodding at Daniel Carnegie, ignoring the glare Paula sent me, and giving Jimmy Baker a small wave. He stood up from his chair at the side of the pit space and walked over. "You look worried. What's going on?"

Before I could respond, Cecilia returned, shaking her head. "I saw her with some people, but someone stopped me before I got three feet and asked what I needed. He told me she was busy on something critical for the race, and they'd have her get back to me."

"The young woman next door?" Jimmy asked.

I nodded, not liking the situation she described. My mind raced as I tried to come up with a way to liberate Lara without an outright confrontation.

"Why don't I take a slow walk past their tent?" Jimmy offered. "I've wandered up and down pit lane enough, that won't seem unusual. Maybe I can talk to those delightful Russian gentlemen again—linger a bit, see what's going on."

"Be careful—"

Jimmy stopped me with a hand on my shoulder. "I promise." Then he was off.

Holly passed him as she ran up. She stopped next to me and Cecilia, scanned the pit lane in front of the tent and swore, breathing hard. "Haven't found them yet. Leaving messages for James also." She turned and ran out of the tent again.

Jimmy returned, looking concerned. "I couldn't get in. I think they're taking her somewhere."

I looked over his shoulder to see four big men exiting the Benchmark tent, a tiny blonde barely visible in the middle of the scrum.

Chapter Fifty-three

"Lara!" I shouted, my voice actually audible due to the lack of cars in pit lane or on the front straight.

I ran toward her. I thought I saw her head turn my direction, but it was hard to see past her captors or guards or whatever they were. All I saw were four identical navy blue polo shirts stretched tight over thick chests and bulging arms.

Vinny Cruise stepped out from the Benchmark tent, stopping my forward rush, holding his hands up. He glanced back at the men and jerked his head the opposite direction, away from me. I saw the men confer, point down pit lane, and start to move that way.

I started to step around Vinny to follow them. He moved to block me.

"Can I help you, Kate?" he asked, in a pleasant voice.

"I need to talk to Lara."

His smile seemed smug. He crossed his arms over his chest. "I'm afraid this isn't a good time. She's not feeling well right now."

I started to push past him, but he reached out with frightening speed and grabbed my left wrist. It felt like being caught in a vise.

He transformed as I watched him. Some expression—disappointment or regret?—flashed across his face, and then he changed. The congenial, friendly, lighthearted man I'd commiserated with about family issues disappeared. A muscle clenched in his jaw as he looked quickly right and left, then back to me.

I froze. I'd expected to see the mark that committing multiple murders left on him, but his eyes weren't devoid of emotion. Nor was the expression in them crazy or deranged. What I saw scared me more than that. Vinny looked frantic and desperate.

Do I hit him? He's a murderer. Do I scream? Would anyone hear? My heart pounded.

He tightened his grip on my wrist. I winced as he dragged me forward a step.

I struggled to free my wrist, but he only clamped down harder, and stepped to my right, wrapping his left arm around my waist. He twisted my wrist hard and then released it, reaching for something in his pocket as I reacted, pulling my wrist to my chest and cradling it. By the time I got through the pain, he was pressing something sharp into my side and pulling me forward.

I dug in my heels, and that's when I felt his knife slice through my windbreaker, cut through my polo shirt, and jab into my side. I flinched and drew breath.

"They have knives also, and they'll use them on her. Come along quietly, my *friend*." His breath felt hot against my cheek, and I shuddered, understanding I'd been tragically wrong about Vinny's character.

I took a single step forward. *I could run and get help—but would they hurt her?* I felt the knife at my side poke me again. I couldn't squirm away without him digging the knife in. I felt cold sweat all over and took two more steps. A dozen different escape options occurred to me, and with my third step, I realized I wouldn't endanger Lara or myself.

Two more steps. *At least I can still see the thugs around Lara.*

Vinny shoved me forward with his hand in the small of my back. "Faster."

"Kate." Salvation in the form of Holly's voice.

I think Vinny might have tried to hustle me forward, but he wasn't bulky enough to block me the way his quartet of muscle blocked Lara—we were close to the same size and well matched for panic and determination. I was able to turn in his creepy embrace—scraping his knife along my side—to see my personal rescue squad: Holly, Scott Brooklyn, and an SGTV cameraman. I knew Holly had explained the situation because the camera sat on the operator's shoulder, pointed at me, recording.

I'd never been so glad to see a camera in my life.

Holly spoke again. "They're ready to do the on-camera with you and your sister."

I read the apology in Holly's eyes as she made the relationship public, but the secret was no longer important to me. I elbowed Vinny in the gut and jerked out of his grasp.

This time Vinny did look blank. Defeated.

I gave him a smile that was more about baring teeth than any joy. "That's right, *Julio*. I need to speak with my sister now. You don't get to hurt anyone else."

I waved at Holly and Scott to follow me, and we moved around Vinny without interference this time. I put a hand to my side to check for blood, but didn't see any. I started to run.

"Lara," I called.

The group of men surrounding her were only two pit spaces away from the exit into the Fan Zone. I shouted again.

I could see her trying to turn around and respond, but the men kept walking. I caught up to them as they reached the exit. The men surrounding her kept trying to hustle her away—until they heard me.

"The television crew is here, Lara," I shouted.

The men finally saw the SGTV camera aimed at them.

I took advantage of their hesitation to reach in between two men, grab Lara's hand, and pop her out from between the monoliths. Fear, relief, and delayed shock played over her face as she stumbled toward me. "They have a gun," she whispered.

My breath caught. *Worse than a knife.* I focused on the four men. "See that red light on the camera?" I asked them.

The closest one grunted. I kept talking. "Camera's rolling. Live on television." They wouldn't know the second part was a lie.

I put an arm around Lara's shoulders and walked her toward the camera, away from danger, speaking quietly in her ear. "We're going to use this interview to get away from them." I looked her in the eye. "Can you handle it?"

She took a single shuddering breath and agreed.

"Good." I turned to Scott and planted a smile on my face, trying to ignore the wall of thwarted muscle behind me and the smarting pain in my side. "We're ready for the interview."

Scott must have been briefed by Holly, because he made a big show of checking the shot with his cameraman. He turned to us. "I'd rather do this down in your own tent, Kate. Let's take this to Sandham Swift."

Scott and Holly led the way, and the cameraman followed us, filming the whole time. The five of us paraded past the four goons, every step taking us farther away from them and from Vinny and the Benchmark tent. I glanced back only once, after we'd passed the quartet of thugs. Vinny stood with them, all five watching us. I knew they wouldn't be there long, however, because I saw cops converging on them from farther up pit lane and from the Fan Zone. Vinny/Julio had nowhere to run.

I turned around before my face could convey any of my triumph.

By the time we reached the Sandham Swift tent, I could have wept from relief. I stopped and hugged Lara. "We're safe. You're safe," I whispered.

At the sound of a throat being cleared, we broke apart. Scott stood in front of us, a smile on his face.

I frowned. "You're not going to insist on an interview now?"

"I'd like to, but I have to run cover the end of the race. You have to promise me an exclusive after the ceremonies." He listened to something in his radio earpiece and spoke again. "SGTV helped you escape from a killer. I figure you can both do an interview with me about it. Plus some on the family backstory—even if SGTV doesn't use that, I know another outlet that will."

That's when I understood the full cost of Lara's rescue. SGTV and Racing's Ringer would publish my family connections. I looked at Lara, nineteen years old, smart, and related to me. Safe.

I spoke to Scott. "I'd better not owe you after this one."

"We'll be square."

That's something.

My father barged into the tent, almost knocking Scott over and barely noticing. James looked distraught and nearly hysterical—until he caught sight of me and Lara standing together, both unharmed. His shoulders sagged. He swayed where he stood. He belatedly apologized to Scott and moved to us.

"You're all right?" he asked.

Lara buried her face in his chest, her shoulders shaking with sobs.

I felt similarly shaky, but I wasn't going to react the same way. I put my hands on my hips and felt my side twinge. "Where *were* you?"

He closed his eyes. "My phone battery died. I finally caught up to the messages Holly left up and down pit lane. Thank God you're both all right."

Lara lifted her head. "They found out Tino—the mechanic—told me there was nothing wrong with that car. They took him somewhere, and they were taking me—" She shuddered. "Kate saved me."

I shook my head. "It was Holly and the SGTV crew." I glanced over to find Scott watching the three of us. He raised his eyebrows and looked from me to my father and back again.

I sighed, knowing what I offered the Ringer. Then I nodded.

He grinned and mouthed, "Now I owe *you*." Then his expression changed to one of shock, and he put a hand to his radio earpiece. He exchanged a look with his cameraman. Both men turned and ran from our tent.

Curious, I walked to the tent opening and looked up pit lane. Scott hadn't gone far. Only one pit space away, in fact, where two uniformed policemen escorted Richard Arena and Monica Frank out of their tent.

Monica looked back and scowled at me. I smiled and waved. Then I laughed.

Detective Latham saw me watching. I met him halfway between us, next to the empty pit space.

He spoke first. "We arrested Vinny Cruise, aka Julio Arena."

"For?"

"The attempted murder of Stuart Telarday and the murder of Foster Calhoun."

"You're sure he did it?" I wanted to believe he had the right guy. That it wasn't my wild guesses and desperation to find someone to blame.

"We're sure. We found evidence on his car."

I went limp with relief. "You found the car?"

"Parked at the airport, across from the track."

"What about the four guys who tried to kidnap my sister?"

"Talking to them also."

"And Richard Arena? Monica?"

"We're talking to them. No charges yet." He shrugged at my surprise and went on. "We'll see what they knew and when. Maybe there will be other agencies involved."

I covered my face with my hands. *It's all over.* I couldn't believe it.

"I understand you got in the middle of things, trying to rescue your sister," Latham said.

I glared at him. "I *did* rescue her. You guys weren't around, and they were taking her away!"

He crossed his arms over his chest. "We were about to move in. Then you got involved."

I wouldn't apologize or be intimidated. I put my fists on my hips. "I didn't see you, and you didn't tell me. She was in trouble."

He shook his head slowly. "Just be careful. Next time there might not be a camera around to save you." He held out a hand, and we shook. "I have to get to the station, but someone will talk to you before you leave. Try to stay out of trouble."

Holly walked up after the Detective left. "The home-wrecker in handcuffs. Satisfying."

I smiled again. Then I remembered the race. "What's going on with the 28?"

"Twelve minutes left. Mike's dogging the back of the third-place car."

"Seriously?" I sprinted for the Sandham Swift pits. "Hot damn!"

Chapter Fifty-four

I got to the monitors in time to see Mike follow a white Ferrari through the Bus Stop, exit well, and stay on the driver's tail through NASCAR 3 and 4 and the tri-oval. Mike set him up perfectly for a pass into Turn 1. Every single person in the pits held their breath as Mike slipped ahead with only inches to spare. The Ferrari stuck to Mike's bumper through Turn 3 of the infield. Through the Kink.

"He's gapping him," Miles said next to me.

I looked around, surprised he was there, and saw Colby on his other side. I reached out to them. The three of us held onto each other as Mike inched away from the Ferrari. As the clock ticked ever closer to a podium result for the 28 Corvette.

Fifteen minutes to go. Holly ducked under Miles' arm to stand between us. Lara and our father stood on the other side of me, Lara closest, her arm around my waist. The Ferrari driver tried another move on Mike. He couldn't get close enough and dropped back even more.

Eight minutes. The Ferrari didn't have the speed to pass Mike, and Mike was a full half-lap behind the second place car. We had third place sewn up…if our new Corvette C7.R would hold together for seven-and-a-half more minutes of racing.

By this point in the race, I knew Mike was hyper-sensitive to any creak, groan, or wiggle. Our racecars ran almost continuously for twenty-four hours, at top speed, high heat, and peak stress. Fourteen cars that started the race wouldn't finish, most due to breakage. Even with a handful of minutes left to run, we could still lose another—it had happened before, as late as the last two minutes of the race. I prayed it wouldn't happen to us.

I felt a hand settle on my shoulder. Our rock-star, Thomas Kendall, stood behind me, his cousin Chris next to him.

Leon Browning, from the 29 car, currently running in sixth place in the GT Daytona class, stepped to Chris' other side and nodded at me. "The car will hold," he told us. "Ian wouldn't have it any different, and this one's for him."

My eyes filled with tears. I felt the rightness of his statement. After the heartbreak of the last twenty-five hours, I didn't think this team could take any more. We *had* to finish. But, like Leon, I suddenly felt sure we would.

"It's for Ian," I agreed. I turned to Holly, Miles, Colby, and the others on my other side. "This one is for Ian."

Miles' fingers tightened on mine. Holly hugged both of us closer.

Colby repeated, "For Ian."

As the clock ticked down, our crew stopped their tidying and packing work. They gathered around us at the monitors. The whole team became a single organism. We breathed as one with every approach Mike made to a corner. We exhaled together as he exited safely.

Three minutes. The 28 Corvette kept flowing through turns and flying down straights as it had done for more than twenty-three hours and fifty-seven minutes. I shook with tension, excitement, and anticipation.

One minute thirty-nine seconds left. The overall race leader flashed under the starter's stand, above the start/finish line. The white flag waved, indicating the last lap. Mike was halfway around the track, which meant one and a half more laps for us. I didn't breathe. Mike continued to make it look easy, and the car continued to perform.

The race clock clicked to zero as the overall leader swept out of the Bus Stop and onto the NASCAR banking for the final time. The checkered flag flew. For the second time in the race, fireworks went off along the back straight.

Our group barely reacted, all eyes now glued to the 28 and 29 cars on the monitors. Mike in the back straight, heading into the Bus Stop.

"Come on, come on, come on, come on," I breathed.

Braking. Left, right turns. Right, left turns. Easy on the throttle. Back up onto the banking. NASCAR 3. Hold it steady, stay high above the prototype limping the final third of a lap back to the flag. Steady. Easy over the bump above the NASCAR 4 tunnel. Charging into the tri-oval.

We all drew breath as Mike pointed the car at the checkers. We whooped and cheered as one when he crossed the line in third place.

I broke another of my rules and cried over the results of a race—but I wasn't alone. I saw plenty of manly tears shed as I hugged everyone around me. Even Jack's eyes looked damp as he climbed down from his pit box after seeing the 29 car cross the line.

Jack looked around and raised his hands. We went silent, though the ambient noise of the track remained high.

"Thank you for your effort and commitment," he said. "We couldn't have done it without every single one of you. This finish is for Ian Davenport. In his honor, we are going to go celebrate."

I looked around at the weary faces of the crew who'd been up all night—from the mechanics who kept the car running, to the hospitality staff who kept us fed and supplied, to the chiefs and analysts who'd monitored us from the pit boxes. I felt a deep welling of gratitude. Endurance racing wasn't merely a test of machinery and driver skill, it was a test of the whole team's ability to focus and perform whenever required. Sandham Swift had come through. Again.

I blinked back tears as I stepped forward to thank Jack.

He reached out for a hug. "Hell of a day, kid, huh?"

I laughed into his shoulder.

"Great drive," Jack went on. "You held onto fast lap of the race for our class. Incredible achievement."

I pulled back in surprise, and he grinned—an expression I'd only witnessed on his face three times. "True. You put in the fastest race lap in the GT Le Mans class. The factory team might have won our class, but you went fastest. Showed them Sandham Swift and Kate Reilly are forces to be reckoned with."

A warm haze of satisfaction and pride swept through me. I didn't care we hadn't won the special Daytona watches for first place—this year, anyway. We'd accomplished something by persevering and finishing under the most terrible of circumstances—finishing on the podium at that. And I'd been fastest. I met Jack's smile with one of my own.

Then Jack straightened. "Time for Victory Lane, Ms. Fast-Lap." He waved the team on and returned to the pit cart to gather his belongings. Around us, the crew put tools away, cleaned up debris, and disassembled shelves and stands they'd used throughout the race.

I smiled, turning for the exit, only to see my father standing there with Lara and someone in an Arena Motorsports shirt. I tensed before realizing it was Ryan Johnston, the only nice person from that team. All three of them were clearly waiting for me.

Now what?

Holly moved to my side as I approached my father, Lara, and Ryan.

"We know you've got to get to the ceremonies," my father began. "But Ryan will need to speak with you. I mean, Agent Johnston."

Why on earth would I want to speak with—

I blinked. "Agent?"

Ryan pulled out a badge. "Federal Bureau of Investigations. Undercover."

I studied him, seeing a nondescript man of average height, average brown hair, and what looked like a well-muscled build under team clothing. Something in his eyes spoke of intelligence and self-assurance.

He held my gaze. "I'd like to talk with you and Lara both about your encounter with Vinny Cruise."

"Vinny? But he's—"

"Really Julio Arena," Ryan confirmed. "As I've explained to James and Lara, that's why I want to hear about the interactions you had with him this weekend."

"Did you know Vinny was Julio?"

"We suspected. But we didn't have any real evidence." He looked me in the eye as he said it. I got the sense he was honestly stating the facts and bracing himself for reaction.

He got one. In a flash, I went from worn out and mildly euphoric to pissed off. "You knew? And you let him hurt Stuart and Ian and Calhoun? You let him kidnap Lara and stick me in the side with a knife?" I heard the screech in my voice and stopped abruptly.

"A knife? Kate, you're hurt?" James put a hand on my shoulder.

I waved him off. "He poked me, cut my jacket. Back to Agent Johnston."

Ryan spoke calmly. "We didn't *know*, only suspected. Without proof Vinny was Julio Arena, we couldn't do anything. No one had any idea Julio would go so far this weekend. We were all slow to catch on, even Richard Arena."

"He had to know his brother was here," I pointed out.

"Yes, but he didn't know about bribery or murder or kidnapping."

"He didn't know? He's obviously up to something himself, if you've been undercover in his team."

Holly spoke up. "You were with the Arena team, not Benchmark."

"We have other ongoing investigations concerning Richard Arena, which I'm not at liberty to discuss. His brother wasn't my primary focus." Agent Johnston looked at me. "Until he went nuts this weekend."

"That's the legal term?" I asked.

"Not exactly." He sighed. "Look, this isn't official, all right? My personal opinion is whatever else Arena is involved in, he kept his racing operations clean. He expected his brother to do the same. He's got a pretty big blind spot where his brother is concerned."

My father shifted uneasily, but didn't comment.

Ryan straightened and reassumed his poker face. "Officially, I'm sorry for your losses this weekend. We weren't sure Julio Arena was behind everything until it was too late."

I was still angry, but yelling at the FBI wasn't a good idea. "You're going to make sure he's put away?"

"Absolutely. You both can help me with that." He gestured to me and Lara. "Can we speak at the Series trailer right after the award ceremonies?"

I looked to Lara, and we both agreed

"Did you," Lara began, then stopped. I squeezed her hand, and she tried again. "Did you get the guys who tried to kidnap me?"

My father looked distressed, but still didn't speak.

"We have them in custody," Ryan confirmed.

Lara relaxed, but she wasn't done. "And Tino, the mechanic who lied for Vinny? Is he in trouble? He's a nice guy, and he felt really bad."

"He's safe, and I believe the local police are talking to him." He softened some. "But I don't think he'll be in big trouble, no. Before any of you ask, the driver of the car is also talking to law enforcement. He may face charges for the collision that killed Ian."

"What about whoever did the bribing?" I asked. "Do you know who that was?"

Ryan frowned. "There are suspects, but again, I'm not sure proof exists." He glanced at my father. "You should get to the podium. I'll meet you after."

I went after him as he exited the tent. "Ryan—Agent—"

He stopped. "Ryan's fine."

"You gave me alibi information for Ed Grant and the cousins on purpose, didn't you? Why?" We were right outside the tent, where my father couldn't hear.

"I knew you were related to them. I thought you might be worried—that you'd want to know they weren't suspects."

"You had that wrong."

He chuckled. "Live and learn. I'll see you shortly."

As he walked away, my cell phone buzzed in my pocket. Buzzed again. And again. I yanked it out. It was Polly, calling from the hospital. She was crying.

Chapter Fifty-five

My world caved in. I crumpled to the ground.

"Kate?" Polly sniffled. "Kate, he woke up! They think he's going to be all right."

I gasped for air. *She's telling me he's alive. She's not calling to tell me he's dead. Alive.* "What?"

"He woke up," Polly bellowed. "Not for long, but he's out of the coma. Come over when you can. Kate?"

I mumbled something in response.

"It's going to be all right, dear."

I thanked her, let the phone slip out of my hand, and burst into tears. I cried with relief that Stuart was alive and the guy who tried to kill him was in custody. I cried for Ian Davenport and Foster Calhoun, who'd never see another day. I cried for myself, for having to let go of so much of my armor—like being mad at Sam, like not acknowledging my father or half-sister. I cried because I felt insecure without those anchors. I didn't know who Kate Reilly was with more family.

Mostly I wept to release the tension, pain, and trauma of the last twenty-four hours.

"Oh, no," I heard Holly say. "Kate, no. Stuart?"

I raised my head to see her crouched in front of me, looking stricken. I smiled at her bleary face. "He woke up. He's going to be okay."

She plopped back on her butt. "Oh, thank God."

I wiped my eyes and laughed. "I know, right?"

She handed me a tissue, then used one to dab her own eyes.

Jack, my father, and Lara exited the tent and stopped short at the sight of us.

Jack's face clouded. "Stuart?"

I grinned at him. "Awake. Alive. They think he'll make it."

Jack exhaled slowly, as if releasing an enormous burden. "Something went right."

I scrambled to my feet. "Jack—the podium—I need to go to the hospital."

He nodded. "Of course. Give him our best."

I felt weak with gratitude and relief. I turned to Holly. "Can you—"

"You take the car." She stood up and pulled the keys from her pocket. "I'll deal with everything here—I'll get your stuff and handle the cops and the press."

"Just go, Kate," Jack said. "None of this is as important as being there. We know where to find you." He nodded to the others and left.

As we followed him up the pit walkway a moment later, I fought contradictory urges. On one hand, I could barely restrain myself from sprinting to the rental car and speeding to the hospital. On the other, I was strangely reluctant to leave the bubble of the racetrack. Reluctant to face reality.

I eyed my father next to me, wondering what he'd face in his own return to reality. A muscle twitched in his cheek. I realized his silence had more to do with holding in fury than disinterest.

I spoke quietly, so Lara wouldn't hear. "From your reaction, you have a pretty good idea of who bribed Vinny—Julio—to take Ian out."

He looked straight ahead, his face blank. "I'm not sure it will ever be proven—it may be Julio Arena's word against theirs—but I have no doubt it was my brother or his son and nephew."

I dodged carts carrying tires, pit boxes, and other equipment as I tried to work out how to respond.

It took three strides, but my father finally exploded. "I can't—simply—I am appalled." He turned to me, stopping in the middle of the walkway. "Kate, I'm horrified at what they've done—to you, to your team, to Ian. I can't—my father—"

I put my hand on his shoulder and started him walking again. "You didn't do it. They made their own choices."

He shook his head. "It's inexcusable. To drag the bank through this—to drag the family through it. Unacceptable. This time is the last straw."

"This time?"

He sighed heavily. "My brother crossed the line once before. The family—he convinced them the ends justified the means. I couldn't convince them otherwise, and to my eternal shame and regret, I went along with family opinion."

I had a bad feeling about what he'd say next.

He looked at me. "That was over you, your mother, and your grandparents. This is not the place, but the time has come, Kate. I need to explain the past to you. Soon."

I nodded, but didn't speak.

"Rest assured," he continued. "This time, I will handle my brother. Even if he goes unpunished by the law, he will not come out of this unscathed." A fierce smile touched his face. "At the very least, I'd say his racing dreams—Billy and Holden's as well—are well and truly over."

It might have been petty, but I couldn't help the satisfaction I felt at his words. "If they were responsible for Ian, they deserve to pay somehow."

"I promise you, they will. I believe firmly in retribution and restitution." The expression on his face was stern, almost frightening.

Check it out, my father can be an ass-kicker. I felt a surge of appreciation and respect for him.

Holly turned around as we reached the gate to Victory Lane. "Kate, wait here for two minutes." She read the anxiety and impatience on my face. "Two minutes, I swear." She disappeared into the gated enclosure, where class winners were being presented with their watches. My father turned to speak with Lara.

Tug Brehan trotted over to me. "Kate, did you hear about Stuart?" While I felt—and almost everyone around me looked— like a bedraggled, exhausted mess, Tug looked neat, tidy, and fresh, if wide-eyed with excitement.

I nodded. "I'm on my way to the hospital."

"Thank goodness," Tug breathed. "I'm so sorry I didn't get to you sooner. It's been a little…" He swiveled his head from side to side.

"Believe me, I know."

As the second place finishers in GTD were called to the podium, Tug focused on my face again. "So I heard. I'll be talking with the law soon, myself."

I wondered if he'd had any role in my cousins' schemes. Or Vinny's. "How well did you know Vinny, Tug?"

He ran a finger under his collar. "Not as well as I thought. Or perhaps I should say I knew Vinny but not Julio?" He whispered the last name.

"How about Billy and Holden with the Arena team?"

I saw a flicker of fear in his eyes before they turned bored. "Casual acquaintances. We've shared a beer or two over the seasons." He paused. I could almost see the wheels turning, connecting the cousins with me and with Vinny/Julio.

As if he'd flipped a switch, he turned into the professional pleaser. "They're representatives of a sponsor, after all, so it's my job to be friendly and helpful." He finished with a smile.

"'Being helpful' is why Ryan was paying you off?"

His smile never dimmed. "I'm not sure what you're referring to, Kate."

I studied him. I no longer believed anything he said.

Tug kept smiling. He glanced around again, shooting his cuffs. "Any support or help I've rendered our teams or sponsors is no more than my duty as part of the race operations team. Which is precisely what I will tell the police when I see them."

That's how he'll play it. "You'll be in charge until Stuart returns?"

He jolted and flicked his eyes back to mine. "That's my understanding. I hope his recovery is swift."

"Will Elizabeth stay on with you in his absence?"

"I hope so." He smiled at me again, full power. "Stuart's shoes are so big, it will undoubtedly take both of us to fill them. Now, if you'll excuse me, I have to run. Congratulations on your finish."

My father murmured in my ear as Tug walked away. "I confirmed Tug spread the rumors about Stuart wanting small teams out of the Series."

"You don't say."

"Perhaps you will pass that along at an appropriate moment."

I agreed, wondering how soon Stuart would be ready to deal with that kind of news. I checked the time. *I need to go.* Just then, Holly reappeared with Mike, Miles, and Colby in tow. I hurried to my co-drivers, opening my arms wide for a group hug.

"Way to finish, Mike," I stepped back and looked at him. "Great drive."

"Great car." He looked worn out, but he smiled ear to ear. "Great team—incredible co-drivers." He blinked and lost the smile. "And it was for Ian."

I took Mike's hand. "He'd be pleased and proud."

"Holly says Stuart's awake?" Miles asked.

"They think he'll be okay." I looked at my three partners, my team. "I'm sorry to leave and not celebrate with you, but I need to go."

Colby hugged me. "Stuart has to come first. We'll celebrate later. Go."

I nodded at her, tears forming in my eyes again. "I'll see you all later. Thanks, all of you." I waved and set off up pit lane.

Colby was right, Stuart came first. But I was headed into the unknown. I knew my relationship with him wouldn't be the same as it had been before his accident. We loved each other. But I traveled for my career, and he'd face a long recovery. I wondered what would change when we didn't see each other once a month at a race weekend.

I was achingly relieved he was alive and awake. I simply didn't know what the future would bring.

I looked back to see Lara and our father watching me leave. They waved, and I held up a hand in return. *I wonder how these relationships will go, too. Will I regret opening myself up to them?*

I had no way of knowing. But I'd reached out, and there was no going back.

To receive a free catalog of Poisoned Pen Press titles, please contact us in one of the following ways:

Phone: 1-800-421-3976
Facsimile: 1-480-949-1707
Email: info@poisonedpenpress.com
Website: www.poisonedpenpress.com

Poisoned Pen Press
6962 E. First Ave. Ste 103
Scottsdale, AZ 85251